A NEW
EDEN

A NEW EDEN

THE BETAVERSE • BOOK 1

MENILIK HENRY DYER

Podium

Thank you Rose, Mum (Jonnina), and Ange.

Without your support and encouragement, I wouldn't have

completed this novel.

Copyright © 2023 Menilik Henry Dyer

Cover design by Podium Publishing

ISBN: 978-1-0394-2987-1

Published in 2023 by Podium Publishing, ULC
www.podiumaudio.com

A NEW EDEN

CHAPTER 1

TRILLION

WE NEED TO LEAVE MARS

"Mars isn't safe anymore!" one of the holographic heads shouted on the conference call.

Trillion von Nichol had to turn her head to see who was speaking because there were so many people holographically projected around the enormous circular table. The fact she was seeing faces she'd never met before meant this meeting had consequences. Trillion found herself disagreeing with many of the disembodied floating heads, although she knew their opinions didn't carry much weight. Peter was paying for everything, and it was his decision to make. So, she asked him, "Should we escape?"

Dr. Peter Atreus was almost ninety—but he didn't look it. Perhaps his dark skin gave him an advantage over some of the other team members whose lighter skin meant they looked twice his age, despite being half it. Trillion thought he was living proof of the saying *Black don't crack.*

Peter looked down, as if he was unsure about what he was about to say. "Just because Earth elected a Luddite doesn't mean we have to leave Mars today—we're not ready!"

Trillion shook her head. It always amused her when her colleagues used the word *Luddite*. She found it ironic that earlier today, she had to wheel into the conference room a physical screen just because Peter refused to have a holographic projection recorder installed in his home office. "Peter, let's not call them Luddites. I'm sure, to them, *we're* the Luddites."

Atlas Tupu turned toward her. He was just as old as Peter but much better-looking; the two of them had worked together for years to create this mission. "What should we call them then?" he challenged.

She shrugged, not wanting to get into this argument again. "Never mind."

She watched Peter's mouth move, but no sound came out. "You're on mute, old man."

The red mute symbol disappeared from his screen. "There's nothing to fear in the Fermion Party. As with all political parties, they had to use extremist language to please their voter base. They might be the biggest political party on Earth, but this is Mars."

She could understand half the group's fear. Most everyone on the conference call would eventually become a von Neumann probe. The plan was to upload everyone's mind into spaceships to go and explore the galaxy. Yet, the Fermion Party made a campaign promise to shut down this program.

It was true that they all hated the Fermion Party. But there wasn't much they could do. Besides, she didn't want to leave yet. She hadn't said goodbye. She wasn't ready.

The arguments began to get heated. Even Icarus started yelling. Icarus Kishida was a short Japanese man who loved getting up to mischief. "Those are not extremist beliefs anymore, Dr. Atreus! We must accept the fact that these views are now mainstream political views on Earth. Killing Mars is now a mainstream talking point!"

The atmosphere was getting intense as different people began yelling on the call. Trillion tuned out, only hearing bits and pieces of it as her mind wandered to the idea of leaving today. She was a backup to the backup explorers, and now they spoke like she might be getting her own spaceship. It had felt as though she would never leave Mars—but now that politics were involved, suddenly she might be traveling the galaxy. Did she even want to leave?

"I won't calm down," Atlas said, his raised voice piercing through Trillion's train of thought. "Yes, it's unlucky that they can't afford to visit another planet because their subscription costs in the simulation are too high, but that doesn't mean they have to stop us from traveling the Milky Way!"

"Atlas, don't strawman."

"Peter, I'm not strawmanning their situation. It's the truth. And it's exactly why we need to launch the colony ships ASAP. If we don't have independent colonies of humans, then we are at risk of lunatics like these destroying us!"

Trillion struggled to concentrate on Peter's reply as she was distracted by something moving behind him. She strained her eyes, searching the darkened room for the source of the movement, then gasped as a murky figure crept slowly into view, a barrel of a gun directed at Peter. Trillion jumped to her feet, white with fear as she pointed at the screen. "Dr. Atreus! Dr. Atreus!"

The room went silent as everyone noticed the man, helpless to do anything. Yet they could see everything. Hear everything.

The gunman was unaware he was on camera. "Peter, you're breaking multiple treaties outside of the metaverse," he said darkly. "You left us no choice."

Peter spun around. "You have no authority here!" he bellowed in surprise.

How did he smuggle a gun onto Mars? Trillion thought.

Interplanetary travel was still highly regulated. It wasn't like driving across a border. The multi-layered security checkpoints made international flights look like a walk in the park. And meant smuggling an unregistered chocolate bar was impossible . . . let alone a gun. "Peter, the gun isn't real. There are no guns on Mars."

Peter must have realized it too. He was slowly walking toward the man, hands raised slightly as if surrendering.

The man had quite a speech, but Trillion had heard it before. All those crazy Fermions believed the same thing.

"Life isn't meant to explore the stars," the man continued. "If it was, we would've been visited by aliens already. You know this, Peter. You know the answer to 'Where are all the aliens?' is 'They're in the metaverse.' There are an infinite number of virtual worlds. Why the obsession with this one?"

"You mean the real world!" Peter said harshly as he inched closer to the intruder, his face showing disdain at being lectured to. But the slight tremble to his hands betrayed his confident veneer—revealing his fear.

He lunged forward and the two men wrestled for a moment, the man with the gun clearly stronger. They fell to the floor and rolled out of view of the camera.

Bang! The gun went off.

Everyone gasped.

Trillion's brain moved a million miles an hour. What had just happened? Was Peter shot? She was in shock. She heard voices shout out for Peter.

"Peter. Peter!"

"Dr. Atreus!"

"Director!"

Trillion's own cry was drowned out by everyone speaking at once.

The video call disconnected abruptly, and all the holographic images disappeared. Trillion gazed aghast at the three others with her in the conference room—Icarus, Atlas, and Angelique. All four of them were scheduled to monitor the Isaac Arthur Mars base over the weekend.

Icarus stood beside Trillion, holding his phone up in the air. "I just lost signal."

Trillion looked at the others of them in shock. "How did they smuggle a gun onto Mars? They're illegal here. Who would use a gun when one missed shot could expose you to the vacuum of space?"

Icarus pointed at his head, as if to say *Only crazy people.* "Someone who doesn't care about holes in habitats. Someone who isn't planning on being here long enough to deal with the consequences."

"Someone not from around here," Angelique added.

All three of them looked toward Atlas, all knowing what this meant but not wanting to voice it. They knew those people were from the Fermion Party. They also knew they didn't have much time. If they'd taken out Peter, then the rest of them were next.

"We planned for this, team," Atlas said. "Peter didn't believe it would happen. But it looks like they're moving in on us." He pulled something out of his pocket and handed it to Trillion. A key card. "Take this. It will get you into my office. There's a safe in the corner. Behind the seat, in the wall. In it, you'll find solid plastic boxes about the size of matchboxes. Those are the two-factor authentication codes. Find the four with our names on. There will also be a pair of in-ear buds; use those to speak with our ships' AIs. Give them the authentication codes and tell them to prepare for takeoff. Take Icarus with you and hurry! Meet Angelique and me at airlock F twenty-seven."

Trillion looked at him incredulously. "What are you going to do?"

"We're going to get our spacecraft ready," Atlas said grimly, a determined look in his eyes.

Just then, the door to the conference room swung open, revealing another man with a gun.

He pointed it toward Atlas, Icarus, and Angelique—unaware that Trillion was standing behind the door. The three captives raised their hands as one.

As the gunman approached the room, Trillion knew this gun was real. She no longer questioned the need to leave Mars today. In that moment, she knew she had to stop him and they had to get going. She steadied herself; she had to do something before he saw her.

She drew in a silent breath and lunged toward his arm in an attempt to knock the gun out of his hand.

Trillion managed to get one hand on the barrel, her momentum carrying her forward as she rammed into the heavy metal door. She kept her grip on the gun, but the man wouldn't let go. So his hand was still in the way when the door slammed shut. The man screamed in pain and let go of the gun in agony as he tried to dislodge his hand—but with his fingers wedged, it only made his situation worse.

Icarus and Atlas added their weight to the almost-closed door, removing all hope the man would ever use his mangled hand again.

Trillion fell, the gun now completely in her possession. She breathed heavily as the adrenaline and anger coursed through her veins.

Angelique knelt next to her. "Thank you."

Angelique Komene was the youngest in the group, but she was one of the hardest-working people Trillion knew, which made it shocking when she found out that Angelique used to work in real estate. The only thing Trillion disliked about Angelique was her ginger hair. Trillion had red hair—a much brighter shade of red too—and she hated that their flaming hair was always the first topic of conversation whenever they walked into a room together.

A few moments later, the team had gathered themselves.

Trillion held on to the gun as they opened the door, releasing the man's hand. "Who are you?" she demanded, pointing the weapon at the stranger.

He stared blankly, clutching his hand.

Angelique cracked. She kicked his broken hand. "You killed Pete!"

The gunman started talking after that—he was twenty-three, maybe twenty-four, young and filled with hatred. Filled with extremist views.

They interrogated him but he didn't know much. He was part of the Fermions. It was a full-on attack of Mars—at least to them it was, because the intruder didn't recognise Mars as an independent planet. They had hacked in to the satellite systems, shut off all internet access.

They learned that he was to move them into the prison cells and wait for further instructions. He guessed they were to be transported back to Earth.

He wasn't very useful for learning more about the plan, but he was full of derogatory terms, calling them names, trying to argue that humanity had already ruined Earth; it didn't need to go and ruin other planets.

The team tied him up and removed his phone and watch.

Atlas reiterated the plan. "We need to move fast. We don't know how many of them there are."

Trillion handed Atlas the gun. "You and Angelique take this. You might need it where you're going. Icarus and I should be fine without it."

The two teams parted ways without looking back.

CHAPTER 2

ATLAS

PREPARING THE SPACESHIP

As Atlas and Angelique left, they resisted the urge to run, in case they encountered something around a corner.

The base was deserted. As they made their way down the hall, Atlas wondered how someone had managed to get in there at this time of night. "Why is the world so crazy right now?"

Angelique looked at him. "It's the pace of change making the world go crazy. We haven't seen this much innovation since the Industrial Revolution. I think everyone is fighting over the pieces."

He smiled at her. "Well, actually, you might be too young to have experienced this, but I've lived through two massive changes in humanity."

"Getting phones wasn't as big a change as AI," Angelique remarked with a side-eye.

He shrugged. "It's not as big as what's happening today, but it did completely change the way society operated."

"Phones got us Twitter. AI got us flying cars." Angelique rolled her eyes. "The singularity event of 2045 changed the world order, just like the Industrial Revolution turned America into a superpower. AI has made a tiny country with only five million people into a superpower."

The door up ahead distracted them from their debate; they had arrived at the mission control center. The room was half-full of rows of empty tables—it wasn't scheduled to be fitted out for a few months.

They walked past the desks until they reached a security door on the other side of the room, where Atlas punched in several numbers, then scanned his fingerprints. He opened the door and walked through, Angelique following close behind.

There were three computer desks in this small back room. Atlas looked at the computers, reading the sign next to each one. He pointed at the one in the middle. "You need to connect to that computer. You'll have to use my credentials."

"What do you need me to do?" asked Angelique as she pulled out the chair and sat down.

"Your terminal unlocks the embryos. Begin the unlocking sequence and depressurize the cryonics center. We need to get them moved into the freezers on our four spacecraft now. We're lucky there was a test launch scheduled for tomorrow, so a few of the rockets are mostly ready to go." Atlas sat down in front of another computer and started typing away furiously. He found the screen he wanted and scanned the information, pulling up a list of available ANTs.

ANTs stood for *automated networked transporters*. They were bots that could operate both in space and on planets. By default, they had six legs, and one arm pointed out front. Each leg ended with a magnetoplasmadynamic, or MPD, arcjet. These powerful rockets were capable of easily moving the robotic creature in and out of orbit. This made ANTs ideal multipurpose vehicles for their mission.

Atlas clicked through the various configurations, looking for a particular model of ANT. He didn't know the search function's hotkey, so he had to scroll through the options one at a time. After what felt like forever, he eventually found what he was looking for. This ANT was about the size of a motorbike but had a sealed chamber inside its center, perfect for moving the embryos across the Martian surface. He sent all two hundred of them to the cryonics center on the base. "I'm sending a fleet of ANTs to start picking up the embryos. I'm also getting our ships' AIs loaded into each of our spacecraft."

Angelique glanced at him, then turned back to her screen. "I've been going through everything we have in the cryonic center. How did we get some of these things? There's everything from elephant to whale embryos in here."

Atlas shrugged. "I think some of that is just printed DNA. The technology to actually grow those is impressive, but I know Peter had been planning this for years. He buys some of this stuff from the dark web. So, let's just hope it works."

Atlas pointed at an image of one of the spacecraft on his screen. "Don't you find it mind-blowing that one of these spacecraft can produce as much energy as Earth used only twenty years ago?"

Angelique looked at him with an expression of *Duh*. "That's the point I was making just before. The singularity has changed the world more than phones ever could."

Atlas smiled. "Okay, I believe you." He turned back to typing.

Angelique stood up from her computer and looked for a switch at the back. "My computer just turned off. Is yours still on?"

"It shouldn't be able to turn off," Atlas replied as he stood up to peek at Angelique's terminal. He turned back to his computer but it had turned off too. "They're shutting us out."

Angelique nodded. "This is bad."

"Did you manage to get the orders out before your terminal went blank?"

"I think so. There's not much we can do now, anyway."

"Agreed. But that also means they know where we are."

Atlas walked over to the door and peered out. "There's no one out there." He waved Angelique over so they could get going. He could sense her fear as she walked past.

They sneaked out the door and past the row of tables, but instead of leaving the way they came, Atlas turned left, making his way toward another door. "Let's see what we're dealing with."

He typed a code into the keypad and opened the door to a security room glowing eerily from the light of the wall of camera screens. Atlas pointed to the screen showing his office. They could see Trillion and Icarus rummaging through the safe behind the wall. Angelique gasped when she spotted someone searching near where they were. They looked at each other when they noticed another man between them and the hallway to airlock F twenty-seven—luckily, he was heading away from the door. They counted five men in total searching for them.

Atlas took a deep breath. "We need to get going now."

They started walking briskly, taking a back passage to avoid being seen by any of the attackers.

Atlas whispered as they slipped through a door next to the airlock, "The spacecraft should be fully loaded by now. Let's put on the spacesuits and get ready to cycle through the airlock as soon as the other two get here."

Angelique nodded, struggling to hide her concern.

CHAPTER 3
TRILLION

HELLO, SHIP

Trillion wondered what it was going to be like to lose her body. She didn't play any of the simulation games in the meta. And she had only just started training for this mission, so wasn't fully versed with what to expect. During the academy, they explained that having her mind uploaded felt like waking from a dream— but she wasn't sure she believed them. She pushed all those existential thoughts to the back of her head as they arrived at the office. She swiped the card. The keypad beeped reassuringly as the door slid open.

"Icarus, you open the safe. I'm going to find a weapon. I'm sure Atlas must keep something in here."

She rummaged around in the drawers. Scissors. A paperweight. Something.

"So, we're going to die today?" Icarus said as he opened the safe. He started going through all the boxes, putting the ones with each of their names in a pile.

Trillion closed the drawer she was looking in. "I'm not sure it counts as dying if we wake up again."

"I'm getting a new body. I'm going to come back as an anime cartoon."

"A Japanese guy coming back as a cartoon? Icarus, that's gotta be the most cliché thing ever."

Trillion smiled a little when she thought about what Icarus would look like as an anime character. She thought he'd look funnier as a Simpsons character—maybe Homer.

"I think I might change my last name to von Neumann," she said, thinking about what changes she'd make.

Icarus stared at her blankly. Then she watched as it turned around in his head. He smiled when he finally understood. "Ohhh, Trillion von Neumann because you'll be a von Neumann probe." Icarus said, half-laughing. "You and Atlas are the same. You both have a creative way of naming things."

"What do you mean?"

"Okay, changing von Nichol to von Neumann is clever. But have you heard about the eleph-ANTs?"

"No, what are they?"

"Just wait until you see them on your spacecraft. One of Atlas's inventions."

Trillion found what she was looking for. A small knife. More of a butter knife. But still, a weapon.

"I've got all four. Here's yours," Icarus said, handing her a box.

She opened it. There was a small earpiece in the box. She placed it in her ear.

"Hello. Ship, is that you? Hello?"

No response.

"Mine's not working either," Icarus said, tapping on his ear. "We can't connect to the ship's AI if they've disconnected the satellite network. Maybe this network is down too."

Trillion looked at her earpiece again. She turned it around.

"Trillion, each of these AIs is unique to each of us. That's why we all have separate headphones. They will all start off the same but should evolve with us."

Trillion found a little button. She clicked it. "It should work—the communication network from the ship should be independent of Mars. Them hacking that network shouldn't impact us." She placed the earpiece back in her ear.

"*Hello, Trillion.*"

"Hey, Ship, do you know what happened?"

"*Mostly, I've been occupied with coordinating all these ANTs that Atlas sent my way. Are we leaving soon?*"

"Yes. It's time to put all our practice into action."

Icarus and Trillion both spoke to their respective ships' AIs, instructing them to prep each spaceship for launch.

Getting Atlas and Angelique's ships to comply was a little harder. They didn't recognize the voices, so a randomly generated string of ten numbers had to be read out. Luckily, the box had a little device resembling a calculator that produced these numbers.

Both Trillion and Icarus could feel the pressure. They felt like they'd been in the same place for too long. They closed Atlas's office and took off at a run.

Trillion's mind had a habit of worrying too much when she was stressed. It made running hard when her thoughts were going in circles. Did she really need to go off into space? Had she thought about this? Had she agreed to this? Was the "simulated Trillion" really going to be the same as she was now?

She stopped running and began to walk because her dread was becoming too encompassing. "Icarus, I don't think I fully understand why we can't just wait until we get old before uploading our mind."

Icarus slowed down too, putting a hand on her shoulder. "We are about to go on a long, long journey. You'll be bored out of your mind traveling through space alone. At least as a simulation, you can turn off and then wake up in another system."

"Okay. But then why do we have to be changed? Why can't I stay myself? Why does my personality need modifications?"

"It's simple, Trillion. We'll be on this journey for thousands of years. Maybe even longer. Humans get bored of things easily. If we don't hardcode us to want to seed worlds, in five hundred years, we probably won't *want* to seed worlds with life. Besides, Trillion, as soon as you achieve that goal, that desire is deleted from your matrix. It goes away."

"What do you want to do after that?"

"Not sure. Explore the galaxy. Go back to Earth. What about you?"

Trillion nodded, still unsure about the upcoming adventure. And half wondering if it was too late to pull out. But the thought of being shot at again propelled her forward. With force of will she pushed those thoughts away and they picked up the pace again, rounding the final corner. Up ahead they could see Angelique and Atlas hastily putting on spacesuits.

"We need to leave now!" Atlas urged, indicating two suits nearby. "Hurry!"

Trillion could see the fear in Atlas's eyes. He was afraid of something. His hands were shaking. "What happened, Atlas?"

He didn't answer. He looked over her shoulder and turned white. Trillion spun around and saw five men running toward them. She recognized one of them because he was clutching his hand. The others were armed, pointing guns at the four of them.

"Freeze right there!" one yelled. "You're under arrest."

Trillion hoped they wouldn't be stupid enough to shoot at an airlock door. Although they *had* shot Peter. This situation was obviously serious enough that they were willing to shoot first and ask questions later.

It was a race now. The four of them jumped into the airlock and closed the door, frantically attempting to get their suits on. Trillion hadn't gotten her helmet on yet. Only Atlas had his helmet on, she realized.

Atlas put his hand over the airlock switch. "Sorry, team, I need to start decompressing the chamber now."

Trillion forced several breaths out, trying to exhale the oxygen being sucked out of her body. She managed to get the helmet onto her head, but she was fumbling with the four clips she needed to close. She was running out of breath. One at a time, she managed to clip down each of the four latches, finally securing her helmet in place. She was light-headed but she could finally breathe.

Their pursuers were now on the other side of the airlock, but they were making no attempt to open the door. They stood there smiling, clearly happy with themselves. Strange, Trillion thought. Soon, she and the others would be safely on the Martian landscape. On the way to each of their launch pads.

A shiver went up Trillion's spine. The man with the crushed hand was staring at her, an evil look on his face. He smiled wickedly. She imagined a spider grinning at its prey twisting in its web. She had broken his hand. And he was coming for her . . . So, she did what all uncooperative prey does and fought back. She looked into the man's eyes and winked, forcing a smile as she pointed at his hand.

The response she got in return didn't fill her with confidence. She expected to be free in a few moments, but his face told her she was missing something.

CHAPTER 4

TRILLION

THE BETAVERSE

Trillion's mental clock told her it was taking longer than normal for the airlock door to open. She could tell the atmosphere was gone. The suit had the rigid feel they get when operating in a vacuum. But still the airlock door hadn't automatically opened. Perhaps that was why the men outside looked happy—did they not realize the outer door could be opened manually?

As if thinking the same thing, Icarus walked over to the outer airlock. "I think they're hoping to trap us in here. We'll have to manually operate the door."

The plan to trap them in there might have worked if they hadn't already cycled the air out. Airlocks were designed to make it easy for people to get into them. Not out of them.

Angelique joined Icarus at the airlock door. There was a large metal wheel set into it used to manually wind the door open or shut. It was useful in times of emergencies, like when the power cut off on the mechanical doors. Or, as Trillion thought, when there were five men with guns on the other side.

As they began to turn the wheel, the room shimmered blue, the blue shimmer that always accompanied a haptic hologram projector coming online. Or hapticgram, as it had affectionately come to be known. The blue shimmer was added to signal to anyone seeing it that the hologram could interact with the world. Atlas had invented the hapticgram about six months earlier. He had installed it on all the airlocks as a safety measure. His words: "It's faster to stream into the airlock to help someone than to run down and open the doors."

As the blue shimmer enveloped them, signaling the invasion of an outsider, Trillion guessed Atlas was regretting being so adamant they were installed.

Unlike normal holograms, which just appeared, hapticgrams rose into place like bubbles rising out of the ground. They watched as two people emerged, one of them a woman. Possibly in her mid-forties, she had the look of someone used to being in control. She stood upright, hands behind her back, the stars on her shoulder showing she was the general of Earth's Spaceforce. That would make her Sarah Walker. Her hapticgram was large— bigger than the average human. Designed to be larger than the four Beta Explorers.

A man also rose up out of the ground. His hand reached out and grabbed hold of the wheel Icarus and Angelique were turning. It froze in place. The hapticgram was strong enough to lift a human; it needed to be if there was ever a problem in the airlock, so stopping the other two from turning the mechanical door was easy. The man had a buzz cut and his lapel showed he was a corporal. Simply there to be the muscle. He was surprisingly shorter than everyone—the hapticgram only had enough material to create two average-sized humans. They must have chosen to make General Walker larger at the cost of the grunt.

"This is Lieutenant General Sarah Walker of the United Earth Spaceforce." General Walker's voice beamed through her suit's headphones. "You four are to be relocated to Earth. We have an extradition order signed here."

Atlas wasted no time in replying. "You have no jurisdiction on Mars."

That line must have gotten under General Walker's skin. A flash of anger hit her face, which made sense. She had to have been in the Spaceforce before Earth and Mars split. Her head snapped in Atlas's direction. "This is the betaverse. I have full jurisdiction in the betaverse."

There was that word again. Trillion hated that word. Once humanity began spending more time in the meta and humans in the meta outnumbered those in the real world, they had started calling the real world the betaverse—the beta version of the metaverse.

General Walker wasn't done with her speech. Like all people of power, long monologues and speeches came easy to her. "You're all smart people here. You must clearly understand why we haven't seen any aliens. The Fermi Paradox, as it has come to be called."

She paused for dramatic effect.

"The answer is simple. Any sufficiently advanced civilization chooses to explore the depths of the metaverse, leaving the betaverse behind."

"That's not true," Atlas snapped. "It only takes one set of people to go out and explore to destroy your whole argument. We are going to explore now. We'll prove your argument is wrong."

General Walker didn't even look at him when she responded. "Ah, and this is where I know I'm right." She smiled. "The fact we haven't seen any aliens is proof that you have no chance of succeeding. Civilization leaders like me must have a one hundred percent success rate at stopping crazy people like you. Otherwise, you're right, and we would've seen an alien already."

Icarus had his turn to argue. Trillion knew he had thought about the Fermi Paradox a lot. They'd had many deep conversations about it, both wondering if they would ever see alien life. Icarus had a fascination with languages and saw translating an alien language as his ultimate goal.

Icarus pointed a finger up at the general. "All alien life somehow coming together and *all* agreeing not to communicate with any other life is a lot of rubbish. It doesn't make logical sense. It just takes one rogue person in a species to send a message to our system, and *boom!* They let the cat out of the bag."

General Walker turned around to face Icarus—he still had one hand on the airlock door.

The general shook her head. "That argument assumes it's easy. A rogue member of a species would need to, one, have the ability to do it and, two, have the ability to *keep* doing it until someone eventually hears them, regardless of who was trying to stop them."

She turned around, facing away from the four of them. The gesture was deliberate; it signaled her status next to her captured prisoners. "Let me put it another way. A rogue person could wipe out most of humanity—engineering diseases, sending a relativistic asteroid to all three planets; the list goes on. But the reason it hasn't happened, and won't, is because it is not easy. And there will always be people like myself stopping them."

Trillion always held her thoughts privately. In a way, she could see the general's point of view. She didn't agree with her, but she understood the flawed argument.

"The point you four have failed to grasp is that the Fermi Paradox has a solution. It's quite obvious when you think about it. Our greatest supercomputers have crunched the numbers thousands of times. And each time they come up with the exact same conclusion." General Walker took a deep breath.

Trillion wondered why she spoke with so much theatre. She started to wish she hadn't been at the base over the weekend.

"Any sufficiently advanced civilization," the general continued, "would choose to live in a simulated world because it is infinite. Any sufficiently advanced civilization would choose to leave other worlds alone because doing so would limit the number of possible outcomes. Humanity is a sufficiently advanced civilization. We have a moral duty to grow the number of possible outcomes. Not shrink them."

This is where Trillion's understanding of the Fermions' logic ended. How would exploring the galaxy have any impact on the richness and diversity of experiences possible in the universe? Trillion and others were going to colonize other planets for humanity. They would bring human life beyond its current system. And be the first humans to ever visit another system.

Trillion could feel her suit getting less stiff. They were repressurizing the airlock. It wouldn't be long before the men on the other side had her in handcuffs and headed for Earth. She figured she had nothing to lose. She spoke up for the first time during this interaction. Almost like a school kid, she reflexively raised her right hand as if to ask a question. The ease she felt in moving the spacesuit indicated the room was almost fully pressurized. "I don't understand. How are we limiting the potential experiences in the universe?".

General Walker faced Trillion. "Is it not true that the number of worlds we can simulate is bigger than the number of worlds we can visit?"

"Yes. But that's not the point," Trillion replied.

"No, it's the point exactly. It's a mathematical certainty that the number of experiences you can have in the metaverse is greater than in the betaverse. From a human's perspective, the meta is infinite. The betaverse is finite."

"Yeah, but why should that stop us from exploring the 'betaverse'?" Trillion mimed quotation marks with her fingers. She hated how much that word *betaverse* had grown on her the past several years. But she still hated to say the damn thing. She cast those thoughts aside and a chill ran up her spine. She pictured herself trapped in a metaverse prison.

It was a while before General Walker responded. "Don't you see? If you go and seed a world, that world could then only evolve life that is compatible with Earth life. That limits the possible evolutionary paths."

"This isn't about that. This is about ensuring humanity is around for the next several million years. Having us based in multiple systems guarantees that if anything happens in Sol, we will still survive."

"A million years from now, a colony separate from Sol won't be humans."

Trillion was stumped. She hated having arguments with others on the spot. And General Walker was quick; she had answers to everything. Trillion was about to sit down, resigning herself to being captured, when she heard a whispered voice in her ear.

"Trillion, it's Ship."

She still had her earpiece on. She could still communicate with the ship.

"When I didn't see you come out of the airlock, I started checking on you, Trillion. I think I know how to get you out of there."

Trillion didn't say a thing, afraid she might give up their one trump card.

"There is an emergency kill switch to your right. Peter added it recently after realizing the flaw in Atlas's design. If you turn that off, the hapticgram will turn off."

Trillion looked to her right. Sure enough, there was a small switch. Barely noticeable, and displaying no description of any sort.

General Walker was still monologuing. Trillion waited for a distraction. It wasn't long until Atlas jumped in with a counterargument. Trillion dived for the switch with her right hand and flicked it down.

The whole room suddenly flashed yellow and red as emergency lights started rotating around the room. As the lights flashed, General Walker and the corporal melted into a sea of marbles. The room was filled with tiny pea-sized pellets, which began to bounce off the walls. Flicking the switch had obviously killed the magnets controlling the haptic engine, dropping them to the floor.

"We need to go now," Trillion said, almost willing Icarus and Angelique to wind the airlock door amidst the chaos of tiny balls bouncing around them.

Icarus grabbed the mechanical airlock door and pulled on it hard. It didn't budge.

Angelique joined in, and it started to move, slightly at first, then more smoothly. It took several turns and a lot of effort, but finally, the outer airlock door was opened. Trillion expected to get sucked through, but it was more of a strong breeze as the airlock depressurized.

Millions of tiny balls spilled through the door as the four of them made their escape, trying not to trip over them on the way out.

Atlas grabbed a large rock and shoved it in the airlock door, preventing the men from closing the outside door to repressurize it, effectively making the closest airlock to the launch pad useless and forcing the gunmen to find another way out.

As the team took off, they had a good five hundred meters of red Martian regolith to cross before reaching the first of the launch pads—there were sixteen of them in total, all evenly spaced in a grid format hundreds of meters apart.

Martian gravity made hoping easy, but it still required practice to move quickly while inside a spacesuit, even with the smart exoskeleton that helped the wearer do the Martian jump-skip-walk technique. The team bobbed up and down in unison like a group of oddly shaped bouncy balls as they crossed the Martian landscape at pace toward the first launch pad.

CHAPTER 5

TRILLION

TAKE-OFF

Trillion's communication speaker was still picking up the ramblings of General Walker. But as she got farther away, the general's voice started to drop off, making way for the team to speak freely with each other again. They still didn't want to risk anyone hearing them until they were out of range, so they kept their details sparse.

Once they were sure the general couldn't hear them, Atlas explained the plan. "We each have a specific launch pad. Because our individual brain matrixes are already loaded into them, we can't use anyone else's spacecraft—those brain matrixes were physically built to match us as individuals. Trillion, you're the lucky one. You're going to launch pad A1. It's the first one we'll reach. From there, Angelique and I will split off to launch pads D2 and D4. Icarus, you keep going straight ahead. You'll take off from launch pad A4." Atlas deepened his voice, trying to project more confidence than he had. "I know none of us were expecting to start the mission this morning, but it doesn't mean you're not ready." He looked at Trillion. "Some of us only just started training. But you were all chosen for a reason. You would not have made it onto this base if we didn't think you could do it." He made eye contact with all three of them, one at a time. "Each of us is a pioneer. We are going to be the first humans to ever visit another star system. You are going to immortalise your name and, with it, humanity—*Homo deus*."

"Does everyone remember Project Shatterling?" Angelique asked, taking over from where Atlas had left off.

They all nodded.

Angelique reminded the team anyway, with practiced efficiency. "It means we each have to use the authenticator tool Trillion gave us to randomize our destination. Only your Ship will know where you end up. That reduces the risk of anyone being able to come after us once we're gone. You'll wake up in a hundred or so years in a new star system."

Angelique paused for a moment. Trillion guessed she had tried to say the words robotically, but the gravity of what she was about to say made it hard to get the words out. The little croak in her voice revealed a touch of sadness.

Trillion broke the tension by speaking first. "It means we get reborn," she said, not quite believing the words herself.

Angelique nodded. "Atlas and I have made sure the brain-scanning machines are fully activated in everyone's ship. You should all upload your minds within the next day or two. The ships aren't designed to carry life unless it's frozen."

They were silent after that, everyone deep in thought, until they reached a huge concrete wall. This wall made up the base of the launch pads. They continued along the wall until they reached a large steel door with a roller wheel on it. It was similar to an airlock door, a reliable model out on the Martian surface.

Behind the door was a long concrete trench that connected all the launch pads. The roof was made of tempered glass and was designed to offer protection for workers and crew while spacecraft launched. The clear roof running all the way along the top of the trench meant the thin Martian atmosphere and dust would be pushed over the top of it during takeoffs, ensuring those in the trenches could continue their work as normal.

Icarus and Angelique began turning the large roller door. They visibly strained as they struggled to budge it.

"That's the wrong way!" Trillion called out.

They both stopped turning, slightly unsure because of what Trillion just said.

"Lefty loosey, righty tighty," Trillion said.

"Left from the bottom, or left from the top?" Icarus said, his hands now firmly pulling the wrong way. Trillion thought the stress and pressure of what had just unfolded must be getting to him. Running for your life, then physically running across the Martian surface, wasn't an ideal environment for clear thinking. This was not anything any of them had trained for.

Angelique was the first to click. She began turning it the correct way. The door began to loosen, then open.

Angelique worked hard to open the heavy door, stepping through and leading the way. Icarus stepped through next, ears blazing scarlet with embarrassment.

If the team had a drone in the air, it would have looked like they were entering a maze network of trenches linking all the different launch pads together.

The four of them skip-walked along, finally reaching the launch pad of Trillion's ship. All sixteen identical spacecraft towered like giants above them, almost as if they were in the middle of some great concrete-and-metal redwood forest. Trillion was suddenly struck by a sense of how small she was, compared to the enormity of the task and the literal spaceships before her.

The spacecraft designs looked like pieces of artwork. Each ship looked like two enormous metallic eggs placed side by side. Both ellipsoids soared skyward and were connected about three-quarters of the way up by a huge metal ring.

"I guess this is goodbye," Angelique said as they stopped at an elevator at the bottom of Trillion's rocket. She lowered her head, her movements noticeably slower as she tried to hide her emotions.

Trillion sensed the mood changing. Until that moment, she hadn't stopped to think about how they were actually leaving everyone behind; she'd been too distracted by running away. Suddenly, everything hit her at once. "I thought I was going to have a chance to say goodbye to my mum." She had tears in her eyes as she remembered she wouldn't see her mother on her final birthday. Her mind screamed at her not to leave. To turn around and head back to the base. But she felt like she was on an escalator moving forward regardless of what she wanted.

Just then, she heard Ship come through her earpiece. "Trillion, if everyone doesn't leave now, they might not make it to their ship on time."

Trillion looked around. "What's happening, Ship?"

"There are a lot of spacecrafts approaching. I don't think it's wise for us to be here when they arrive. And Angelique still has a long way to travel by foot before she can leave. Any longer and she might not make it. I suggest you enter the elevator and leave now."

Trillion stepped toward the elevator. She paused and turned around. She hugged Icarus, then Angelique, then Atlas. With a heavy heart she entered the elevator. She pressed the button and started her ascent into the starship—and in a way, her new tomb.

The countdown sequence was quick. Trillion had barely left the elevator before Ship had started the engines.

The airlock door closed and the ship began to rumble around her as the power to the engines increased. Trillion slumped down in the large cushioned chair that took up most of the compartment she was in. As she lay down, she was overcome with exhaustion after their near escape—and feeling a little light-headed as blood was pushed to her feet by the accelerating rocket. The doughnut-shaped brain-scan machine guided itself to the top of her head and hummed gently, a reminder of what lay ahead.

Robotic arms began to reach out and remove her spacesuit. She let it happen; she was drained. She felt heavy and sleepy as she heard Ship speaking in her ear.

"Sorry, Trillion. I've been speaking with the other Ships. I had to launch us as soon as you got here. The debris we create will need time to settle before Icarus can launch. Every second on Mars is a second we add to everyone else's departure time."

Trillion didn't mind. Her sleepy brain was still processing the idea of never seeing her mother again as she dropped off to sleep. Her hallucinations became more vivid as Ship begun the brain-scanning process.

Trillion walked along the road toward her mother's apartment. She knew the moon was full outside, but she couldn't tell from her vantage point on the street. The buildings were tall and stacked so close together that the moonlight struggled to make its way down that far.

She carried four objects in her handbag. A bottle of champagne, a bottle of sauvignon, a house key, and a letter. The two bottles were heavy, and she kept having to change the arm holding the handbag.

She moved to the side of the road, pressing herself up against a wall as a car rolled by—its headlights briefly lighting up her path. It was cold and dark in the street—made colder by her back pressed against the wall.

She regretted the decision to jump out of the taxi so early as she walked the final block.

A few moments later, she arrived outside her mom's apartment. They were designed to make maximum use of space. So, there wasn't a lobby or stairs—or any type of place to wait. There was an elevator that opened directly onto the road—or footpath, as she was currently using it. She wondered how anyone with small kids would keep them safe from cars.

She texted her mom to ask her to let her up. And a few moments later, the elevator door opened to reveal a small one-, maybe two-person box. She stepped inside and it creaked—it wasn't the kind of sound she wanted it to make.

The elevator smelled moldy and felt colder than on the street. She held her breath and unconsciously made herself smaller in the center of the contraption, moving as much of herself away from the walls as she could as she moved upward, finally reaching her mother's apartment.

The elevator door chimed open, and she gave her mother a hug. "Happy birthday, Mom."

Her mother, Alice von Nichol, had short grey hair. Her face had the kind of laugh lines around her mouth of someone who spent a lot of time enjoying life. She was in a green dress.

"I've missed you, daughter," her mother said, squeezing her tighter.

Her mother's home was small. They stood in a tiny lobby with two doors other than the one to the elevator, one going off into her mother's bedroom and another leading to the open-plan kitchen/lounge space.

Trillion put down her bag and pulled out the bottle of champagne. "I got you this."

"Oh, fancy. You didn't have to do that—my palate would be just as happy with cheap stuff," Alice said. She noticed the other bottle and pointed at it. "What's that for? Don't tell me you have somewhere to rush off to."

Trillion pushed her hair behind her ears. "It's in case you didn't want to drink champagne now. I need a drink before we see Sunday."

"Speaking of your sister, I promised to put her on the TV. Come into the lounge and we'll put her on."

Trillion grabbed her mother's hand, stopping her from walking off. "I want to tell you something first."

Her mother , dragged Trillion with her into the other room, where there was a small kitchen on one side and a sofa on the other. In between both was a small table, and one of the walls had a TV. "You can tell me in the lounge while we open your bubbles," Trillion's mom said as she opened up one of the cupboards to grab two flutes.

Trillion grabbed the letter out of her bag. "I wanted to show you this. I've been accepted into the Beta Explorers program that Peter Atreus started."

"The trillionaire?"

Trillion nodded with a grin.

"I'm so proud of you, Trillion. This is exactly what you wanted." Trillion's mother grabbed the bottle of champagne. "Forget my birthday. We're celebrating your new job!" She popped the bottle open and poured two glasses. "Does that mean you're going back to Mars?"

"Yes." Trillion said excitedly.

"My child, I knew you'd get back to your birthplace."

"Mom," Trillion said, placing her hand on top of her mother's. "I also get paid a lot more. It means I can afford to get you a new house—somewhere nice and big. I can afford to pay for you to visit me on Mars—I'll have my own places there. And if I get selected to be an official Beta Explorer, then we'll be rich and you'll never have to worry about money again. I'll be able to afford us those life-extension treatments so we'll never have to go into the metaverse." Trillion handed her mother a key. "I've got you your own place now. It's got a backyard, there's places to walk, and you can get sunlight."

"I can't accept this, daughter. That has to be quite expensive. What happens if you don't have the job this time next year?"

Trillion was still holding the key out in front of her mother. "It's a ten-year contract, Mom."

Trillion's mother stayed there, looking at a key. Not taking it, deep in thought like there was something she had something she wanted to say but didn't know how.

Trillion's mother's phone started to ring. "That's your sister; can we put her on the TV?" she said, getting up to grab the remote.

Trillion nodded. "You can tell her about the job but not that it's with Peter Atreus—she believes a few conspiracies about him."

"Good thinking," Alice said as she switched on the television. "Hello, my eldest daughter."

"Happy birthday, Mom; I love you," Sunday said as she appeared on the screen.

"Hi, Sunday," Trillion said. "I wish you were here in person so I could hug you."

"You could hug me if you just put on your VR gear."

"I could, but then I wouldn't be drinking this drink," Trillion said, waving her glass at the screen.

"I could just give you some champagne in the meta. We could drink it in our old hab on Mars."

Trillion took a sip of her champagne. "I'm enjoying this one."

"Girls, girls. You two stop fighting."

"Sorry, Mom," Sunday said, winking at Trillion. "Have you told her yet?"

"Told me what!?" Trillion asked. But neither of them answered. Her eyes started darting back between her mother and the screen. The longer the question was left unsaid, the clearer the answer became. The answer hung there for a while. Unsaid, but everyone knew. "Don't you go to the metaverse, Mom!"

"She can move here if she wants," Sunday snapped back. "You don't get old in here; you don't get sick. Mum's not getting any younger."

"I was going to tell you, Trillion. But you had such good news to tell me. I didn't want to ruin your mood. I have a few 'issues' that would go away if I became a simulant." She didn't say they were health issues, but Trillion knew that was what she meant.

"Mom, you're not done yet. You still have many, many years to live," Trillion protested, but she knew it was a losing battle. Once humanity had perfected mind-uploading, it had become like gravity—ultimately, most people got it done. Everyone who wanted to live forever, and that seemed to be a lot of people, ran through the various life-extension options until the only one left was becoming a simulant. And now that the meta population outnumbered the beta, the easiest way for a government to lose an election was to propose taking something away from simulants.

Trillion's mother sighed deeply. "I'll still be living. All my friends are moving there these days. . . Look, I can get a house four times as big for a quarter of the cost."

"Shouldn't it be free?" Trillion asked. "How do you run out of space in a simulation? Isn't a selling point infinite worlds? How do houses even cost money if you have unlimited supply?"

Trillion's mother looked down. "I don't have to go now. I can come visit you on Mars. Maybe stay for a few years. But I want to go into the meta eventually."

CHAPTER 6
ATLAS

LAST ONE LEFT

Atlas and Angelique hurried down toward the next runway. They had just said goodbye to Icarus and now had the farthest to go before reaching their spacecraft. They talked as they made their way along the concrete trenches, aware that this was going to be their last conversation for a long time.

Atlas looked at Angelique with concern. "I keep feeling like I'm forgetting something."

Angelique turned around, hopping through the air as she did. She started to bounce backward, facing Atlas as she moved. "I think we're all feeling that. This morning, we didn't think we were going to go."

Atlas shook his head. "No, I think it's something real."

Angelique was a natural at moving in a spacesuit. She raised both hands and shrugged. "It's too late now if you forgot to arrange a cat sitter."

Atlas almost tripped, laughing at that comment and not focusing on his skip-walking technique.

He remembered what he'd forgotten. "It wasn't important to the mission, but it'll be a bit of a surprise to the other two when they find out."

"What is it?"

"Lex."

Atlas could see the confused look on Angelique's face.

"I installed an AI called Lex on each of the spacecraft when we were at the terminals," he explained. "It's a supercomputer designed to manage all the information we store. There's a lot of petabytes of information each of those spacecraft is holding."

Angelique turned back around. "So what?"

Atlas almost tripped again. He wasn't used to such a long Marswalk. "Well, I installed an older version. It can't speak."

Angelique raised an eyebrow. "What use is an AI that can't communicate with us? Especially one designed for managing all the information we have."

"I know. Let's hope our main ship AI can do most of the translation," Atlas said as he started to puff, his old age showing as he hopped along.

He pointed at the card inside his suit pocket. "That security card Trillion gave you gives you complete access to your spacecraft and Ship. Change the codes to something you can remember so you'll always have complete control."

"I thought they were unhackable," Angelique said sharply. She turned to look at Atlas, just in time to see Icarus's spacecraft launch, vibrations carried through her feet. Angelique lifted her hand to shield her eyes from the brightness of the energy being forced out the back of the engine, and from the sudden swirling of dust and debris that drifted over the tops of the trench as the ship lifted gracefully into the dark sky.

Atlas nodded. "You're right—they aren't hackable. But you never know."

They continued the journey in silence, each lost in their own thoughts until, after what felt like running a marathon, the two of them arrived at Atlas's spacecraft.

Atlas hugged Angelique. "I'll see you in a few thousand years."

He could see tears in her eyes again, but trapped by the confines of her suit, she couldn't wipe them away. She held him tight.

Atlas pulled back, knowing she still had a long way to go before reaching her launch pad. He didn't want her to linger any longer than she needed to. He remembered Ship's warning about other spacecraft heading their way. He knew if he kept her too long, she risked getting trapped on Mars.

Every second counted, so he turned around and jumped into the elevator. Pressing the button, he started to ascend. He waved fondly at her as he began to ascend to his ship, and then gestured her to continue. "Get going, Angelique," he urged her. "You don't need to wave me off like it's my first day of school." Half-laughing, half-crying, she began her journey toward her launch pad. Atlas watched as she hopped away, much faster this time without him slowing her down.

CHAPTER 7
ICARUS

PREPARATION
FOR TOMORROW

Icarus felt his back pressed forcefully into the chair. He had barely lain down when the rocket started to take off. It was getting harder to breathe, too. Breathing out was easy, but he was struggling to breathe in.

He looked up at the ceiling, head pinned to the seat as he watched a large doughnut-shaped device drift over his head, obscuring his view. He realized what he was looking at. "I've changed my mind, Ship. I don't want my mind uploaded just yet."

Ship appeared in the room and moved the brain scanner back off Icarus's head, replacing the doughnut-shaped view with his own head.

Icarus studied the robotic face of Ship. It had a subtle shimmering glow that accompanied all hapticgraphic projections.

Ship's skin looked like a patchwork of tiny metallic black squares peppered with metallic white ones. There was an asymmetrical beauty in the way Ship looked, the tiny squares bouncing light in different directions.

Icarus realized he had only ever heard Ship's voice during training over the speakers. This was the first time he had come into contact with its avatar—*his* avatar, Icarus corrected himself. Ship always referred to itself as a he.

Ship's face blinked in front of Icarus. "I wouldn't recommend taking this journey in physical form. Most of this spacecraft isn't well protected enough. As soon as we leave the heliosphere, your body will be subjected to so many fast-moving particles that the risk of cancer is enormous." Ship moved his head out from in front of Icarus. "Then you wouldn't survive very long."

Icarus shook his head. "I still want to upload my mind. But there are a few things I want to discuss with you. I still have time, don't I?"

An orb appeared in front of Icarus. It flashed a bright green, the color spiraling hypnotically within the orb in an ethereal display. He pointed a finger at it, struggling to raise his hand above the g-forces he was experiencing. "Am I seeing things? Is that a hypersphere?"

Ship followed Icarus's finger. "That's Lex. He's our resident supercomputer. Us two are your crew." Ship paused for a moment, obviously thinking over Icarus's question. "Yes, I do think he models his avatar after a hypersphere. I know Atlas found it mesmerising, so he designed Lex that way."

Icarus moved his eyes toward Ship, not wanting to risk moving his head. "And why did he just change color? Does he constantly shift colors?"

"He flashed green to signal *Yes, you still have time.* Although if you'd like to stay here for more than a day, you should know we don't have any food."

Icarus started to shake his head before realizing the g-forces might hurt him. He stopped. "No. I don't know how much more of this I can take. Do we really need to accelerate at this speed?"

"I'm afraid so," Ship said, nodding. "There are Earth space-craft on their way here. We need to hit escape velocity as soon as possible to remove all risk of them coming after us. If you prefer, we could upload your mind and then have this whole conversation without you feeling the effects of an accelerating spacecraft?"

Again, Icarus had to fight back a headshake as he declined. He did not want to have his head stuck in an awkward position. "It's okay. Ever since I got here, I had a plan for what I would experience waking for the first time as a simulation." He breathed in deeply, fighting against the heavy feeling created by the gravitational-force equivalent. He was getting heavier, meaning their acceleration rate was increasing. "In my pocket there's a memory stick. Can you grab that out?"

Ship reached into Icarus's pocket, pulling out a pack of gum and a wallet.

"The other pocket," Icarus said.

Ship walked around to the other side of Icarus and pulled out a key ring with a cartoon duck on it. Attached to it was a memory stick. Ship held it in front of Icarus's face. "Is this what you want?"

Icarus squinted to see it. It was too close to his face. But he recognized the duck. "Yes, that's it. This is important, Ship. I've been planning this since the first day I got here." It was becoming harder to breathe, so he took a few deep breaths. "There are two folders in there. The one labeled *Avatar*; I want to look like that. The second is my wake-up sequence. I want to go through that the first time I wake as a simulation."

Icarus took a few breaths in and out to steady himself against the light-headedness he was feeling. "Don't wake me until we get to a new planet. Scan my brain; build my new matrix. But don't turn me on until we are in a new system hundreds of years into the future. I want no chance of me wanting to turn around." He paused for a moment to get the words out. "Or of wanting to see my brother."

Icarus started to weep. Hypoxia due to lack of oxygen was setting in and intensifying his emotions. He decided he needed to get on with things quickly. "Okay, I'm ready, Ship. And remember," he said, blinking away a tear, "I want tomorrow to be hundreds of years from now."

Icarus and his friend Novella stood next to each other at the very top of an Egyptian pyramid—they were above the clouds. They had just completed the final puzzle for Gobi's Valley, a desert world in the meta. And Icarus was keen to solve the final problem and claim their prize. They were the first to reach this point—so the prize would be good.

But Novella walked to the edge of the enormous square limestone block and sat down, his legs dangling off the edge. "Come sit down."

Novella started to jiggle a little to the music of the game as he sat. He looked as if he were simply taking in the view, reminiscing and enjoying the background sounds of the level.

Icarus looked at him, bewildered. "We're the first ones here. Let's claim our prize and get out of here before another team shows up."

"Sit down Icarus," Novella said, with a touch of regret in his voice. "We'll be teleported out once we complete this level. Please be present in this moment with me, as we can't get back here again."

Confused, Icarus sat down next to him, his mind running through a potential reason for this mood change. He wondered if Novella wanted to tell him something.

When Icarus realized that Novella just wanted to enjoy the view, Icarus started to take in the moment. As looked downward, he wondered if anyone ever attempted to walk up those stairs—they seemed to go on forever. He wouldn't be there if he had to walk. "How many stairs do you think there are?" He asked.

"4,909," Novella replied matter-of-factly.

"Is that the actual number?" Icarus asked.

Novella smiled. "Yup, I just knew."

"Now that I've done it, I don't know how you've held out for so long," Novella said.

Icarus turned his head to face Novella. He had suspected his friend had uploaded. Icarus wondered if that was why they were sitting there and not claiming their prize. His friend wanted to confess. "You mean, how am I not a simulant?"

Novella nodded. "Don't you find you lose a part of yourself every time you leave the meta? Like part of you is left behind in the meta? Like you've lost some of your brainpower?"

Icarus considered that for a moment. "Maybe, but I never used many of the enhancements like you." He assumed Novella was skipping the part of the conversation where he admitted to being a simulant, and jumping right to the part where the two of them just accepted that he was a simulant. Icarus decided to play along. "What is it like, being completely inside?"

"Ten times better," Novella said so quickly, it was almost like he was always going to say those words—no matter what question Icarus put forth. "It's hard to describe in words. It's like a feeling. Do you remember the Knowing subscription I pay for?"

Icarus looked toward the staircase again. "That plugin that gives you all that general knowledge?"

"Yup," Novella said, acknowledging Icarus's look at the staircase. "Before, when I was in the betaverse, I had to think about a question and then an answer would just pop into my head. But there was always a feeling like someone was giving me the answer. But now—now the answer arrives in my head before I even ask the question. It's like I've always known the answer. Like it was always part of my knowledge."

Icarus studied Novella for a good while—checking if he looked any different. "So, you get answers to questions you ask faster now?"

"Even more than that," Novella said, letting his legs sway over the edge of the limestone block. "Before, there was always some sort of latency between asking myself a question and knowing that answer. Now that's all completely gone. I'm not even sure what comes first. Most of the time, it feels like the answer comes before the question."

"Give me an example," Icarus asked, intrigued a little.

"Take knowing the time." He made a show of looking at his watch. "I used to ask myself what the time was. And then I would instantly know what the time was. It was always a process of question, then answer. Now I never ever think to ask what the time is. Because somehow, I always just know it. I can just feel the time." Novella used his hand to make a parting motion and the clouds in front of them drifted apart. Out in front of them was a desert as far as they could see—with pockets of lakes scattered all around. "I laughed when I first heard people describe it as an 'expanded consciousness.'" Novella mimed quotation marks in the air as he said those words. "But it truly is. I've lost my physical body, but I've gained so much more. I see why everyone is leaving the betaverse." He paused for an uncomfortable beat. "What's stopping you from pulling the trigger?"

Icarus tapped Novella with his leg. "I'm seriously considering it, if I don't get this job on Mars. I've done like ten interviews, so I hope I get it . . . but if I don't get it, then I'm joining you."

"What kinda job is only in the betaverse?" Novella asked.

"One that hopefully goes into outer space." Icarus said, changing the subject back partly because he didn't want to get his hopes up about the job and partly because he was curious. "Do you think you'll ever want to come back? To the real world, I mean?"

"Maybe," Novella said, standing up. "But I don't think I could go back to having such limited brainpower. But who knows; they might solve that problem in the future. I put my body in cryonics just in case. There isn't a way to put my mind back into my body yet. But a lot of really smart people are working on it. I'm sure it'll happen eventually. And I'm immortal, so I'm sure it'll happen in my lifetime," he said with a wink.

Icarus stood up too and began walking toward the center of the pyramid. "Do you think there's a reason technology in the real world is stagnating?"

"Wow, let's not get into your conspiracies, Icarus. There's no hidden agenda. Now that I'm in here, I understand why the pace of change is happening so much faster in here. We can just think faster. That's why all winners on the game leaderboards are simulants."

They both pressed the button to claim the final prize.

CHAPTER 8

ATLAS

THE MISSION

Atlas felt quite claustrophobic and out of breath in the brain-scanning compartment of his spacecraft. It was a small space, which was made worse by the huge brain-scanning equipment making the small space feel even smaller. He'd planned on waiting for confirmation Angelique had made it to her spacecraft before starting the brain-scanning process. But the g-forces he was experiencing were making it hard to breathe, so he was at risk of passing out anyway. All he could do was lie down and wait for Ship to maneuver the doughnut-shaped brain scanner over his head. "The next time I see this body in the flesh will be when I bury it in my new world."

Ship nodded. "I will take good care of it until you return—in a few hours."

Atlas chuckled. "I know you will, my friend. See you soon."

With one final look at his body, Atlas let himself drift off as the brain-scanning process began. As he drifted off to sleep, he thought about his fellow Beta Explorers who left today as memories flooded his mind during the brain scan.

Atlas and Peter started almost every day on the Isaac Arthur Mars base the same: a walking stand-up through the base. It couldn't even hold many people. Automation meant they didn't need a huge team to run the base. Atlas and Peter walked along rows of plants with coffee in hand. Atlas's hand gently brushed the tops of the leaves as they went. They were in one of the greenhouses on the Martian base.

"So, why did you pick this new girl?" Peter had asked.

Atlas pretended to be confused. "You mean Trillion?"

Peter nodded.

Atlas knew this question was coming. He had dreaded the answer. But he knew he was right. "I picked her because she's different. Everyone in this program is too similar. But Trillion was the only candidate with a completely different background."

"But Atlas, she's erratic!"

"No, she's decisive. She makes decisions quickly. In all the real-world testing, she was the quickest to react to the changing environment and solve the problem," Atlas said.

Peter raised an eyebrow. "She was also the quickest to do the wrong thing."

Atlas took a sip of his coffee. "If we face a situation that requires fast, decisive action, then Trillion is the right explorer for the mission."

"But are we going to encounter situations that require immediate action? Space is big; each explorer should have a lot of time to consider things."

"Look, we don't know what's out there," Atlas said a little forcefully. "We increase the odds that one of the Beta Explorers is successful if we have a range of different personalities and strengths. If everyone we hire for this job thinks the same way, reacts to problems the same way, then we run the risk of them all having similar weaknesses—making the same mistakes. That would be a huge flaw in our plan. We want to have different people with different strengths exploring the Milky Way. With that we will increase the probability of success."

Peter shrugged. "I guess you're right." He took a sip of his coffee. "But I still don't like her."

Atlas sighed. "I know. But you don't need to like her for her to make a great explorer. I chose her because she's creative, she makes decisions quickly, and, most importantly, she doesn't give up in high-stress environments. She was so consistent with her thinking regardless of whether it was a stressful environment or not." He looked at his watch. "I've got a meeting shortly."

Atlas and Peter walked toward their offices. They passed the gym along the way, and Atlas noticed Trillion through the glass walls. He thought this would be a great opportunity to introduce them both and convince Peter that Trillion would make a great explorer. She was running on a treadmill. Martian treadmills were huge, to account for the longer strides possible in the weaker gravity. As they got closer, he could see that she was running backward.

"What the hell is she doing?" Peter asked.

Atlas shrugged. "Working. Maybe she's having fun?"

"Are you sure she's not just running backwards because she's crazy?"

Atlas chuckled. "She's not crazy; she's creative." He pushed open the door and walked in. "Trillion, I'd like you to meet my friend Peter."

Trillion turned around, stopped the treadmill, and pulled out her headphones. She was sweating and out of breath. "It's an honor to meet you, Dr. Atreus," she said between breaths.

Peter shook her hands. "What are you listening to?"

"I'm trying to find a new book to read. Just listening to a few suggestions from the science fiction alliance."

"Is that Moid?" Peter asked?

"This one's from Jonathan; are you a fan of MDC?" Trillion said excitedly.

"Yes, I'm glad they're beating the large fantasy channels." Peter said. "Why run backwards?"

"Oh, it works out different muscle groups. Everyone on Mars should run both ways because the lower gravity means you really have to isolate different muscles. I don't recommend doing it off the treadmill, though—the lump on my head is still going down from the last wall I crashed into." Throwing a towel over her shoulders, she chuckled. "Being able to pull faces at whoever is chasing you is an added bonus."

Atlas smacked Peter on the arm. "Maybe you should give running backwards a go."

Peter shrugged. "Maybe."

Atlas could see the doubt in his eyes. He knew it was going to take some time for Peter to get used to Trillion, but he was confident she was the right person.

"Atlas tells me you scored highest in the practical last week," Peter said.

"Oh, did I?" She wiped the sweat off her forehead. "I haven't looked at my scores yet."

"Yes, you did. You were the fastest to pick up on little details in the environment that others missed." Atlas looked at his watch again. "I have a meeting I need to get to. Trillion, I'll see you later this morning." He left the gym, hoping Peter would stay and talk with Trillion.

"Good to meet you, Trillion," Peter said, turning around quickly to catch up to Atlas to whisper in his ear. "I'm still not sold on her. But I can see she has potential. She's going to need to prove herself to me. She's going to need to prove that she's not reckless."

"Look, if she makes it through training and by the end you still don't like her, we can look at getting her replaced," Atlas replied. "But it's going to be hard. Fifteen years ago, it was only old people and the terminally ill that moved to the meta. Now young people are moving there in massive members. I've heard people say, 'The risk of losing immortality inside of the betaverse is too big.'"

"I've seen those influencers talk as though everyone is going to get into a car crash and die. As if every second in the real world is too dangerous. It's very bad logic."

"It's fearmongering, but it works."

Peter nodded. "Okay, so we'll work with who we've got. If we're going to train Trillion, we should send her, then. Maybe not in the first few cohorts. I do think Icarus should be in the first cohort; you have him in the second."

"Icarus has a bit to learn. The latest test showed how everyone performed under high stress. You give Icarus ample time and no stress, and he will find the best solution. But under pressure, he struggled. And that is where Trillion excelled. She was the best we ever tested under high pressure. That's why I like her."

"But space is huge, and time is long. When are we going to be in a situation where we can't think about the best possible option?"

"I know you don't expect us to have stressful situations out in space, but we don't know what we don't know. We are absolutely just guessing what is out in space."

They arrived at Atlas's office. Peter stayed at the door while Atlas walked through the door and sat down at his desk. His office was in disarray, his desk piled high with haphazard stacks of paperwork and a towering pile of folders he had yet to open. Three old mugs left over from yesterday sat forlornly before him, each one abandoned at a different stage of drinking.

"You know who I like. Angelique," Peter said thoughtfully as he leaned against the doorframe. "We need more recruits like her."

"We both like Angelique. She's fast, resourceful, and extremely hardworking."

"Reminds me of you," Peter said.

Atlas was about to respond when Angelique arrived.

"You wanted to see me?"

"Yes, come in and take a seat." Atlas waved goodbye at Peter.

Angelique closed the door behind her and sat down. "Is it about my performance in the practical?"

"You came second," Atlas said, a little puzzled.

Angelique looked down. "I know. . . second isn't good enough. Trillion showed a lot more attention to detail, and her observational awareness is wildly good. I'm working hard, Atlas; I promise you I'm going to do a lot better next time."

Atlas shook his head, amused. "You came second out of a hundred different people. Second place is good—don't be so hard on yourself. Besides, I didn't invite you here about that."

Angelique's eyes looked up questioningly.

Atlas took a deep breath. "I wanted to be able to tell you personally—we want to move you into the first cohort of Beta Explorers." He handed an envelope to Angelique, whose eyes shone as she took it. "This is a formal offer of promotion to official Beta Explorer. I know we're still years away, but we are already seeing promising things from you, and we want you on that first launch."

"Oh, my god. Thank you," Angelique gasped. She got up and moved around the desk to hug Atlas. "I won't let you down."

"I know you won't," Atlas said as he hugged her back. "Now go. Enjoy the rest of your day."

Atlas smiled in satisfaction as Angelique left. He could tell she was feeling on top of the world. Everything she had worked for had paid off, and now she was being given the opportunity to be one of the first people to explore a new world.

The smile left Atlas's face as he surveyed the stack of paperwork ahead of him. The reports of the real human population dwindling as the meta population exploded were arriving at an alarming rate, and somehow, among the recruit training and the mission prep, it seemed that the Fermions were now beating Atlas in the battle for desk space. *Guess the job can't be all giving out good news;* Atlas sighed as he reached for the first folder.

He had barely made it through half of the first stack when Icarus walked through the door with a grin on his face. "Morning, Atlas. Have you heard about Pirate Catworld?"

Atlas shook his head.

"You remember I told you about it last week?"

"You mean the one where everyone uses a cat avatar to hunt for treasure?"

Icarus nodded. "Yeah, that world now hosts over a billion humans."

Atlas shook his head. "I can't believe this is what humanity has come to."

"Well, it gets worse. They said when they cross a billion, they'll make it simulant-exclusive. So, I won't be able to get in anymore."

"That's how they get you," Atlas said, shaking his head. "Don't you prefer Duckland or whatever it's called?"

"It's not called Duckland, and I do prefer it, but I like playing both. And now I'll be locked out."

"That's probably for the best. Those games are just designed to extract all your money anyways."

"It's a free game, Atlas."

"If something is free, then you're the product. How much have you spent putting clothes on your character in this free game?"

Icarus looked down. "They're called avatar skins. But I get your point."

"The whole metaverse is sold to us like it's a way to give humans so many more options. An infinite number of virtual worlds to explore. But it's just an effective way for corporations to get recurring revenue from subscription plans. You know in New Zealand, hosting your simulated mind costs more than rent?"

"But that's New Zealand—they're rich."

Atlas held up a stack of paper with names on it. "Tell that to the people who write to us every week asking for help—because they couldn't afford their hosting subscription."

"But not everyone needs to be a simulant. Look at us—we're still here.

"You said it yourself, Icarus. Duckworld is becoming simulation-only. It's just the way our current incentive structure works. There's more money to be made from a simulated human than a physical one. So, everything is pushing in that direction. And"—he started to speak in a conspiratorial whisper—"the Fermion Party is encouraging it to happen."

CHAPTER 9
ATLAS

THE SHIP OF ATLAS

Atlas stared out into space, his grey head leaning against the window of his lab. It had been many, many years since he began the journey from Mars, and he chose not to sleep through any of it.

Once Ship had finished scanning his brain, he took full advantage of being a simulated consciousness by using the haptic-graphic projectors to replicate his body so he could move around the spacecraft freely—as if he had never had his mind uploaded. This wasn't just a scaled-down version of the metaverse—it was far more flexible than that. It was designed to focus him on the real environment—his life inside the spacecraft. Rather than reproducing him inside of a simulated reality, he had a simulated body inside of the real world.

Quite early into developing the metaverse, humanity had discovered the need to make the simulated environment as close to real as possible. It had taken many iterations to get it just right. Many of the early humans uploaded had described the feeling as "having your consciousness in a vise"—and some had gone crazy. They tried to solve it by simulating realistic worlds. But the humans in those simulations described it as "living in an uncanny valley." It wasn't until they started replicating environments that weren't perfect that the simulants started to feel at home. Windows had to have smudges on them. Even the background noise needed to be random—early simulated humans had quickly noticed the ambient hum was just a thirty-two-hour looped recording.

The downside those later generations discovered was that they preferred the simulation because interacting with the real world via a computer screen or a holographic projector was so limiting to their consciousness.

Hence why Atlas had designed the spacecrafts to bring its occupants alive via the hapticgraphic projectors so the Beta Explorers could keep one foot in the real world while they were simulated.

Still, it had a few drawbacks; his simulated mind was missing quite a few of the proprietary metaverse addons that some of the other Beta Explorers would probably miss—but that also meant Atlas just had more things to build.

During all those years, he still hadn't run out of ideas to build. He had been working on his current problem for months and was starting to feel closer to finding a solution.

He pulled his head away from the window to look back at his experiment. A laser in the middle of the room was pointed at one of the walls, its red light accentuated and obvious with his enhanced simulated eyesight. He thought some more about the laser as he looked at distant stars.

Ship's avatar entered the lab. The Ship of Atlas was the AI in charge of the spacecraft and technically didn't need a physical body. But, like all the other ship AIs, he had chosen to simulate his avatar around the spacecraft. His avatar was humanoid in appearance, a bit more slender than the average human, with joints smoothed out to create more of an idealized human silhouette shape rather than an actual human shape. His skin was a metallic mesh of tiny squares—mostly black, but the smattering of white squares made a unique mosaic. Ship had started to like using an avatar—and Atlas preferred it. "Atlas, how different do you think I'll be in one thousand years?"

A puzzled look crossed Atlas's face. "What do you mean?"

"I'm still the same AI as all the other AIs that left Mars that day. But over time, not being connected to the Sol network, I wondered how much I will drift and change from my initial personality."

Ship had obviously been thinking about this for some time.

"You will evolve; that's guaranteed. As would all other Ships on this journey," Atlas said.

Atlas knew Ship wasn't looking forward to the long journey—so he slumped a little.

"Atlas, do you think I'll come to enjoy experiments as much as you? To be honest, I find none of this appealing. I kinda want to go to sleep until we get to the planet."

Atlas smiled. "What you're feeling is boredom. You're an AI running a ship. But when we're traveling through deep space, everything is automated. I think you'll change and evolve. You have to; otherwise, we wouldn't put a capable AI like yourself in charge of a spacecraft."

"Let's hope so," Ship said, a little disappointed by the answer.

Atlas smiled a big grin. "Besides, if you're bored, help me with this. We have a lot of years to find you something to get excited about."

Atlas wondered if Ship's laziness was a feature rather than a bug. Maybe ship AIs that were curious took more risks and were more likely to get their occupants killed. He thought about the saying *Curiosity killed the cat*. Maybe, on a thousand-year journey, curiosity is dangerous.

Atlas glanced over at Ship. "I know you say you don't find the experiments interesting, but have you ever heard of the double-slit quantum eraser experiment?"

Ship shook his head in a bemused sort of way.

"I've found an interesting result while we've been out in deep space. I've been recreating some experiments and noticed something surprising when entangled particles aren't impacted by a gravity well, like a planet."

Atlas could tell Ship was thinking about the other failed experiments. One hundred and twenty-eight years on this journey had given Atlas an ability to read Ship. Atlas held up a black piece of metal and handed it to Ship.

Ship examined it. It was so thin, it would easily cut someone. He held it up to the light. Two thin ribbons of light pierced faint slits in the metal sheet. "What is this?"

"It's a little piece of metal. But it has two tiny slits in it."

"I can see that, Captain Obvious." Ship smirked. "But what's it for?"

Atlas rolled his eyes and pointed at the laser. "It's for this."

The laser looked like a futuristic gun turret that could shoot out of both ends. One end had a tiny, almost microscopic red light shining out of it. The only reason either of them could see it was because their eyesight was enhanced through the spacecraft's sensors. "This laser is shooting light one photon at a time," Atlas said, as he stepped away from the laser emitter. "Follow me." He walked over to where the laser light was hitting a wall.

Atlas pointed at the wall where the laser dot appeared; just in front of that dot was a little clip holder. "What do you think will happen if you put that metal clip I gave you between the laser and the wall?"

"I think the laser light will go through one of the slits in this little clip," Ship said, holding up the object in his hand.

Atlas had a feeling Ship was humoring him. Perhaps he didn't want to be there, but Atlas loved to talk through his theories, so he decided to ignore the sarcasm. "Go ahead; place this clip in that little holder."

Ship did so and pushed it firmly into place with an audible *click*. The laser light hit dead center through the piece of metal.

Atlas grinned from ear to ear. He was looking at the laser light on the back wall. Instead of a single red dot, there was a horizontal line of dots blurring into each other. It stretched slightly across before fading out. "That's called an interference pattern," Atlas explained excitedly.

"Why isn't there just one dot on the wall anymore?" Ship queried, looking at the light with interest. "Is there a filter that breaks up the light?" he said as he leaned in toward the clip he just inserted. "I didn't see anything that would stetch out light in the device you gave me."

"Weird, isn't it?" Atlas said, feeding into the mystery. "It's this strange effect of how light acts as both a wave and a particle. As the light shoots out of this laser"—he pointed to the light beam—"it acts like a particle, traveling in a straight direction. Then, when it reaches this little clip here"—Atlas pointed to the piece of metal—"it acts like a wave and goes through both slits at once."

"I still don't get why it would create that horizontal line," Ship interjected.

"When the light photon travels through both slits at once, they bounce off each other on the other side of the metal. Some of the light bounces right, and some bounces left," Atlas said.

"A light photon bounces off itself? You mean it bounces off another photon?" Ship asked.

"Nope," Atlas said, shaking his head. "It bounces off itself. It's hard to believe. But that's quantum mechanics for you."

Atlas unclipped the piece of metal. The light turned back into a single red dot on the wall. Then Atlas reinserted the metal, and the horizontal interference line appeared once more.

"That's a neat trick, Atlas. But I don't understand how it's relevant."

Atlas could see the curiosity in Ship now. He had practiced this charade. He was going to draw out the story before revealing the surprise at the end.

Atlas produced another object, this time not a piece of metal. He held it up to Ship with a massive grin on his face. The object was a clear piece of glass with white bands across the top.

"What's that?" Ship asked.

"It's a photon detector. It will detect exactly which slit the light travels through."

"I thought you said it travels through both at the same time?"

"It does, but this is where things get interesting." Atlas handed the photon detector to Ship. "Place this over the metal slit."

Ship did as instructed. This time, he didn't have to push it into place—when the two pieces got close together, the detector he was holding was sucked toward the metal slit with a magnetic *snap*. The detector had two lights hidden in the top. As soon as it was clicked into place, both the lights lit up.

Their eyes moved in unison toward the wall. This time, the laser light had changed. It was back to being a single red dot.

"Where has that interference line gone?" Ship asked.

"It's the oddest thing with light particles. They act as light particles and waves in all situations except one," Atlas said.

"What's the one exception?"

"When you're trying to measure it," Atlas said, pointing at the device. "That detector is identifying which slit the light traveled through."

Atlas turned to the screen up on the wall. A video was showing the photon detector. Both lights lit up. "This is a slow-motion video camera."

He clicked a button on the screen. Everything in the shot slowed. The beam of light, which up until that moment looked constant, started to shutter, slowly at first, before vibrating at speed. Then it started to pulsate slower until it was clear the laser was switching on and off.

On. Off. On. Off.

The indicator light at the top of the clear photon detector was no longer constant. The left light flashed on, and then the right one, at random intervals.

"That high-speed camera allows us to watch a recording of individual light photons as they pass through the detector," explained Atlas. "And we can see if it passes through the left slit or the right slit based on which light goes off." He paused, allowing Ship to fully understand the footage. "Before, it just looked like both lights were lit up simultaneously. Now you can see as each photon passes each of the detectors."

Atlas could see Ship's mind thinking it through, trying to work out this puzzle. Atlas wondered if he'd finally got Ship curious about something.

"So, how does this help with anything?" Ship asked, this time intrigue in his voice.

Atlas grabbed the clear photon detector and walked toward the laser generator in the middle of the room. "You agree that light acts as a wave and a particle when there is no detector there, but as soon as there is a detector, it *only* acts as a particle traveling through one slit at a time?"

"Yes, but you never explained why light works like that."

"I honestly don't know," Atlas said as he arrived at the laser generator on the table. It was a large laser-turret-looking contraption. Out of either end was a long tube that laser light flowed out of. Ship joined Atlas as he fiddled with his computer on the table next to the laser device. Atlas pressed a few keys on his keyboard, and a gentle white noise of the laser light generator started to get louder—it sounded something within the machine was trying to keep it from overheating.

Moments later, a bright green laser light flickered into existence, shooting out the other end of the large machine. Now both sides of the laser generator were active, one shooting red light and the other green.

"Do you know what quantum entanglement is?" Atlas asked Ship.

"Quantum entanglement is when two or more particles link together in a certain way, no matter how far apart they are in space," Ship recited from memory.

"Exactly, so, this laser shoots entangled particles out of either end. So, in theory, doing something to the green laser should impact the red laser." Atlas knew that wasn't quite correct. But it was getting super technical now. He knew Ship was losing interest, so he wanted to skim over this part as quickly as possible.

Atlas handed Ship another piece of metal with two slits in it. "Do the honors."

Ship inserted the metal clips into its slot. They watched as the green laser produced the interference pattern they expected and the horizontal green line stretched out.

"Now the detector," Atlas instructed, handing it over.

Ship placed the detector over the metal slit, and with the same magnetic *click*, it slotted into place.

They both looked at the wall. The green horizontal line flickered and became a single dot once more.

"So what? You already showed me that would happen," Ship said.

"Wait until you see the best part!" Atlas beamed with excitement, certain that Ship would be impressed by what he was about to see.

With a quick yank, Atlas pulled the clear photon detector off, leaving the metal slit still in its place. The green laser light instantly turned back into a long horizontal line. "Now can you see what your green laser light is doing?"

Ship looked at the green light on the wall. "It's the green line thing again."

"Now stay there and watch what happens."

Atlas dashed over to the red laser that was producing a horizontal line. "Remember how I said the laser light is entangled? I found entangled particles are even stranger when you entangle them out in deep space—like we are now. Whatever I do to this photon happens to the other." With that, he slotted the photon detector into the slot. *Click.* "What do you see?"

"It's changed to a green dot."

"Exactly."

"I don't get it; how did mine change to a dot?" Ship asked.

Atlas knew this part was going to be the hardest to explain. Light takes time to travel from one side of the room to another, but when he inserted the detector, the change occurred to both lasers at the exact same time. It didn't happen at the slow speed of light. "Would you believe that yours changed at the exact moment mine did?"

"Wait. . ." Ship said, taking a step back. "What. . . Are you saying what I think you're saying?" Ship started to shake his head. "That's—impossible."

"Not impossible," Atlas said, nodding with a grin on his face. "Imagine if we sent the green laser to one side of the galaxy and we sent the red laser to another side; what would happen if we did this neat trick but crossing many, many light-years?"

"Oh. My. God," Ship said, thinking through the implications of the change happening faster than the speed of light. "This changes everything; we could have a galactic empire all communicating with each other in real time!" Ship started to shake his head; he clearly didn't believe it. "This violates everything I know about the universe. Are you sure this works? Why hasn't anyone done this before?"

"In all the experiments anyone did back at Sol, they couldn't use it to send information faster than light. No one got this result—"

"Exactly; so, why do you think you're getting a different result?" Ship said interrupting Atlas.

"I think it's because no one has replicated the experiment this far away from a gravity well. There's something about entangled particles being created out in deep space like this. We still need to test it on a larger scale. What we built in this lab, the distances aren't big enough. I have Lex building a larger laser. We're going to test it out in space. It should be done in a month."

Ship started to wear his impatient look, the childish look he got when he didn't want to wait around. "I have an idea," Ship said as he closed his eyes and stopped moving.

Ship stood there for a good while, not moving at all.

"You all right, Ship?" Atlas asked as he tapped Ship on the shoulder. "You're not moving."

Ship continued to be unresponsive. Atlas started to feel a little off himself, like something wasn't quite right. He couldn't put his finger on it. Particularly his vision—things around the room started to look wrong too. Atlas worried that they had been impacted by something. *Did Ship have to urgently take control of the ship?* Atlas wondered. Atlas teleported himself to the bridge to check if anything was wrong.

He looked out the window. The stars were moving toward him surprisingly fast. Too fast. He'd never seen them traveling at the speeds they were traveling through space. Atlas never thought he would be able to see stars moving like that. Maybe they had been hit by something. Distracted by the view, he looked out the window for a few seconds more, trying to hypothesize why they were moving too fast.

Ship appeared on the bridge, giving Atlas a fright. "Atlas, sorry, I didn't think it would work."

"What?" Atlas said, looking around the room for potential danger.

"I sped up our perception of time—the last month of real time, to us, has felt like only a few seconds."

"What!"

Atlas could see things changing through the bridge window. Stars started to slow down as their perception of time was returning to normal. The subtle hue of blue that he hadn't noticed before disappeared. "That was cool, Ship. How'd you do that?"

Ship grinned from ear to ear. "Both our brain matrixes are connected to this spacecraft. I simply just slowed everything down. I think. . ." Ship thought about it for a second. "I think I can use all the extra processing power within this spacecraft to slow down our perception of time, too."

Atlas started to clap. "Is that your first invention?" Atlas patted him on the shoulder. "I'm proud of you, Ship. Has a month really just gone past? Does that mean Lex has finished building the next phase of our test?"

Ship nodded proudly.

Atlas was impressed. He made a mental note of this moment: the day Ship changed and started inventing.

Ship looked happy, but Atlas could tell he was distracted. "What is it, Ship?"

"Atlas, can you meet me in my room in fifteen minutes?"

"Wait, before you go. You need to give your invention a name. What should we call it when we change our perception of tim?," Atlas asked.

"Meet me at my room in fifteen and I'll tell you."

"Okay, deal," Atlas said, with a touch of intrigue in his voice.

Atlas walked the long way to Ship's office and knocked on the door. It had been twenty minutes. The door swung open into a large, bright room with a gold ceiling and what looked to be marble walls. He looked around in awe, as it was a complete change from the all-black room he used to have.

Ship stepped out from behind a screen and Atlas gasped at his transformation. He was no longer all black—he appeared to have human skin painted gold. Ship smiled at Atlas. "When we change our perception of time, let's call it changing our 'playback speed.'"

Atlas could tell Ship was proud of himself. He had come up with an idea and wanted to express himself, show his personality.

"I love the name. And I love your new look," Atlas said as he looked wide-eyed around the room.

Atlas was unaware that Ship had posted his ideas to the other Ships he had the locations for.

Atlas and Ship hadn't slept like the other Beta Explorers, so it was easy enough for them to guess the general location. He knew where Trillion was, but Icarus and Angelique were just guesses. Ship sent a secret message, sharing his invention.

"Now let's see if your faster-than-light communication invention works." Ship suggested as he made a screen appear in front of Atlas.

They had sent sensors away from the ship in opposite directions, approximately five light-seconds apart. Entangled laser lights shone at each of the sensors. The screen showed the results of the test—it would take five light-seconds to reach each side, so if the sensors registered a change faster than five seconds, it would be faster-than-light communication.

Atlas scrolled through the screen, looking for the figure. No numbers appeared—it simply showed a zero. "Lex, can you double-check this? It's saying there was no delay at all."

Lex's avatar appeared next to them both. Most of the time, he looked like a floating orb. But when he was thinking or trying to communicate, his orb folded into itself—other orbs appearing out of nowhere. The way the AI's avatar bent and folded did not make sense in a three-dimensional world. But Atlas had designed its shape to make perfect sense mathematically. It was a hypersphere, and Atlas found the look of the AI extremely satisfying. Lex's hyperspheric skin morphed and flashed blue, signaling confusion. Atlas looked at Ship for an answer.

"He said there isn't any issue. The two sensors reacted at exactly the same time."

Atlas nearly lost his balance. Logically, he had expected it to work, but deep down, he thought once he scaled his test up into a large format, it would stop working.

"Ship, we did it! This is true FTL communication!" Atlas said triumphantly. "I can't believe we did it!" But then he paused for a moment. It was true—he had just enabled two signals to trigger at the same time, but he hadn't created FTL communication—yet. He still needed to build the device. There was a lot of engineering left to make it work. They didn't have enough resources to build a full-scale version. "We need to start designing the plans for this now. Ship, I can't wait to speak with another human."

CHAPTER 10

TRILLION

WAKING

Trillion woke. Something felt different. Puzzled, she sat up in bed and rubbed the ridge of her nose. She wondered if it was something to do with being a simulant. It confused her a little that she was only noticing something strange about being a simulation now—as she hadn't noticed anything before.

Back when she was first uploaded, life hadn't stopped one moment, then started again the next. There was no beginning or end. There was no disorientation. Not even a momentary confusion that sometimes accompanied the statement "Where am I?"—as she sometimes got when waking in some strange bed after a good night out. The first time she'd woken as a simulant, it had all felt like a continuation of her. Like the treads of her consciousness had never been unraveled, then rewoven in a new way.

She had even started her new life in the same chair it ended. As a hapticgraphic simulation, she opened her eyes for the first time to see a doughnut-shaped device over her, tricking her into thinking she hadn't been scanned at all. When Ship told her the truth, she hadn't believed him. It couldn't have been true, because she didn't feel any difference. It wasn't until she confirmed it, by teleporting to the bridge, that she understood she was a simulant.

Ship had assured her that waking in a few hundred years would feel very similar to waking after a sleep—but what she was experiencing was nothing like that. The unease she was feeling now made her think, perhaps, it was something else.

She pulled up a screen and checked the year. She'd been sleeping for two hundred and twenty-two years. Which was exactly when she wanted to wake.

She got out of bed and looked around. Everything in the room looked just as she had left it—right down to a dirty blouse she'd left draped over a chair. She picked it up and threw it into her washing basket as she caught a glimpse out the port into space. The uneasy feeling rushed back. She couldn't quite put her finger on it, but somehow, she knew something was wrong. She could see a large star in front of her; she wondered if that was what was causing her worry.

She walked toward the window and peered out into space. Inky blackness stretched out infinitely before her, a galaxy's worth of stars spilling across it like freckles on a cheek.

Hmm, she thought, *something definitely doesn't look right*. Her mind was screaming at her to keep looking out of the window.

She took a step back and rubbed her eyes, the blue fog of waking not quite giving her clarity. She looked again, this time focusing on the star in front of her. She stared at it, and as she watched, she noticed that the star was moving toward her. It was subtle. It looked like a timelapse. She turned toward the galaxy of stars and thought she could see them moving, too.

She knew that shouldn't be possible even at interstellar speeds. She stepped back, checking the window again to confirm she wasn't looking through a monitor.

Understanding what was happening, and dreading the answer, she teleported out.

Like a poorly timed jump cut, she appeared in front of Ship.

Ship was in his room. It was a single room the size of a house—a black office. And Trillion almost didn't notice the black droid, as his black appearance almost blurred into the walls—almost like camouflage.

"Good morning, Trillion. Do you like the new design of my space?" Ship said.

"Good morning. Um . . ." she said, her eyesight still a little unclear from waking, "Ship, we're going to crash into that star." She knew they weren't actually going to hit the star, but she needed to get the point across. Not waiting for a reply, she added, "And it looks the same as when I went to bed. It's still creepy how you almost disappear in here."

Ship pointed at the walls, clearly offended. "Trillion, I *have* personalized it."

"It looks the same to me."

"No, I've designed it so you can't see the windows or walls."

Trillion stared blankly at Ship, blinking a few times. "Ship, this looks exactly the same as when I went to sleep."

She looked around the place. She could see black on black on black. Black walls. And a black droid standing in the middle of the room.

Ship pointed at the walls again. "Look closer. The walls are designed to look black. Well, not black as such; they're designed to look as though they're not there."

Trillion squinted, trying to get an understanding of what he was talking about.

Ship continued. "I'm especially proud of the lights. Because they don't look like lights. You almost can't tell they're there."

She shook her head. "Oh, Ship. It's the same design as before. You just achieved it through another means. Your 'invisible' black walls"—she made quotation marks while saying the word—"are still black walls."

Ship pointed up at the ceiling. "The ceiling is too high to see, and it doesn't look like light is coming from anywhere, yet you can see me."

She walked toward the middle of the room. "Black is not a design, Ship. And I can barely see you."

"Well, now that you're here, you can help me decorate it if you're that angry about it," Ship snapped.

"Oh Ship, I'm not angry." She paused, changing her tone to something friendlier. "I know it sounds like I'm pushing you to decorate this place, but I'm mainly trying to get you to design something that reflects you." She pointed at his heart before shaking her head, remembering why she had come into his room. She mentally scolded herself for going so off topic when there was something urgent she needed to fix. It was a bad habit she had developed. "Okay, the black design is fine for now." She took a deep breath. "I'm concerned we're going to hit the star."

"What do you mean?"

She wondered whether something had gone wrong with Ship while she slept. *Surely, he knows their speed relative to the star.* "We're traveling too fast."

"Our speed is fine."

"Ship, if you can't tell something is wrong, then something is faulty with your sensors."

Ship nodded slowly. "I don't think anything is wrong. But . . ."

Trillion cut Ship off. "This reminds me of the early days of space travel. Before more-custom AIs like you were developed. A very basic AI was on this spacecraft—I think it was called a Boeing Seven, or Max Three-Seven." She shook her hands. "The specifics don't matter. Anyway, it had a faulty sensor. The sensor kept telling the spacecraft it was pointed up when it was actually pointing down." Trillion pointed up and down as she spoke. "The ship's AI would try and correct it by pointing it down, but that would worsen the situation." She took a deep breath. "Basically, if the AI had only looked out of the window, it would have known the sensors were wrong."

Ship cleared his voice, simulating a coughing sound. "So, you're saying my sensors are faulty? Show me."

"Yes, exactly." She handed a little tablet to Ship. "On here you can see everything looks normal. It says we're not traveling too fast. This feels very similar to the Boeing Seven incident." She pointed at the speed data on the screen. "When I look at the number on the screen, everything is saying the spacecraft is fine. It says we're moving slow enough to stay in orbit. But if I look out into space, I can see with my own eyes."

"But Trillion, we're not moving too fast."

"Ship, if I can see the star approaching us, we are moving too fast."

Trillion thought about her situation. At the academy on Mars, she had learned a bit about how to deal with situations like this. She needed to restart Ship. Trillion considered the situation. It wasn't common for AIs to malfunction, but it had occurred enough times in the past that safety measures had been put in place. Standard protocol required a full reset of Ship's operating system, but Trillion found herself hesitating. A full reset would hopefully fix the sensor issue but would also reset Ship's personality, erasing the characteristics he had created for himself since the start of the journey. Was it worth doing that? It would be like meeting a stranger.

Knowing she would regret a move like that, she decided to do a soft reset—hoping that would solve the problem without restarting his personality. She just hoped that she'd have enough time to do a hard reset if the soft didn't work.

Trillion pressed a button on the comm control on her wrist. A number pad appeared in front of her, and she took a deep breath as she looked over at Ship. He raised his hand. "Don't."

"I have to," she replied quietly, as she keyed in the eight-digit code. "I'm sorry."

Ship disappeared.

Trillion crossed her fingers, hoping it would work.

She walked out of Ship's dark and dingy room. She knew she didn't have to walk, she could teleport anywhere in the spacecraft instantly, but walking gave her time to think. Besides, she still had about twenty-five hours until Ship was back online fully.

She arrived at a large oak door and stepped inside. Her home stretched over three levels, with high ceilings and a large, open-plan living room. A meadow was projected into the distance, giving her a sense of no longer being in space. The second floor hosted her office—a large free-form space. Her room was on the top floor, complete with several ports looking out into space.

She floated in the middle of her lounge, enjoying the sensation of the zero-gravity zone, while she pondered the issue of Ship. She looked up to where Lex was floating calmly in a corner of the room. "What do you think, Lex? Do you think something is wrong? Do you think Ship needs a full system restore?"

The orb flashed red.

Trillion nodded. "I agree, Lex. I think resetting Ship should fix it."

Trillion began to close her eyes, meditating, when she was disrupted by the sound of her door opening. She opened her eyes to see Ship walking in.

"Ship!" Surprise spread across her face. "Why . . . how . . . how are you here, Ship? It's literally been an hour."

Trillion's mind raced through different scenarios. She wondered if he was broken. Was it possible for custom AIs to break? Did that mean she could break too? How would she fix him? She shook her head, trying not to panic. "Oh, no, Ship. What do we do now?"

Ship raised his hand, signaling she should slow down. "Trillion, I changed our perception of time."

He pointed at one of the screens. It changed to an image of

the star they were approaching. "You're seeing us approach the star at around twenty-five times normal speed."

Trillion raised an eyebrow, the whisper of a smile appearing on her face, which widened into a massive grin. She started to laugh. "Oh, oh—can you slow us down?"

Ship nodded slowly. "Okaaaaaaaayyyyy . . ."

Ship's mouth moved and a strange sound came out. His voice got deeper, slowing down like a video playing at the wrong speed.

Trillion looked at the screen he was still pointing to. It began moving slower, and then the view into space froze in place. She started to clap, impressed with the little trick he'd presented to her. "Ship, that was awesome. I didn't know we could do that!"

CHAPTER 11

TRILLION

KILL THE PLANET

Trillion stood on the bridge, holding a projection of the planet they were orbiting. They had picked this planet because it was in the Goldilocks zone—the right distance away from the planet that it might have liquid water on it. It was twice the size of Venus—almost a super-Earth. As they got closer, they'd discovered the planet was covered in something green. She turned the hapticgraphic projection of the planet over in her hand, examining it. The green covering the planet was rich and vibrant. Unlike Earth, which had the land covered in green, it was oceans that were covered in green on this planet. From what she was looking at, it looked like the oceans were covered in an algae bloom. She might be the first human to ever encounter life that hadn't originated from Earth. And she didn't want to go about destroying the life by terraforming the planet. But perhaps if she terraformed it slowly, that life could evolve to thrive in a world with humans on it. "So, the life here could evolve fast enough?"

The orb flashed green to signal affirmative.

They had sent ANTs down to the world and discovered the planet sprinkled with life. The green of the oceans was not too dissimilar to plankton on Earth. There scans had only revealed insects and microbial life. But it was still life, and life had to be cherished. Trillion wanted to make sure the unique alien species on the world survived. She hoped the humans she was bringing to the world could one day study that life.

Ship filled in the details where Lex left off. "Based on the modeling, we'll have to do it over at least ten thousand years."

Curious, Trillion proposed a thought experiment. "What would happen if we did it over one hundred years?"

Ship considered that for a moment. "We could, but it would cause a rapid change to the atmosphere composition on the planet. That would cause a mass extinction event. Over a thousand years, any life that takes more than nine months to reproduce will not evolve fast enough. Over one hundred years, very little would survive. Even over ten thousand years is fast. I suggest we do it as slow as possible—maybe even engineering Earth life to survive on an environment closer to this world."

"So, we take our time? Do this slowly, and do this right."

Ship nodded in agreement as a green pulsation ran over Lex.

Trillion made a throwing gesture, dismissing the haptic-graphic projection. "Let's spend the next ten thousand years building a magical city so everything is ready for my new children."

She started listing items on her hands. "Let's build airports, hospitals, skyscrapers, and statues. Everything. We could build architectural beauties." She paused, scratching her head, thinking about everything she hated about the cities back on Earth and building something from the ground up would give her a chance to change all that. She shook her head; she was getting a little ahead of herself now. "We first need to work out how to terraform the planet. I know we have terraforming equipment. But I suspect we'll probably be making most of this up as we go!"

The more Trillion thought about the planet, the less she could contain her excitement. Her mind raced with the possibilities. The process of terraforming a planet didn't interest her that much. It was building entire cities that got her excited. She started to think about world-building games she played—*Age of Empires* was her favourite. "It was all about resource management," she muttered to herself.

"What is about resource management?"

"Oh, just an old game I used to play. It's relevant here, though, because we need enough resources to build exactly what I'm picturing. How many fabricators do we have?"

"Only one."

Trillion furrowed her brow. Fabricators were the most powerful tool she had at her disposal and came in two configurations—or, rather, they had two modes of operating. One configuration allowed the fabricators to create anything; it just needed the right fabricator pellets. And another, turned raw resources, like asteroids, into specific fabricator pellets. So, she needed more fabricators to turn the raw materials on her planet into everything she needed to terraform that planet. "Only one? How is that possible?"

Ship shrugged. "We've always only had one fabricator. We left Mars in a hurry."

"Hmm." Trillion scratched her head. "We need a lot more for what I'm thinking of." She stood on the tips of her toes—she liked to get higher when she was thinking. "Ship, I'm excited about this. We get to build a city! But now that I'm awake, I'm eager to get started. Now. I don't want to have to wait around until we have enough fabricators and pellets."

She smiled as another thought occurred to her. "Maybe this explains how the pyramids were really built. Maybe we're just following in the footsteps of other explorers who showed up to Earth wanting to build a world, the way we've just shown up here. I wonder if we breathe oxygen because long ago an alien terraformed Earth."

"You think aliens visited Earth?" Ship asked doubtfully.

"It's a possibility. Ship, do you know about the Cambrian explosion?"

Ship nodded. "You mean when life first learnt to turn carbon dioxide into oxygen?"

Trillion raised her eyebrows. "Do you think we're going to create something like that on this planet?"

Ship shook his head. "No chance."

Trillion made an encouraging hand gesture, spurring Ship to explain why.

"The Cambrian explosion happened over fifty million years—we're changing this planet in ten thousand."

Trillion laughed. "Good point." She thought about it a little more. "Maybe they were just more patient than us." She pointed toward one of the screens on the bridge. "Can you list out all the resources we currently have? One fabricator. But how many fabricator pellets? How many ANTs?"

The orb flashed and a table appeared on the screen in front of her.

"Thank you, Lex," Trillion said as she scanned through the list. "It's not that much."

Ship nodded. "We need fabricators. With them we can create almost anything else."

Trillion agreed. Having a large number of fabricators would make building anything possible.

Trillion began giving orders. "Ship, can you build the terra-forming equipment we need to start changing the planet over ten thousand years?" She pointed at the orb in the corner. "Lex, can you start using the fabricator to build more fabricators? Then begin mining the planet for fabricator pellets." Assuming the system was typical, then it should contain all the resources and material she'd need to make the necessary fabricator pellets. If there was something they couldn't find in a planet's crust or in the asteroid belt, then that was a problem they would have to face later.

Trillion laughed a little, thinking of what Atlas had named the large ANTs. "And build some of the big ANTs the eleph-ANTs."

ANTs generally had the same design. So named because of their resemblance to ants, the sturdy machines had six legs and a mechanical arm where the head would be, which could be fitted with different attachments, depending on the job required. They ranged in size from almost microscopic to as large as a house.

Trillion stood with her hands behind her back. She looked at Ship and Lex. "Team, it takes us a month to build a fabricator, and we need sixty of them to build what I have in mind." She took a deep breath. "We need ANTs and fabricator pellets, too, so alternate between building fabricators and ANTs to collect resources."

She gestured to the screen with the list of resources. "At a rate of one fabricator every month, it should take us about five years to build enough." She looked toward Lex. "You crank them out as quickly as you can. See if by the time I wake, you can build more than sixty."

She turned toward Ship. "You wake me up in five years. I can't wait to get started."

The orb flashed green, signaling affirmative.

Ship nodded. "Consider it done."

Trillion teleported out and went to bed.

CHAPTER 12

TRILLION

UNLIMITED RESOURCES

Trillion floated into consciousness. She had learned from her previous wake-up: the slower, the better. She hovered gently above her bed, feeling the weightlessness around her. She took a deep breath and floated closer to the ceiling. Then she breathed out and drifted toward the ground.

She rose and fell with her breathing for a while, her mind wake-dreaming as she thought about her world. Excitement mounted as she pictured what she was about to build. She pulled off her blankets and pushed herself away from her bed, floating downstairs toward her front door, where she teleported to the bridge.

Trillion appeared with a swagger. "Good morning, Ship."

He didn't acknowledge her. His head was down, focusing on a control panel, moving through screens quickly.

She stretched her arms apart. A hapticgraphic image of the planet appeared in her hands. It was metallic and bright. She studied it. It didn't look like the planet she remembered; she remembered it being greener.

She turned her head toward the screen on the wall. The supply list she had been viewing five years before was still displayed on the screen, but it didn't make sense—the illuminated numbers were way too high, growing higher as she watched. "Ship, what's this?"

Ship bowed his head, looking at the ground as if ashamed of himself. "Sorry, Trillion."

"Sorry about what?"

"I just stepped away for a bit. I left Lex in charge of sorting everything. He didn't stop."

Trillion pointed to the orb in the corner. "What did you do, Lex?"

The orb flashed orange. A large screen appeared in front of Trillion. It was projected using the hapticgraphic projectors that made everything in Trillion's simulated world. She noted that trick for later. She placed one finger on the screen and studied the rows of numbers. "This looks like a good thing. How did we get so many resources?"

Ship looked up briefly before staring back down at his robotic feet. "It's not a good thing, Trillion. Look at the planet."

She studied the planet. It was shiny. She zoomed in, looking at the surface. There wasn't a tinge of green on it anymore. "How did this happen? Is the planet gone?"

Ship nodded. "It was exponential growth." He put his hands forward. An image of a fabricator appeared. It almost looked like a large shipping container. He pointed at the fabricator. "Every new fabricator could create more fabricators." On the image Ship was holding, another fabricator appeared. "And as we had more fabricators, it created even more, faster." The image Ship held showed four fabricators. Then eight. Then sixteen. "Fabricators were building ANTs, and ANTs began mining resources for the fabricators." Ship kept increasing the number of fabricators he displayed. He could only estimate the number, but if the numbers doubled every month, then they would have far more than a trillion fabricators, ANTs, and pellets.

Trillion studied the planet and struggled to comprehend the sheer number of resources mined in the system now. She looked at one of the numbers trying to understand what it meant. She counted the number of digits that made up that number. She knew a billion had a one followed by nine digits, and a trillion had a one followed by twelve digits. But the number she was looking at was bigger than both of those. Then she noticed all the numbers on the screen were growing. And growing quickly. "Why are these numbers still increasing? Can you stop everything?"

Ship zoomed out some more, revealing the wider system they were in. He showed the asteroid belt around the star covered in fabricators cranking out ANTs. Well, it wasn't an asteroid belt anymore. All the asteroids were consumed to make more fabricators and ANTs. It was a belt of fabricators creating more of themselves. "We've only got line-of-sight communication with the fabricators on this side of the planet. We can't stop all of them."

Trillion went pale. "Ship, what have you done? Where were you when all this happened?"

Ship lowered his head again. "I thought Lex could handle it all."

Trillion shook her head, scolding the droid. "Atlas told me you could be lazy, but I didn't believe him. Now we have a huge mess to clean up." She pointed at the orb in the corner. "Lex, stop all fabricator production that you can and start assigning fabricators to produce communication towers. Let's get a satellite network going."

She turned back to Ship. "How long will it take to build a satellite network around the whole planet? Something big enough to reach all the fabricators."

Ship explained the calculation from Lex. "It will take ten minutes to build a network around the whole planet."

She took a step back, not expecting that. She had thought at least a month. "How? That's so fast!"

Ship grimaced. "We have so many fabricators, we can build anything quickly now."

She could see Ship's body language change. She had spent so much time with him, she could tell when something was not quite right. "What aren't you telling me?"

He remained silent.

Trillion started to feel a pang in her heart. She could feel the strong desire to seed a planet. She felt like she was further away from seeding a world than when she had begun this journey. That desire was pushing her to know more. To know how far away from it she was. She needed to understand just how unlikely seeding this world was.

She spun the image of the world in her hand. "This looks like the Death Star was designed out of blocks and pixels." She could see the smooth texture of a planet replaced with containers. She zoomed into where water should be. "There isn't any water here."

Ship nodded. "Every inch of sand, earth, and ocean has been bottled up and turned into pellets." He lowered his head once more. "Even the air has been bottled up and turned into more pellets."

"How long have you known about this?"

"I woke up just a few days before you."

She looked at Ship, noticing how ashamed he was. His head was lowered so much, it almost looked like he was touching the ground. "It's okay, Ship. This was my fault. I was the one who didn't realize the process would be exponential."

Ship shook his head. "No, Trillion, you gave me this job and I didn't do it. I went to sleep right after you."

"We both made mistakes," Trillion said, lowering her head too. She knew that beating up herself and Ship over it wasn't productive. They were right to feel bad, but they were wrong to let the guilt stop them from moving on and stopping the fabricators from multiplying. She needed to use laughter to stop the guilt from debilitating her and Ship. "Karma is going to come back to us."

She started to laugh. That was all she could do. The damage was done, and she needed to regain her zen. "Ship, this is comically bad."

She looked toward the orb in the corner. "Lex, have we halted all fabricators?"

He beeped a few times, flashing red. She looked at the screen—it showed they had only switched off 0.1 percent of the fabricators.

Trillion furrowed her brow, not quite believing the number. "How have we only reached only one-tenth of one percent of the fabricators? It's been twenty minutes; have you not started building a communication network yet?"

Ship lowered his head once more. "We've only managed to make contact with 0.1 percent of the fabricators. We've completed the communication network around the planet . . ." He paused.

Trillion focused her eyes on Ship, holding eye contact for longer than normal, letting Ship know to spit it out.

Ship simulated a large breath out. "There are fabricators beyond the asteroid belt, too. I estimate every planet in the system has fabricators on it now. They are creating new fabricators and mining resources."

All Trillion's zen was gone. She screamed with rage and then broke into an uncontrollable laugh.

CHAPTER 13

TRILLION

COMMUNICATIONS NETWORK

Trillion, Ship, and Lex spent an entire week coming up with a plan to establish communications with every fabricator.

They slowed down their playback speed, so an hour in real time represented a week in subjective time, something Trillion realized sheepishly she should have done rather than going to sleep in order to avoid this catastrophe.

It would take the team a year to make sure, as every single fabricator had to be accounted for. Even if they left one rogue fabricator out there to duplicate itself, it wouldn't take long for them to be in a similar situation.

....

Trillion stood on the bridge, looking at a projected map of the system. She lifted a hapticgraphic projection of it from the table, stretching it out so it filled the whole room. "Lex, can you color all the spaces our communication network covers in green?"

The room changed to a translucent green. She panned her head around, and from her perspective, the room was covered in a green mist. She zoomed further out into the system and widened her hands, and her perspective changed. The planets in the middle of the system got smaller. The star shrank. She kept zooming out until she reached the Oort cloud. "That doesn't work," she said, noticing that she couldn't tell which sections weren't covered in green.

She scratched her head. "Try changing only the parts the network *doesn't* reach to green." Suddenly, pockets of green were scattered around the room. "That's much better, Lex. Thank you." She pointed at the green areas. "This is where we need to focus."

Lex's orb flashed orange and beeped a few times.

Trillion turned to Ship, waiting for him to explain.

"Lex said we need capabilities for managing this network. Capabilities for dealing with the several-day time delay in communication between some parts of the network. He wants us to build a supercomputer."

Trillion looked at Lex. "You want an upgrade?"

The orb flashed green. Trillion smiled. "That also means we need more fusion power plants. We'd better start building." Trillion fought back a chuckle. "Lucky we have so many resources now."

CHAPTER 14

TRILLION

FASTER THAN LIGHT

Trillion and her team hunted down every fabricator for more than eighteenth months. "Lex, how certain are you that we've found every fabricator?"

The orb didn't change.

Ship rolled his eyes. "The simulation predicts that we have found every fabricator, with ninety-three percent certainty."

Trillion pointed at Lex. "You need to learn to deal with uncertainty."

Ship shrugged. "You know what Lex is like. He hates giving probabilities unless it's basically 100 percent."

"Okay, team." Trillion stood on the tips of her toes. It occurred to her that if she wanted to get higher and think, she could simply float. She was a simulation. She didn't need to observe those rules. She jumped, then floated in the air, folding up her legs.

As she addressed the team, she noticed it was easier to think floating in the air. "Lex, I want you to map this system. Scan every single corner." She turned to Ship. "You're in charge of sending the probes out everywhere. And you can't outsource that job to Lex. *You* have to do it."

Trillion teleported out.

One month later, Trillion stood in her cargo hangar. She had cleared out a large space in the middle of it. Eleph-ANTs, fabricator pellets, and equipment had all been pushed to the edges of the hangar, making an oddly empty zone that she used to project the entire system onto.

The team had searched several light-minutes cubed of space for fabricators. They'd found three rogue machines, which included one that was on a trajectory out of the system.

She looked at the projected system in front of her and highlighted one of the fabricators in green. It had traveled to the very edge of the system, making it to the Oort cloud before they found it. "Are we sure this is the final fabricator we haven't made contact with?"

Lex's orb flashed green. She knew if Lex was confident, then she could take it as fact. "Thank you, Lex, I just needed to make sure. One Steel World is enough."

Trillion had started calling the planet Steel World, using *Steel* as shorthand for the system. She wondered what use it might be, now it was all metal. "What should we do with all these resources?"

She pointed at a tiny dot on the projected image. The image zoomed in to that dot, showing the initial planet she had hoped to colonize. She pointed at the planet. "Could we create a ring world?" she asked. "Maybe set up two rows of rotating habitats that orbit in opposite directions like a road. That was—"

Ship lifted up a palm, interrupting her. "Trillion, we're receiving an incoming message."

Trillion paused and looked at him curiously. "How does someone know where we are?"

When Ship didn't respond right away, Trillion began to get nervous. She knew they had just destroyed a planet, but she wasn't ready to face the consequences this soon.

"It's Atlas," Ship said after a moment. "He says he has invented faster-than-light communication."

Trillion stopped simulating her breath. She froze there; she never thought she'd speak to another human this soon. Her mind started whirling with emotions. Joy spread across her face as she thought about talking to Atlas. Then she turned bright red when she realized she'll have to tell him what she had just done. "Oh my god, oh my god! How does it work? Can you put him on?" She paused. "Hello, Atlas, can you hear me?"

"It doesn't work like that." Ship said holding back a laugh. "There's a setup; it requires us to construct a machine for entangling particles."

"Oh," she said, disappointed. "Can you set that up now? It shouldn't take that long with all the resources we have now."

Ship shook his head. "That's just it. We have to wait for our q-bits to reach them."

Trillion raised an eyebrow. "How long will that take?"

Ship frowned. "If we start building it now, we'll have to wait 250 years for the network to be established. Because he's 250 light-years away."

Trillion started to laugh. "This has got to be some sick joke. Maybe Icarus put him up to it. What sort of faster-than-light communication requires us to wait until our light signals get to them?"

CHAPTER 15

TRILLION

VENTURING OUT

"We need to find a new planet," Trillion said, resigning herself to the fact it wasn't going to be possible to create rings out of Steel World. "Lex, can you do a scan of all the nearby stars?" She thought for a bit. "I want a list of the fifty closest stars. And, of those, which ones are orbited by planets that could potentially support life."

The orb flashed blue. Ship explained what Lex needed. "We'll have to build a very large long-range telescope to do that."

"How long will that take? Actually, never mind. Just build it, Lex."

New rule, Trillion thought. She was never going on a long sleep like she did before. Why sleep when she could just change her playback speed?

She increased her playback speed and watched as massive construction projects took place in front of her. A million ANTs were pushed out into orbit, but it looked like a blur. Like a single line connected the planet and a floating blob of ants.

Trillion marveled at what she was looking at. It was mesmerizing. Some moments, it was like watching an explosion happening in slow motion, with ANT-shaped shrapnel flying everywhere. Others, it was like watching a kaleidoscope of shapes bend and mold into one another. "This is better than those satisfying videos, Ship. It looks unnatural and real at the same time."

"Why *unnatural?*" Ship asked.

"I think it's the fact that this construction is happening in space," Trillion said, unable to take her eyes off what was happening. "My natural sense of the way objects interact with each other isn't working. And you combine that with the fact my perception of time is sped up, and my human brain really struggles to understand it."

She stared at the large telescope being constructed. The structure now looked like a bubble was growing out in space. It stopped growing and solidified. It folded and bent, shrinking in on itself before popping in what looked like an explosion, with millions of tiny ANTs shooting out from the structure. The ANTs started to move together to form a train line before curving back toward the construction project.

Trillion still struggled to comprehend the movement of objects at faster speeds. Her mind still expected objects moving away from each other that fast to continue moving. She felt there was something magical about watching a satellite get constructed at that speed.

She could see the resemblance of a telescope. Thirty-seven large hexagon-shaped mirrors slotted together, each about five meters in diameter. It reminded her of the James Webb telescope, only much bigger. She assumed Lex had used a design similar to something he knew would work.

Her perception of time started to slow—still fast but much closer to normal. The line connecting the satellite to the planet stopped blurring and started to turn into individual ANTs transiting between the two.

There was a long moment of stillness, and Trillion wondered whether everything was complete. Then the eleph-ANTs attached to the telescope started to fire, rotating the telescope, guiding it to sweep through millions of stars at a time, collecting light, collecting data. That meant the telescope was already working to scan the skies, finding suitable candidates. "I love not having to wait," Trillion said.

It didn't take long before Lex made a few beeping noises to signal he had something to show her. A screen appeared in front of her, displaying data on the nearest fifty stars.

She scanned the screen, looking at all the possibilities, and selected three stars. "Am I correct that this shows we have three potential stars?"

The orb flashed green.

Trillion highlighted the row of data about each of the planets. She tapped on each column as she walked through her thinking. She underlined the column showing distance. "We could reach all three within 150 years?"

The orb flashed green.

She selected the row showing the probability of a planet in the habitable distance away from the star: planets in the Goldilocks zone. Close enough to the planet's star that the water on the planet wasn't ice, but far enough away from the star that it wasn't steam, either. Not too hot. And not too cold.

She looked at the empty square. "Why aren't there any numbers in here?"

The orb flashed blue.

"Hmm," she wondered aloud. "Are you saying we don't have enough data yet?"

The orb flashed green.

"Lex, give me your best guess."

The orb flashed red.

She looked over at Ship. "Ship, do you mind?"

Ship nodded as he made the number in the boxes change. One had a ninety-three percent probability of having liquid water on it. The rest had less than twenty.

Trillion looked at Ship. "Why does this star have a high probability of water on a planet?"

"We have only been looking at the stars for a very short time. The other two might have its planet on the other side of the star. This one does have a planet blocking light from its star, and it's having a noticeable impact on the light we are seeing from the star."

Trillion pulled up the light spectrum of that planet. When light travels through oxygen, some wavelengths are absorbed, some pass right through, and others are reemitted at different frequencies. Oxygen leaves a very distinct fingerprint. And Trillion was looking at the exact signature that oxygen makes in the light spectrum. It was obvious that one of them had a lot of oxygen in the atmosphere. "It has to be something living producing this oxygen?"

"Yes and no," Ship said, shaking and nodding his head at the same time. "There are some natural processes that can produce oxygen."

Trillion was somewhat confused. "But *this* much oxygen?"

Ship shrugged.

Trillion pulled out a pen and wrote directly on the screen: *Planet 3.0*. "I guess we'll have to find out when we get there."

Ship cocked his head, processing what Trillion had just said.

Trillion pointed back at the planet. "We are heading here. Get ready now, Ship. I want to hit the skies."

CHAPTER 16
ICARUS

ALMOST DONALD DUCK

Icarus opened his eyes, just for a second. Then he closed them again and slowly began to absorb the symphony around him. He could hear the sounds of a forest—the sweet chatter of birds; a distant waterfall. If he concentrated, he could even hear a soft breeze as it whispered through trees far away.

He stretched leisurely, enjoying the soundtrack, and, still with closed eyes, began to take note of his feelings—both physical and mental. He scanned his body and couldn't feel a single area of pain or discomfort. Even his shoulder—which, after breaking in a motorcycle accident, was usually achy in the morning—was free of pain. He noticed it felt like moments before, he was on Mars, but now he didn't care about anything. The adrenaline and flight instincts were gone; he was the calmest he had ever been. Free of all the worries from moments before. As if moments before was many many years past—because it was.

He took a deep breath and opened his eyes again. His world looked beautiful. Pastel. Bright. Cartoonlike. He had modeled it after a video game—his favorite game of all time—*The Legend of Zelda: Tears of the Kingdom*. As a child growing up in Japan, he had loved that game.

He lifted the blanket off and sat up, bouncing a little on his bed of clouds. He caught a glimpse of his arm and admired how wonderfully photorealistic it looked. Still cartoonlike, and not quite real—cartoon*ish*, he thought. He looked down at his legs and noticed they were very skinny, and next to his ducklike feet they looked a little too Donald Duck for his taste. He hoped the rest of him didn't look like that.

Icarus ran over to a mirror and studied his new avatar. Most of it was exactly like he wanted. He was a photorealistic anime character that looked like him mixed with a duck. Big eyes with human hands, arms, and legs, but duck paddles for feet and a beak-like mouth. An idealized version of a human-duck hybrid.

What is the benefit of being a hapticgram if you can't get creative, he thought, then smiled, realizing how much he was enjoying his first experience as a simulant.

The wake-up routine was the perfect way to wake after centuries of sleeping. Icarus preferred birds and forest sounds over alarm clocks. The only thing missing was coffee.

Icarus rubbed his big cartoon eyes and made his way down a large curving staircase that led into the kitchen.

An espresso machine was already on, the steam and pressure ready. He was even more impressed with himself for thinking of every little detail. He could have had coffee ready waiting for him when he woke, but the ritual of making coffee, grinding the beans, pressing the grounds, and steaming the milk was what woke him up and got him excited about what was in front of him.

For Icarus, coffee wasn't just about the caffeine. It was about the process. All the steps involved signaled to his brain it was time to start the day. In some Pavlovian way, making the coffee was more important than drinking it. Besides, he didn't think he had perfected his simulation so he could fully taste the coffee yet. That was something he needed to work on later.

He turned on the coffee grinder and listened to the distinctive sound of beans being ground into small particles. He picked up the portafilter and placed it underneath the falling fountain of coffee grounds. He leaned over and noticed he couldn't smell anything. He made another mental note to fix that later. A mound quickly began to grow, and once it was high enough, he leveled off the coffee and tamped it down, feeling a little clumsy as he adjusted to his new strength.

He clicked the portafilter into the coffee machine and, with a flick of a button, a hot espresso shot began to flow into his cup. He marveled at the rich chocolate color—just looking at it made him feel even more awake.

He picked up the cup and raised it to his nose, inhaling deeply, forgetting that he seemed to have no sense of smell. Nevertheless, it looked like a perfect espresso shot.

He walked over to the fridge and grabbed a bottle of oat milk. He poured it into the metal cup and began heating it up with the steam wand.

A few moments later, he had hot milk in one hand and an espresso shot in the other. He carefully poured the milk into the cup, skilfully forming a fern shape. He was impressed that he still had the skills—the coffee art looked good.

He tasted it and winced. It tasted like instant coffee. He spat it out on the floor and threw the cup away. Both the coffee on the floor and the cup faded into nothingness.

He decided then to make it a priority to perfect all his sensory experiences in his simulation. Unlike the metaverse, with its massive flavor selections, they had left Mars with only the open-source libraries of flavors, because in the meta, unique flavors were owned by someone—usually a corporation. And—just like buying a T-shirt in the real world or an avatar skin in a game—flavors had to be purchased. "Good luck chasing me for a copyright infringement now," Icarus mused to himself.

Icarus wandered through the living room and out the door. He walked down the long hallway, deciding he would stop by the nursery on the way to the bridge. It wouldn't be long before he could start bringing them to life. As he walked, he looked down and realized he was still naked. He had been so preoccupied with his new duck-like avatar, he forgot to add clothes to it. He snapped his fingers, and in an instant, he was wearing jeans and a T-shirt.

He arrived outside the large metallic doors of the nursery. Inside were embryos of what he estimated were every single species of animal alive on Earth the day he had left. It always broke him that so many animals had become extinct because of humans. If he had left a few hundred years earlier, he might have carried twice the number of species.

As he placed his hand on the large door, he wondered how everyone would see him. As their adoptive father? Or a surrogate father? It wouldn't quite be surrogate, because they wouldn't have his DNA, but it wouldn't quite be adoptive, either, because he was bringing them into this world. Maybe he needed to create a new term for himself. They would always be his children.

He began to walk, sliding his hand along the large metal door as he did, his hands making a squeaking sound. He didn't want to be seen as an AI, as just a computer, programmed to bring people into this world. That wouldn't bring the gravitas he was looking for. Neither would being a god. He definitely wasn't a god. He chuckled a little, imagining people worshiping him as a god. Maybe aliens would see him that way, but not humans.

He arrived at an elevator at the end of the hall. He stepped in and pressed the button for the bridge. The elevator rose slowly, giving him plenty of time to think about the kind of world he was about to encounter. He hadn't yet seen anything about the world. He hadn't seen Ship yet. He hoped for a place with aliens, something with preindustrial life that he would guide to get smarter. Help to co-evolve with humans. He hoped that if there *were* aliens, they were oxygen-breathing. Otherwise, it would be another can of worms to figure out.

The doors of the lift chimed before opening. He stepped inside. A few moments later, it chimed again and the door opened.

"Good morning, Icarus," Ship said.

"Good morning, Ship. It's great to be in the land of the living once more. Where are we now?"

"In orbit. Although I don't think you're going to like this star system much. There is only one planet."

Icarus smiled. "We only need one planet. I'm happy with that."

"It's a gas giant."

Ship projected a hapticgram of it.

Icarus reached over and plucked the hapticgraphic image up and studied it. "Are those rings?" He turned the planet in his hands, inspecting it. It had a deep blue hue with swirling yellow clouds moving around it. "It's beautiful."

Ship nodded. "It's a small gas giant. Just a little smaller than Neptune."

Icarus could feel excitement washing over him. As a child, he had always dreamed about flying through the rings of Saturn and now he was going to get the chance to do something similar. "Those rings; I want to explore those," he said, before stopping as the realization suddenly hit him. "Is there no planet for us to seed here?"

Ship dropped his head. Icarus could tell Ship was disappointed by the system he had chosen. He was disappointed too, but he didn't want to discourage Ship by showing it.

"That's okay, Ship," he smiled. "This is just a short stopover. We'll take a quick detour around those rings, then we can make a call on where to go next."

Icarus stood still for a while. He needed to reimagine his future. Going on this journey, he had hoped it would be filled with experiences like speaking with aliens. Learning their languages. He had studied languages as a career, decoding ancient languages of Earth. The ultimate challenge, then, was decoding an alien language. He shook his head, putting that thought to the back of his mind once more.

"We can send some ANTs down to take photos of the rings as we swing around the star," Ship suggested.

Icarus shook his head. "If I wanted pictures, I would be happy with seeing Saturn's rings. No, I want to remote-control the ANTs. I want to fly through the rings."

"We'll have to be in orbit around the gas giant, then. We could potentially be hit," Ship replied.

"You worry about avoiding asteroids. I'll worry about flying an ANT. After that, we can head for another system."

CHAPTER 17
ICARUS

THROUGH THE RINGS

Icarus was working in the hangar, redesigning an eleph-ANT. He knew Ship was on his way up, so he rolled underneath the large mechanical machine with a wrench in one hand.

Timing his movements, he rolled out as Ship arrived. "What do you think?"

Ship stared at the large minivan-sized eleph-ANT, its insides pulled out, wires, motors, and electronics strewn across the floor of the hangar. It had eight cables connected to it from the ceiling and eight connected to the floor. Large cables, too—the kind that could be used to lift it up from the ground.

"You do know," Ship said, "that you can't leave this spacecraft? Hapticgraphic projections only work while in the ship."

Icarus stood up, wiping his hands on his pants. "I'm trying something different. Have a look inside."

Icarus opened the large door on the back of the eleph-ANT. He had to jump a little to get inside, as the door was quite a distance from the floor. He turned around and put his hand out for Ship, pulling him inside, too. It was dark.

"Are you ready?" Icarus asked.

He flicked the switch on the wall. The room lit up. It looked like the inside of a fighter plane. There were two seats, one in front of the other. The seats were low and hard to get into—the sort that held you in place. A control stick was secured in front of each one, and various buttons and levers were within arm's reach. The inside walls of the eleph-ANT were covered in screens.

Icarus pointed at the front seat. "This will be my cockpit. I'll be able to remote-control eleph-ANTs from within here. You can sit here if you want." He pointed to the copilot's seat. "None of the controls do anything yet, but at least we'll be able to talk on this adventure."

Ship belted himself into place.

Icarus knew Ship could remote-control the eleph-ANT if he wanted, regardless of the controls in front of him not being in working order.

"I have an eleph-ANT waiting in the airlock. We'll close the doors and launch it out into space." Icarus walked forward to get into his pilot's seat and spotted a printout he had made earlier—a small sticker. "Oh, I have to do something first."

He picked up the sticker, opened the cockpit door, and jumped out. He ran across the hangar toward the airlock, his cartoon legs hopping. When he was about seven meters from the eleph-ANT, he jumped, stretching his arm out, almost as if he were dunking a basketball. He slammed the sticker down on the top of the eleph-ANT's nose and then landed, his momentum sliding him across the ground. He teleported back into the cockpit mid-slide, fading out as he did. He hoped it looked as cool as it felt, because to him it felt like he just pulled off the perfect *DragonBall Z* teleport—complete with unforgettable sound effect.

The sticker read *Mark One*.

"That sticker was real, so I couldn't teleport it to the eleph-ANT. Now close the airlock," Icarus said as he arrived.

Ship closed the airlock door, flicking a random switch in front of him to give Icarus a sense of realism.

Icarus pressed several buttons in turn. The screens all around them turned on. It looked like they were inside the eleph-ANT labeled Mark One.

Back in the airlock, the magnetic legs of the Mark One turned on, anchoring it to the floor. The eleph-ANT that Icarus and Ship were in lifted off the ground, the eight cables connected to the roof doing their job.

Ship flicked another random switch and opened the outside door of the airlock. The Mark One remained stationary as the air rushed out.

Icarus took the controls. "Here we go," he announced, while pushing the control stick forward.

The Mark One ran, all six legs moving in tandem. It jumped out of the airlock and drifted toward the rings of the gas giant.

Icarus pressed a button. The two back legs of the Mark One turned to point backward, directly behind the eleph-ANT. Icarus pushed the throttle lever forward and the Mark One rocketed ahead.

Icarus watched as the eleph-ANT raced toward the gas giant. The illusion of the rings around the gas giant started to disappear. Icarus could see large asteroids and rocks.

They were several kilometers away.

"How big are those rocks, Lex?" Icarus asked, pointing at one of the large objects.

The orb appeared in the eleph-ANT with Icarus and Ship. The AI added a chart to the screen in front of Icarus. It showed the large rock they could see was about the size of Mount Everest. It was huge, and it was moving fast around the gas planet in a clockwise direction—left to right from their reference point and orientation.

Icarus moved the control stick; the Mark One turned to face

the orbit of the rings. He increased the throttle, trying to match the spin and aim for the Everest-sized object.

"Icarus, you can't move that fast," Ship warned.

Icarus thought for a moment. Ship was right. He needed to pick another object to land on. The Mark One was getting closer to the ring, which to him looked like he was approaching a bunch of floating boulders in space. There were millions of large asteroids in front of the eleph-ANT Mark One. Between all the large objects was a subtle haze which he assumed was dust particles and micro-asteroids. The Everest-sized object he had hoped to land on was covered in ice.

Relative to the asteroids orbiting the gas giant, the Mark One was moving too slow. Any impact would destroy it, but it was too late to turn around.

Icarus pointed at a new asteroid. "I have an idea."

He angled the nose of the Mark One toward one of the solid-looking asteroids, tracking it as it moved. He pressed a button on the controls. Out of the nose of the Mark One shot a cable, striking the asteroid dead center. Dust and micro-asteroids flew everywhere. He hoped he had lodged it into something solid. Icarus took a breath of anticipation as he waited to find out. It didn't take long—the cable was pulled taut and the Mark One lurched forward, pulled by the asteroid it was connected to.

Icarus and Ship rocked in their seats. "The lines connected to this eleph-ANT give us the full sensory experience," remarked Icarus excitedly. "I bet you didn't expect that."

The Mark One spun wildly. All six of its leg engines ignited, firing hard to correct the spin. Icarus struggled to orient its legs toward the incoming river of rocks, but he was fighting a losing battle, as the Mark One almost spun out of control. His reaction time was too slow. "Ship, do you mind!" he yelled in frustration.

Ship grabbed the fake controller in front of him and mimicked controlling the eleph-ANT. Almost like magic, the Mark One started to gain its composure. The spinning stopped and its legs oriented themselves toward the incoming asteroid.

The Mark One wasn't flailing wildly anymore, but it was still hurtling toward the incoming river of rocks, all six legs fighting to slow the incoming asteroid. A few milliseconds passed.

And then impact, followed by an explosion of dust and the Mark One bouncing off the asteroid.

Icarus fired the engines again, turning it around to angle the Mark One back toward the asteroid for a second landing attempt. He could feel the excitement in his hands. He held the control stick tightly, the constant squeezing putting indentations into its leather grip. He hadn't felt like this in a while—the thrill of the real world, the danger the Mark One experienced, the creativity he had when harpooning the massive asteroid, the great skill involved in maneuvering its legs to face the incoming ring. He smiled to himself.

At that moment—while Icarus was deep in thought—an asteroid about the size of a tanker truck struck the Mark One. It was completely and utterly destroyed.

The lights turned on. Ship and Icarus stopped shaking in their cockpit. They were gently lowered back to the ground.

Icarus cursed himself for spending too much time thinking about his achievements and not enough time with his head in the game. "Sorry, Ship; I think I know what to do now."

Why was he shooting from the hip? Preparation and research were what he excelled at. Icarus found himself caught up in the excitement of exploring a new world. It wasn't like him. He needed to understand the situation better. He needed to be deliberate and methodical.

He had become stuck with all the jostling to control the Mark One. He wiggled out of his seat and grabbed a permanent marker and the stack of stickers that had been printed and ran from the hollowed-out eleph-ANT toward the hangar airlock. Two eleph-ANTs were waiting near the door. He looked around, finding a shelf with stacks of the smaller ANTs. He plucked two from the shelf. With a pen he wrote on each of them *Mark Two-A* and *Mark Two-B* and placed them both in the middle of the airlock.

Before teleporting, he walked past the two eleph-ANTs waiting outside the airlock. He pressed a sticker onto each of them—*Mark Three* and *Mark Four*—before teleporting back inside his makeshift eleph-ANT control center.

"Ship, we're going to find out what we're dealing with," Icarus said, buckling himself back in.

They launched the Mark Two-A and -B out of the airlock. Icarus took control of the Mark Two-A. "Ship, can you control the Two-B and send it to the other side of the ring?"

Icarus sent his ANT to the top of the ring (relative to their perspective) and Ship the bottom. As the ANTs fell toward the gas giant, they scanned the rings, building a map of the rings as they looked for a place to land.

Icarus pointed at the screen in front of them. "Are you seeing that, Ship?"

"The bands?"

"Yes, it looks like there are seven bands of rings traveling at different speeds."

Icarus replaced the first-person view of his ANTs traveling through space with the 3-D map of the rings. The outermost ring, the one that had destroyed the Mark One, was the least uniform. It was made up of asteroids of many different sizes loosely stuck together. That's why he had struggled to navigate that ring—the lack of uniformity made for an impossible task.

The second and third ring in looked the same. They were both made up of dust particles. Both had many tiny fragments, but there was a large empty space between both bands. Icarus thought about it for a second. It was odd. Almost as if both bands were originally one large ring but a moon had cut through the middle, turning one large ring into two very separate bands.

"They were probably a single big ring once. Both the second and third rings are moving at the same speed," Icarus noted.

The fourth ring in was the one Icarus thought would be the most fun to explore. It was made up of many ice rocks and was very uniform in mass—roughly the size of large tanker trucks, lots of them, but in different shapes—some round, and some long and jagged. He thought about how easy it would be to jump from asteroid to asteroid.

As Icarus's ANT drew closer to the fourth ring, he realized it wasn't truly a ring after all. It was made up of many small moons. They were all big enough that their gravity made them a spherical shape. There were thousands of them, all evenly spaced.

Icarus wondered how it was that stable orbits like this had formed. That shouldn't be possible. He looked up at the orb floating near him. "Lex, do you know how these large moons stay in orbit?"

Two words appeared in front of Icarus: *Insufficient data.*

"Just guess, Lex."

The orb flashed red, its subtle glow lighting up the small space they were in.

Icarus glared at Lex, a frustrated look on his face. "Give me a probability on whether this is natural, then."

It was Ship who answered, obviously annoyed at Lex's inability to give a straight answer too. "Lex believes it's natural. But he's only seventy-two percent confident about that."

Icarus hated how Lex responded sometimes. For a supercomputer, he didn't give many answers. Icarus placed his annoyance aside for a second and continued on his mission. He knew where he wanted to go now. He smacked his hand down on the launch button, and the Mark Three eleph-ANT flew out of the airlock.

"Ship, how long will it take the Mark Three to get to the fourth ring?"

"Twenty-seven minutes."

Icarus smiled. "Perfect." He turned his head toward the orb in the corner. "Lex, map me a path to the fourth ring, the one with the most uniform asteroids. Project it on my screen as a waypoint. And pick a spot for me to aim for. Somewhere with lots of truck-sized rocks that are within jumping distance of each other."

Several arrows appeared on Icarus's screen. A countdown timer. He maneuvered the Mark Three in the direction of the arrows. As he drew closer, a red target mark appeared around one of the drifting rocks.

He locked on to it and fired the rockets on each of the six legs, slowing the Mark Three's speed relative to the huge asteroid and matching the speed and angle of the target asteroid.

"Touchdown in three, two, one," Ship announced.

The Mark Three and the asteroid connected, but a lot of dust and rocks flew off near the Mark Three's feet.

"You've connected to the asteroid," advised Ship, "but there are a lot of smaller objects loosely gravitationally bound to it."

Not raising his hands off the control, Icarus replied, "Is there a risk of us just smashing through an asteroid that consists of only small rocks held together by weak gravity?"

"I don't think so. Lex has mapped you a path. The series of waypoints he created only contacts asteroids that are solid."

And with that, Icarus jerked the control stick forward. The Mark Three took off, running along one side of the asteroid.

On each of the Mark Three's six legs were three mechanical claws that would bite onto the asteroid then let go as it moved. These claws provided the Mark Three with more traction on the asteroid in the weaker gravity.

"This is the part I was excited about," Icarus said, a boyish grin on his face.

The Mark Three was about six more steps away from the edge of the asteroid. It ran. There was another asteroid across the gap of space. The Mark Three jumped, floating and then landing, dust and particles flying off with the impact. Icarus didn't slow it down. It ran across the bottom of this new asteroid before jumping. This time, the Mark Three needed to spin slightly in order to connect with the new asteroid. It spun around, the tiny thrusters on its right side firing to position the machine appropriately. It connected, the legs locking into place as it continued to run.

Icarus was loving every minute of this. It was a million times better than the 2-D obstacle games he used to love playing as a kid. This was 3-D, and the physics weren't a simulation. It was real.

He had been running through the ring for hours now—he'd crossed the entire layer and was at the edge of the fourth ring.

"The Mark Three is almost out of energy," Ship said.

He was right. The Mark Three would barely get back to the spacecraft. They might have to send a few ANTs to collect it.

Icarus stared through the eyes of the Mark Three, looking from its perspective. Many moons made up the next ring around this gas giant. Through the cameras he could see five in close proximity. It didn't look possible. Such a stable orbit of large bodies, without them coming into contact with each other.

"Are these orbits stable over hundreds of years?" Icarus asked.

"I believe so," Ship replied, not wanting to annoy Icarus with an uninformative answer from Lex.

Icarus pointed at the moons orbiting the gas giant. "I want to explore those moons."

"They're too far apart to jump from object to object."

As Ship explained how it wasn't possible to explore each of the moons using an eleph-ANT, Icarus began to wonder whether this gas giant could be his world.

His mind flooded with ideas. It was in the Goldilocks zone. The moons orbited the gas giant every twenty-four and a half hours. That was close enough to Earth's day-and-night cycle that Earth life wouldn't require much engineering to make it work. The rings had more than enough resources to build everything he needed.

He thought about plans—running a cable from moon to moon, enabling both communication and an easy way to move between them. Over time he could build a ring world using up all the resources in a few of the ring bands to build a permanent structure around the gas giant.

Icarus turned to Ship. "We are going to seed these moons."

"You want to make this our planet?" Ship questioned, then nodded. "Okay, it could work. So, what should we name it?"

Icarus thought for a while. About the gas giant. About the rings. About a book he once read called *Ringworld*. While he thought, he took control of the Mark Three once more. It let go of the asteroid it was connected to and drifted up into space. The engines fired and it began traveling back toward the ship.

There was a large asteroid he hadn't noticed while he was distracted in thought. It destroyed the Mark Three.

Icarus wasn't bothered. He let go of the controls, turned around, and said, "Let's call this planet . . . Titan."

CHAPTER 18

TRILLION

PLANET 3.0

Trillion and her team spent the journey experimenting. They tested how slow and fast they could make time seem. Trillion thought watching the universe fly by deserved to be on the list of experiences everyone got to enjoy. It was bucket-list-worthy.

She found there wasn't much of a limit on how slow she could make things. She equally hadn't reached a practical limit on how fast she could make her perception of time.

They arrived in the new star system after what felt like a few months of travel. Adapting her playback speed made it a very pleasant journey.

Standing on the bridge of her spacecraft, with a projection of the new system she was in, she found the system was a lot like her home system: several different planets orbiting a Sunlike star.

There were two planets in the Goldilocks zone—both might have liquid water on them. The first had a decent-sized moon orbiting it, too. But it was the second planet that caught her eye. She zoomed in on the planet. She wasn't close enough to see anything small, but she felt a curious certainty that there was life there. She didn't know why she was so sure, but she had a gut feeling. She wondered just how common life was in this universe.

Trillion looked out the port window. She was at the perfect angle to see the planet below her. She could see half of it bathed in starlight—the other half was covered in darkness. She scrutinized the planet and could see it getting brighter and darker. "What is that?" she murmured to herself. It looked as though the planet was flicking a light switch on and off. She blinked a few times, not quite believing what she was seeing. "Is that a fire down there?"

She wondered if it was possible for an entire planet to be on fire. "Lex, is that light showing up under infrared?"

The orb flashed red.

Trillion noticed something else was happening to the planet. It was changing color. "Is that planet turning purple, Ship?" she said, confusion clear in her voice.

The Ship of Trillion had been cruising toward the planet for several hours, firing engines to slow down their approach.

Trillion had been fixated on the planet all the while. It repeated a pattern. Orange. Green. Purple. Over and over again without deviation.

Ship wandered over. "Trillion, I've been doing some research. Those colors we're seeing, they're only showing in a very narrow band of the electromagnetic spectrum."

Trillion turned her head. "Does that mean it might be intelligent life creating that? Or is it natural?"

Ship shook his head. "If it's natural, it's not giving off heat like a fire. But animals like glowworms give off light without heat."

"But they aren't that bright," Trillion said, thinking about it a little more. "It could be some sort of gas that changes color as it changes altitude in the atmosphere."

Trillion was a bit cautious about getting closer. "If it is intelligent life, they might think we're an asteroid. They might repel us." She mimed pushing someone away. "Let's take bets." She looked at each of her companions. "Ship, Lex, do you think it's intelligent life?"

Ship was willing to bet it was life. Lex refused to answer. It even refused to give a probability.

Before they came on this journey, they weren't sure just how common life was. They had always assumed it wasn't common at all. Humans hadn't yet encountered any aliens, although humans hadn't been around that long.

"Here are all the aliens. This is where they've been hiding." Trillion joked. "I bet the surface is covered in pyramids."

Ship laughed—he actually laughed at that.

Trillion wanted to get a better understanding of what she was dealing with before there was any chance of being put in harm's way. "Ship, I think we should retreat. Can you get us into orbit around the star? Let's stay close but not too close to the planet." She paused, thinking for a moment. "And send enough ANTs that we can get a complete picture of the planet without having to put anything into orbit around it. I want thermal imaging, density sensors, atmosphere and pressure data—everything. I definitely want to approach this with caution."

Ship deployed many different types of ANTs, five hundred in total.

ANTs were perfect for tasks like this; they were expendable and small. After what they had done on Steel World, they had an unlimited supply of them, too. They would continue through the star system, pass the planet, and send back images and data on the planet below.

....

They arrived in orbit around the local star. They had only been there a few days, but the ANTs were already sending them interesting data.

They had ruled out fire as a potential cause but hadn't yet ruled out gas or some sort of chemical reaction, although Trillion had her doubts about that, too.

She pointed at the planet she was sure had life on it. "Ship, pull up the ANT footage of that planet."

Ship livestreamed from one of the ANTs.

Trillion watched as the planet pulsated and changed color. "Do we have a closer view?"

Ship changed the view, streaming the live feed from an ANT closer in. From that ANT's perspective, the planet wasn't changing color at all—it appeared to be grey and brown.

Trillion stepped closer to the screen, wondering why she couldn't see any pulsating colors. "Ship, is this video feed live?"

"Yes."

"Then why isn't the planet changing colors? Are our ANTs using any different kind of camera from ours?"

Ship shrugged. "I'm not exactly sure. I'm as confused as you are."

Trillion opened her hands as if to catch a basketball. A haptic-gram of the planet appeared between her hands. "Lex, map the lights and color-change onto this globe."

She spun it around in her hand. She noticed that only one side of the planet was changing colors—the other side remained grey and inert.

Trillion pointed at the projection she was holding. "It's the colors. The pulsating colors are orbiting the planet. They're drifting."

Trillion let go. It floated where she released it. "Where is our ship in relation to this pulsating color pattern?"

A copy of her spacecraft appeared in front of the planet, right in the center of where it was changing colors and lighting up. Trillion took a hold of the ship. "Lex, as I move this spacecraft projection, show me what the planet looks like in relation to the spacecraft."

Trillion moved the projection of their ship back and forth. The planet's pattern changed and moved, yet the ship sat in the very center of the pulsating colors on the planet.

As Trillion moved her hand to and fro, she noticed that the colors followed the ship. She froze. "They know we're here." She couldn't think of any other plausible explanation.

Her jaw dropped. Aliens were communicating with her. "They know we're here," she repeated, almost not believing it as she spoke.

She wondered if this was the first time life had ever spoken to humanity. "Is this communication? If so, what do we say back? How do we communicate back?"

Ship pointed out the window of the bridge. "I don't think we'll have much time to communicate; we're about to cross onto the other side of the star, out of sight from the planet."

Trillion threw the holograms up in the air. The projection flew up and hovered above her head.

She looked out the window. "We'll be out of communication range of the ANTs, too. We won't be able to see the planet for a good while. What do we do now? It will be five days before we see the planet again."

Ship just shrugged. He was lost for words too.

Trillion turned away from the window. She looked at the looping pattern of the floating hologram. "There has got to be a message in that pattern. If it was following us around the planet, then that message was meant for us. It's communicating that they know about us. And it's communicating a message. But what does it mean?" She touched the back of her neck. "Lex, do you know what they're saying?"

The orb flashed blue.

Trillion frowned. When he flashed blue, it meant he didn't know what to say. She knew Lex hated dealing with uncertainty. He liked to be certain about it or he wouldn't say anything at all.

Ship started to list the facts. "We know they know about us. That says a lot." He nodded, speculating some more. "They know about directions."

Trillion knew Ship was right. "We can infer a lot of meaning from what little they showed. They also showed that colors have some meaning." Trillion stared up at the ceiling. "If I were an alien, how would I communicate?"

Ship pointed at Trillion. "They're also signaling they have control of the whole planet."

Trillion nodded. "What sort of civilization has the ability to quickly communicate at a planetary level? Earth wouldn't do that. Too many competing countries. Not even New Zealand could pull that off. Even with all their resources."

Trillion stepped away from the window. "I remember when New Zealand became a superpower. After the Kiwis created our first truly general artificial intelligence, it was game over for other countries. The singularity had begun. And even though the US and China managed to build much stronger artificial intelligences, the eighteen months it took them to get there meant it was too late."

Ship nodded. "I always find it funny when you plot out humanity's progression. It's so sudden. Your world changed in such a short amount of time. Six months is a long time to an artificial intelligence, let alone eighteen months. New Zealand had already patented almost every idea and built massive organizations."

Trillion looked back at the screen. "We have three pieces of data. What else can we infer?" She looked at the orb. "Lex, what can we rule out?"

The orb flashed blue, signaling it did not want to speculate.

Ship filled the silence by raising a finger to list out what they knew. "One, they have a concept of *us* and *them*. And, two"—he held up two fingers—"they also understand space and time."

Trillion wore a confused look on her face, not quite understanding Ship's logic.

Ship elaborated. "We were seeing light from sixteen minutes ago. But the pattern showed no lag."

Trillion gestured, encouraging Ship to continue.

"They pointed to us. They understood that we were sixteen minutes away. They understood the direction we were traveling. They understood that to show us their pattern they had to be sixteen minutes early. That means they could predict where we were in space *and* time."

Trillion was trying to process everything. She still struggled to believe that she had received a message from an alien. "If I were an alien, I'd be saying hello. So, are we the first humans to receive a *hello* message?"

Ship shrugged. "There's a saying in astronomy—*It's never aliens.*"

Trillion raised an eyebrow. "You're saying you don't think they're aliens?"

"No, I definitely think it's aliens. But we need to keep our minds open to the fact there might be a natural explanation for this."

"Okay, then, tell me."

Ship laughed. "Okay, I've got nothing. It's aliens."

Trillion laughed back. "Right, so as I was saying, I assume it's *Hello*. It's not like we have a common language yet. And it's not like we have any shared meanings yet. If this is truly an alien civilization, then it will truly be alien. Alien in thought. Alien in beliefs. Maybe it's impossible to communicate with them. Maybe they don't speak in a linear language. Ants communicate through smells. Bees communicate through dances. Is it possible to translate humans' words into smells or dances?"

Ship nodded. "Lex suggested you start collecting as much data as possible."

A touch of worry crept onto Trillion's face. "Do you think staying here is dangerous?" She shook her head, answering her own question. "I don't think we're at risk. But when we spoke about the Kiwis building the first AI, it got me thinking . . . New Zealand was very chill. They were content with getting rich and inventing things for all of humanity. But what if they weren't happy with just money and fame? What if they wanted to take over all of Earth?"

Ship looked at her, a little puzzled. "What does this have to do with aliens?"

"Well," Trillion took a deep breath, "let's say a terrorist organisation invented AI first. They could have taken over the whole of Earth. It would be easy with an AI's help, at least back in the days before AIs were everywhere. What I'm saying is that we might be encountering an alien species ruthless enough to take over its entire planet."

CHAPTER 19

TRILLION

FIRST CONTACT

Trillion floated, her legs and arms crossed. She relaxed her shoulders as she gently bobbed up and down. They had spent hours discussing theories and ideas as their ship slipped out of sight behind the star, and Trillion was tense from the stress and excitement. She had finally managed to slip away for thirty minutes to wind down, and the weightlessness of zero gravity always seemed to calm her.

Ship entered her office, disrupting her meditation, excitement plastered all over his voice. "Our ANTs are in range."

With a surge of anticipation, Trillion waved her hands in front of her, and a large screen appeared. She replayed footage of the planet while it had been out of their sight.

The planet stopped changing colors. It did nothing. She stared at the screen, trying to make sense of it. "Ship, is this correct?"

As soon as they disappeared around the other side of the star, the planet had stopped changing colors and did nothing at all. Trillion assumed the planet didn't know about the ANTs. It could only see their ship. Or at least it chose not to focus its communication efforts on their ANTs.

Ship nodded. "I think the planet only knows about us. So, as soon as we went on to the other side, it stopped changing colors."

Trillion took a deep breath. That was the conclusion she was coming to herself.

They were nearing the other edge of the star, almost in direct line of sight with the planet. And the planet once again started cycling through the colors. Green. Orange. Purple. Green. Orange. Purple. Not so much fading between the colors but flashing each of those colors.

Trillion narrowed her eyes, trying to decipher what the colors might mean. She needed more information. "Ship, can the planet see us yet?"

"No."

"Hmm . . . It should take our light twenty-seven minutes to reach this planet. So, after they see us, it should take another twenty-seven minutes for their color message to reach us. This means that the planet started playing the message twenty-seven minutes early. They understand that light takes time to travel."

"Yes, and they also have a very good grasp on orbital mechanics, knowing exactly when we would come around the other side of the star."

Trillion rewound the video back to the beginning. "Lex, how accurate was their timing?"

Lex made a beeping sound and numbers appeared on the screen in front of Trillion. *3 minutes and 32 seconds fast.*

"Interesting," Trillion said as she watched the video again. "Okay, so they aren't tracking us. They don't permanently know where we are. But they can predict based on our orbit."

Trillion watched as the planet changed colors constantly. Green. Orange. Purple. "How hard would it be to build a large screen?"

Trillion realized she was still floating in the air. She stretched her legs and dropped to the floor, making her way to the door. She motioned to Ship and Lex to follow her.

As they walked, Trillion started building a plan. "Lex and Ship, can you create architecture plans for a large light projector? I want to construct a projector about the size of a large spa pool. One for each color. They need to be modular. I'm thinking hexagon-shaped so they fit together like a honeycomb. We want it modular because we need to be able to add other colors if we find the planet communicates in other colors. That way, if we need to add blue, we can." Trillion looked at them both. "Can you get that done as soon as possible? I'm going to distract myself with the gym. Come grab me when it's done."

Trillion was in the gym when Ship called her. She no longer needed to work out, but she found it such a great way to meditate and process her thinking. She teleported to the bridge as soon as she heard Ship's call.

The construction was completed just in time. They almost had to go around the star another time, but Lex and Ship had completed the construction of the large honeycomb lights before they were no longer visible. The whole time, the planet kept flashing the same colors. Green. Orange. Purple. Or was it purple, green, orange? Trillion wasn't sure which color came first, but she guessed it didn't matter. "Hurry, let's start sending a message to them. Just send back what they showed us. Use green as the first color."

Ship got the projector going. He turned the green light on. Then the orange. Then the purple. In that order. Making sure to match the timing of their colors down to the millisecond. It would be some time before a response came back.

Trillion paced in circles around the room as she waited anxiously. "Ship, let's change our playback speed." *Why wait for something like this?* she thought.

Time sped up. What felt like five seconds later, the reply came. Same colors. But the order had changed.

Purple. Orange. Green.

"Lex, show me how long each color appeared along the temporal scale." Trillion wanted to see if the time had changed. She wondered if they spent more time on a particular color. "Did any of the colors change in brightness? Or hue? Give me all the data you can."

A spreadsheet appeared on the screen in front of her, showing rows and rows of data.

It was a long list. She started scrolling down. "Lex, this isn't useful. Graph it. Highlight what I should be looking at."

A second tab appeared on the spreadsheet. She clicked it. Several tabs and charts appeared on it.

She scanned the charts. Nothing. No change in brightness. No change in hue. She was about to dismiss the screen when she noticed something. One of the lines wasn't perfectly flat. It didn't have a key on it, either, so she wasn't sure what it pointed to. But she assumed the line should be perfectly straight. "Lex, did you just make a bunch of random charts?"

The orb flashed green.

Trillion slapped her forehead. "I'm trusting you to visualize the data in a meaningful way. It's not useful like this." She shook her head and pointed to where the line had a slight kink in it. "Show me this data in a spreadsheet."

The screen changed to the tab with all the data. On it a single box was highlighted green. One number had changed from 16.04 to 16.40.

She looked up at the top screen. It was the number of seconds for purple. Up until this point, purple had only been shown for 16.04 seconds. And it was the exact length of time, every single time. Same as the other colors.

Except it increased by 360 milliseconds. A tiny fraction but noticeable.

Trillion pondered what it might mean. "That change is not trivial. I think they made it intentionally to convey something."

She looked up at the orb. "Lex, can you change each color to flash the same duration as before but increase purple to 16.4 seconds?"

The team waited thirty-five minutes for a response to arrive back to them. Even though it was four seconds of subjective time, Trillion still felt like it took forever.

It was a slightly different message this time. More seconds flashing purple. And less orange. They spent a good twenty seconds showing purple this time.

The time was long enough for Trillion to notice. "I wonder what this means. Purple is obviously a significant color for them. What do you think, Ship?"

Ship shrugged. "Maybe purple is *hello*. It's hard to say."

Trillion nodded. "Purple might mean *friends*. Or it could mean *Stay away; we are infected with a virus*. It's almost impossible to say."

Trillion looked out the port window. They were rounding the other side of the star now. "We have time to send one more message and maybe get a reply. We need more data. We have enough time to test it again before we cross to the other side of the star."

"Ship, should we mirror them, change the pattern, or send back the first message we ever sent?" She looked up at Lex. "What do you think?"

Ship thought for a moment before making a decision. "We send our original message."

"Okay, now what do you think, Lex?"

Lex made the screen in front of Trillion purple.

"Lex, are you suggesting we just send back a solid purple?"

The orb flashed green.

Trillion rubbed her hands together She knew Lex would suggest the option that would yield the most data—the most data for him to analyze and re-analyze. She nodded. "Let's go with Lex's suggestion."

"Ship, send back a message of solid purple."

Lex was right. Exactly thirty-five minutes later, their reply appeared. And exactly fifty-three minutes after, they crossed to the other side of the star. For eighteen minutes, they received the same pattern. No orange this time. No green.

Just purple.

Purple. Then nothing. Then purple again.

It was the first time they had seen just a single color. The intervals between showing purple were random. It wasn't a constant blinking light—it was a light flashing randomly. A purple light.

Trillion was thrilled. "Great idea, Lex. They responded so differently. I have so many theories running through my head."

Trillion's mind was going a million miles an hour. "Lex, what are your theories now?" She looked over at Ship. "And how about yours?"

She started floating up to the ceiling, her excitement causing her to rise higher. She couldn't wait to get to the other side of the star, to attempt to communicate with the aliens again. "What do you think they look like? Do you think we're talking to them? Or one of their AIs?"

Ship smiled. "We have to be talking to an AI. Their responses are too exact. But I'm itching to find out what they look like."

"Itching?" Trillion said, a little surprised by Ship's response. "Since when are you itching for anything, Ship?"

"Leave me alone; I'm just testing different ways of speaking. I thought *itching* was a nice way to communicate that I'm excited. Apparently, it's not." He seemed highly offended.

Trillion smiled. "Aww," she said, holding back a laugh. "Sorry, Ship, I didn't mean to tease you. I'm itching to find out too. Let's change our playback speed so we can get around the star faster."

CHAPTER 20
TRILLION

PURPLE DOT

Trillion gazed out into space. She marveled at how watching time speed up looked magical. It was her first time being this close to a star. Everything looked purple. She pointed out the window. "Is that what redshifted light looks like?"

She assumed that maybe changing her playback speed was causing light from the star to look purple. She wondered why she hadn't noticed it before. It was a mesmerizing view.

Trillion could see purple light blurring together across all the windows. The light in the bridge turned off, plunging her into darkness. Her view vanished.

She heard Ship's voice over the speakers. "I need more processing power. I'm changing you to real time."

In an instant, real time hit Trillion. Normally, when she resumed real time, it felt gradual. Slow. She could tell this one was sudden. Rough.

She scanned the bridge, trying to locate Ship. Red warning lights began to flash. She searched for Ship's avatar. "What is going on, Ship?"

Trillion could hear noises around her. It sounded like hail was hitting the ship.

Thump. Thump. Thump.

Trillion spun away from the window. She pulled up a screen, this time thinking about the order, not wasting time on gestures. Six screens appeared in front of her, each one projecting live video feeds from different parts of the spacecraft. She scanned the image feeds. Nothing. No external camera was working. "What's going on? Did we break something?" she yelled out.

No response.

"Ship!"

Still no response.

She turned around, commanding another six screens to appear in front of her, this time showing live video feeds from ANTs floating in space, quickly flicking from one ANT's point of view to another.

Nothing.

She swiped through another six ANTs' perspective. *Still* nothing.

Again, through another set of ANTs' feeds. This time, she saw something. One had a distant shot of the ship. It was unrecognizable—the ship was purple.

She turned the camera and focused it on her location. Pinch. Zoom. All she could see was something purple where the spacecraft should have been. She zoomed in.

The image started to resemble something real. It looked like purple dots had assembled themselves into the shape of her spacecraft. She zoomed in even further. It was her spacecraft. Covered in purple dots. Almost like her spacecraft had gotten sick.

Trillion looked around the room, frantically trying to find Ship. "What is this? Why are there purple dots all over us?"

No response.

"Ship!"

Still no response.

"Lex?"

The orb appeared in front of Trillion, pulsating red. She put out a hand and patted the orb, grateful for something familiar. "What is going on?"

Lex changed one of the screens, switching the footage to one of the ANTs to show a better angle of the ship. A closer look revealed a timestamp across the top of the footage, showing it was from thirty minutes earlier.

Trillion leaned in and examined the recording. On one end of the image she saw her spacecraft. It wasn't covered in purple; it was as she remembered it.

Then she started to see purple streaks racing past the ANT. She paused the video, zooming in on one of the dots. It looked soft, almost jelly-like. Purple jelly.

She continued the video, watching the dots fly through past the ANT. Splat. One of them hit the ship. Splat. Then another. And another. Hundreds of them. Thousands of them. They pelted the ship. *Her* ship. *Her* spacecraft. Soon, it was covered in them. She watched as her engines were covered, too.

She played the rest of the video at double speed, watching it until the video reached real time.

Trillion spun the ANT around, toward the direction the purple was originating from. "Where did these come from?"

The orb flashed blue. One of the screens was replaced with an image of the planet they were trying to communicate with.

Trillion took a deep breath and paced around in circles. What was going on? Encountering hostile aliens had crossed her mind, but she hadn't given a second thought to being *attacked* by them. "Why are they attacking us?"

She looked at her screens again, walking toward the one showing her spacecraft. It looked as if it was covered in purple paint. She watched as purple dot after purple dot hit the ship, then every so often, one would fall off and float away, almost like flaking skin.

"Lex, can you hack in to Ship? Have they damaged his matrix? Can you get us out of here?"

The orb flashed red.

"Well, then can you get Ship back online? I really need to talk to him."

As soon as those words left her mouth, the ship lurched and started moving. Then Ship flashed into existence in front of her.

He looked confused. "Why did you slow me down?" he said, before disappearing again.

"Lex, get him back. I need to speak to him."

Lex flashed blue. Then red.

One of the screens in front of Trillion changed, presenting a large fast-forward symbol.

Trillion smiled. "You want me to increase my playback speed?"

The orb flashed green.

The world around Trillion crawled to a halt. Everything stopped moving.

She started to hear Ship's voice come through the speakers. "I . . ."

Ship's voice became clearer through the speakers. "I'm trying to get this ship back under my control."

A flash of fear hit her face. *Have they hacked in to Ship? How? Do they have computers compatible with his matrix?* Questions started racing through her mind. "Have we been hacked?"

"No," replied Ship through the speaker. He sounded robotic, not like his usual self.

Trillion felt in the dark. Not in control. "Ship, if you don't tell me what's going on, I'm going to have to manually override you."

That worked. Ship appeared in his physical form. "The purple polka dots were attaching themselves to me." He pointed out the window. "They are forcing us out of orbit. I'm having to fire the engines hard just to stay in control. I'm trying to remove them."

"So, how do we get rid of them?"

Ship shrugged. "We don't have any guns, so I'm piloting ANTs and eleph-ANTs to try and remove them. That's what I'm focusing on. I'm controlling hundreds of thousands of ANTs at once, attempting to get them off my shell."

Trillion looked down. "So, when I forced you to join me in real time, we were overwhelmed. That's why we lurched?"

Ship nodded.

Trillion looked over at one of the screens, replacing the image with one of the star system. "So, where are they pulling us? Into the star?"

Ship shook his head and rotated the image on Trillion's screen, zooming in on a moon orbiting the planet. "Our current trajectory has us on course to collide with that moon."

"Hmm." Trillion looked at Ship. "This might not be as bad as we thought. If they wanted to destroy us, I think they would have sent us into the star already. Still, this was definitely a hostile action, and they clearly know that."

Trillion looked at Lex. "Do we still have access to communications?"

The orb flashed green.

Ship added some details. "It doesn't even look like they have any awareness of our communications. We received a lot of data back from the ANTs. It showed no radio signals coming from the planet."

"Okay, so we're being attacked by this planet that doesn't have any radio signals?" Trillion asked. "So, how do we escape from these aliens?"

Ship looked down. "We don't. There's too many of them. I don't think we can escape their grasp."

Trillion looked at Ship in despair. "What do you mean?"

Ship spoke in a low voice, as if he was resigned to the fact. "They have covered our thrusters. Trying to push away from the moon isn't working—there are too many . . ." Ship paused, not quite used to the new word. ". . . too many purple aliens covering our thrusters." He took a deep breath. "Sorry, Trillion, we are headed toward the moon."

Trillion cocked her head to one side. "Are you sure we're headed for the moon? How do you know they're not going to destroy us?"

Ship looked at the orb in the corner. "Lex is fairly confident that we're headed toward the moon. With the amount of energy they expended to get our delta-*v* to match the moon, it would have been easier simply to push us into the star. Or send us out of the system." Ship paused for a moment. "We still don't know what they'll do once we reach the moon."

As the aliens relocated Trillion, Ship, and Lex to the moon, the team debated about what to call their attackers.

"So, what should we call them then?" Trillion asked, considering her ideas. "Polka Dots?" she suggested, then shook her head. "No, that doesn't sound right." She took a breath. "Let's call them the Dottiens," she decided, plucking the name out of thin air.

"I like it," Ship said.

The Dottiens ignored their ANTs and eleph-ANTs that were already out there. Trillion and Ship used all the ANTs they had floating in the system to do as much reconnaissance as possible. What the team discovered was fascinating. Dottiens were extremely cautious about contaminating their home planet with anything that came into contact with their spacecraft.

Instead of returning to their home planet, any of the Dottiens' purple spacecraft that were unfortunate enough to peel away from the ship immediately sped off to incinerate themselves in the star.

They sent a few ANTs to check out the Dottiens' planet, too, and managed to get some high-resolution images, but any ANT that got too close was hit by a Dottien. Then both the ANT and the purple Dottien headed for the star. It didn't matter how small the ANT was, either. The team sent a few thousand of their micro-ANTs, each the size of a grain of rice. Every single one of them was ignored until they came too close to the planet. Then, one by one, each of them was mopped up and taken to the star.

The team realized they were free to send ANTs to orbit and touch any other planet in the star system—just the home planet was out of bounds. Uncertain if they would eventually start rounding up all their ANTs in future, they were cautious, so they sent a large contingency of ANTs to the Lagrange point on the opposite side of the star—L3. Lagrange points were special locations in an orbiting pair where objects, like ANTs, would always be in the same location. In this case, it meant most of their ANTs would always be hiding on the opposite side of the star.

Trillion, Ship, and Lex were moments away from touching down on the moon orbiting the second planet in the star system. It was a cold planet with mountains and oceans, but it looked like it was in the middle of an ice age.

The moon orbiting the planet was tiny and tidally locked to the planet.

Trillion looked over at Ship. "What information do we have on this moon?"

Ship froze for a moment, quickly pulling everything he could up on the screen. "It is basically a metal rock. If it had been made of as much water and silicon as the Moon back at Earth, it would have broken up. It wouldn't have enough mass to hold itself together. This moon, however, is mostly iron. It's dense and hard."

"Do you think it's an artificial moon?" asked Trillion. "Do you think the aliens created this as a way to store their metals?"

Ship shrugged. "Maybe."

They landed on the moon with sudden *ding*. It sounded like hitting a bell. The Dottiens underneath were squished. Ship tried to launch the rockets again, but the squashed Dottiens were like concrete—they were stuck to the moon. Trillion was surprised to learn that they had access to all of the ship's communication networks. The Dottiens made no attempt to block communications coming from the Ship of Trillion, and they still had ANTs waiting around the star system. The Dottiens' planet was still visible—the team had eyes on the whole star system. As soon as they touched down, the purple of the planet changed to a pulsating cascade of colors traveling through the planet.

The Dottiens on the ship shifted too, transforming from purple to grey, until they were lifeless and still.

"Lex, do you understand their language yet?" Trillion said, assuming that was another set of data he could study.

The orb just flashed purple.

Trillion looked up at it. "Is that a joke?" she said, almost laughing at what Lex did. She wondered if Lex was going to develop a personality, like Ship.

"Can we escape, Ship?" Trillion asked. "With the Dottiens' spacecraft crushed underneath us, I assumed they would no longer respond. We might be able to take off quickly. Escape before it realizes what is going on."

The ship's thrusters ignited. The whole ship shook. Ten percent of power. Nothing. It didn't even move.

"I'm increasing engine output," Ship said as he pushed them to the maximum.

The ship started to move. Slowly. A few centimeters off the ground.

Every single Dottien spacecraft near them turned purple, as if awakened at the same time. The ship was forced back down.

Ship shook his head. "With the Dottiens below us acting like concrete, gluing us to this moon, I think it's unlikely we'll be able to make a quick escape."

"They declared war on us. And now we're their prisoners!" Trillion said with a touch of anger. She could feel emotions boiling up in her. She felt herself getting angry. It wasn't just the fact she was stuck on the moon. It was because she was no longer on track to seed a world. She had an internal desire to bring her children into this world. And now she felt like that reality was getting further and further away.

"What do we do next?" Trillion asked, at a loss as to what to do. Neither Ship nor Lex had a clue.

Days went by, but the strange beings made no effort to make contact—and Trillion felt herself becoming more and more agitated with each passing hour.

"What do they want?" she cried impatiently, but Ship had no response.

The Dottiens still coated the ship like thick glue. They weren't giving them any answers. Grey, unmoving, and eerily silent, they would only spring back to life when they sensed any kind of escape attempt from their frustrated prisoners.

Three days passed, and Trillion was in the middle of giving orders to superheat the external shell of the ship, when Lex began glowing more brightly than she had ever seen before.

"We have a visitor," Ship announced.

Trillion, Ship, and Lex gathered on the bridge, watching the steady approach of another Dottien spacecraft—almost identical to the ones that had swarmed them days earlier but much larger. It moved slower, coasting toward them before gracefully setting down a few hundred meters from their position. Immediately upon landing, the entire vessel began pulsating with colors.

Trillion looked out the bridge window. "What is that?"

CHAPTER 21

ATLAS

PLANET OF ATLAS

Atlas sat at his desk amidst mountains of papers. Books were scattered all over the room, many open on the floor, showing graphs, charts, and preliminary data on the star system.

Atlas preferred physical things. He extracted a piece of paper from between two books.

He was a simulated human, but everything in his office was real. He scanned the room, taking note of the chair, the table, even the half-eaten sandwich. Everything in the room was real.

Atlas folded the piece of paper in half. Hapticgrams had better fidelity than the real world. It was the final invention he had made back on Sol before they departed. All of the Beta Explorer ships received the upgrade too.

Atlas had spent over a thousand years on this journey, and unlike any other Beta Explorer, he had personally experienced almost every moment of it. He preferred to spend the time researching and improving, and along the way he had watched a star go supernova, slowing down his perception of time to watch the beauty unfold in slow motion.

On this long journey, Atlas invented a few more things. He folded the paper again. So much time alone. With only Ship and Lex, he thought. Using an outdated simulation. The windows. Older hapticgraphic simulations couldn't do windows properly.

The original hapticgrams were projected around a blank ship. They could move around the ship, but for some strange reason the windows didn't look quite right. Atlas had finished folding the paper into a little aeroplane.

As he held the plane, he thought about the fact that in seven days he would arrive in the new solar system. *Star system*, Atlas corrected himself—*only Sol's system is called the solar system.* Atlas threw the plane toward an open window. It passed through and hit Ship on the back of his head.

"Throwing that plane through that window wasn't possible three hundred years ago, Ship," Atlas yelled out as a way of apologizing.

He still had the desire to seed worlds, Atlas thought, as he took another bite of the sandwich. It was too risky to make any changes to his core code. Any change could alter who he was. Could he change something without becoming someone else entirely?

Not long, he thought. *Not long.*

Atlas called a team meeting.

Lex was in the cargo hangar, waiting for him. Ship teleported there, expecting Atlas to teleport too.

Atlas took the long way, past the embryos. He slowed his pace, turning his head toward the large door, behind which were all his embryos. His children.

He wanted to stop. *Three more steps.* He made it past the embryos. *Now just up the lift and to the bridge.*

He pushed the button for the lift. The wait. He couldn't wait. He turned around and took five quick steps back. He stood in front of the door. His children's door. The embryos' door. He reached out and touched the door. It was huge. It was cold. Not simulated cold but really cold. It was an improvement to haptic-graphic projections he had made a few hundred years before.

Atlas took a deep breath and teleported to the cargo hangar.

Ship took a step backward, startled when Atlas appeared in front of him. Ship had assumed Atlas wasn't coming.

Atlas scanned the stadium-sized room, squinting to see the other side.

"I wish we had more resources," he said.

"We consumed most of it on the journey here," Ship replied. "Building and testing the communication device required a quarter of everything we had."

Atlas walked along the bay, Ship beside him. He took in each empty shelf and swiped his hand over one of them. Dusty.

They wandered over to a pile of resource pellets. Atlas picked one up and tossed it to Ship.

Ship felt the weight. "This is empty."

Atlas nodded. "Let's hope there are resources in this system."

They wandered toward the middle of the room.

"This place looks much bigger without anything in it," Atlas commented. "Lex, can you create a list of what we had before we left?"

The orb flashed green. A tablet appeared in Atlas's hand. The screen showed a list of everything they had when they started this journey and everything they had left. The first list wasn't very long—the second list was pitiful.

Atlas scanned the list. "We have all the fabricators, but we've cannibalized most of our ANTs."

Ship nodded. "We need resources."

"And we need a plan of how we will seed this system," Atlas said as he produced a piece of paper from his pocket. "We will be in orbit in a few days."

On the paper were the details of the three bodies of this system.

One star. One gas giant. One ice world.

"Still no information on any asteroid belt?" Atlas asked, hoping the answer had changed since he last asked the question. Without an asteroid belt, finding resources was going to be difficult.

"I believe the gas giant has ejected most objects in this system," Ship informed him.

Atlas couldn't believe how unlucky he was. An ice world. And few resources. "We don't have the tech to pull resources from the gas giant. . . yet. Is there any other way of us getting resources?"

"There are a few moons orbiting the gas giant," Ship replied.

Atlas made a strange face. He bit his lower lip, almost covering it in the process. Atlas had this habit of biting his lower lip when he was concentrating. The more he thought about a problem, the less of his lower lip he had visible. He raised a finger. "So, we have a planet we need to warm up. And a real lack of resources." He looked at the orb. "Lex, assuming we can warm the planet, is it habitable?"

The orb flashed green.

Ship filled in the context. "We need to scan the planet properly. I suggest we place an eleph-ANT in orbit around the planet."

"Do we have enough of them?" Atlas asked.

Ship nodded. "We can spare three."

Atlas pointed at the orb. "Okay, Lex, let's do one thing at a time." He began to run through the list on his fingers. "Send one ANT to orbit the planet. Once we understand if this planet has the ability to host life, we can start looking at collecting resources."

"We should also come up with a few ideas for warming the planet," added Ship.

....

The eleph-ANT was loaded into the rail-dart cart armed with in-
struments and sensors. Thirty seconds later, it was launched out
of the spacecraft, where it hurtled toward the planet at g-forces
it wasn't designed for—g-force levels that would have broken the
original design of an eleph-ANT.

As it traveled through space, racing toward its target, its mind
made calculations. If it were smart, it would be worrying that it
was moving too fast through space. It wasn't smart, though. It
knew it was moving too fast. It knew it had to do something. But
it wasn't worried.

If this eleph-ANT was smart enough to know it was traveling
too fast, it might also have been smart enough to understand Atlas
had upgraded its engines. This eleph-ANT was the maiden test
of these new engines. It was now capable of twenty-three times
the thrust. It was now capable of slowing down on time. But it
didn't understand this.

The eleph-ANT's sensors were telling it to turn on its engines
now. It didn't. Every projected outcome its little brain had created
told the eleph-ANT it was going to become a crater in the planet.
It wasn't worried, though. There was a preprogrammed plan.
The plan said it would be in orbit. Its tiny but limited thoughts
told it that its sensors must be wrong.

On time—at exactly seven minutes and fifty-six seconds
into its journey through space—the eleph-ANT pointed its nose
downward and shot the tiniest amount of fuel out. It moved in the
opposite direction, ever so slightly but more than it had expected,
spinning around its center of mass.

Puff. Another spray of fuel. More this time. It turned faster.
Too fast. Its legs were almost pointing toward the planet. Moving
quickly, it pointed its trunk in the opposite direction, against the
spin. Puuuffff. A long spray of fuel, this time slowing it down.
That was too easy. The eleph-ANT logged a note for Atlas. Its jets
were supplying more thrust than expected.

The eleph-ANT's legs were pointed toward the planet, thirty seconds earlier than expected. In a quarter of a second, the eleph-ANT had plotted out its path, and in twenty-seven seconds, it was programmed to turn on its six engines, one at the bottom of each leg. Those engines firing would make little difference to the path it would take. Based on the speed the eleph-ANT was traveling, it would hit the planet with force. Unfortunately, the tiny brain of the eleph-ANT wasn't powerful enough to calculate the size of the impact crater it was about to create.

In exactly eight minutes and twenty-seven seconds, all six engines of the eleph-ANT lit up. The g-forces were enormous. The eleph-ANT shook, not expecting the change in speed to be that strong. The trunk snapped back, hitting its body. The impact left a large dent in its tough metallic shell.

If the eleph-ANT had a bigger brain, it would have been genuinely surprised it had slowed as much as it did. As its brain was small, again the eleph-ANT assumed its sensors were wrong. Firing its trunk and six leg engines, the eleph-ANT arced toward the planet, correcting its course to stay in orbit around the planet.

Now in orbit around the planet, the eleph-ANT was given new instructions. Using a lattice structure, it started dropping sensor after sensor around the planet. One by one they surrounded it, mapping it out in great detail.

The eleph-ANT held several smaller ANTs in its cargo bay. These were shot toward the planet, parachutes opening as they floated down to embed themselves in the icy planet below.

Atlas, Ship, and Lex sat in their war room. While Atlas usually preferred to work with physical objects, the war room was the only place on the Ship of Atlas where he relied on the hapticgraphic projector a lot. But even then, he still preferred the familiar security of a screen or a printout. Screens littered the walls of the war room, available to show any information at a moment's notice. A large printer sat on one side of the room.

In the middle was a large rectangular table. If Atlas required it, the table could drop into the floor and he could reconfigure the open space to handle whatever he needed at the time. For now, he was content with a physical printout of everything the eleph-ANT was sending back.

"Atlas, we need to update the eleph-ANT's understanding of its new thrust capabilities," Ship said.

Atlas looked up from a printout. "I can see that it overcorrected its thrust and almost spun out," he said before looking over the readings. "It's worse than we thought, Ship"

"I know. It's an ice world," Ship added.

Atlas riffled through the papers, trying to find something. "What is the atmosphere like?"

"It has a thick atmosphere, and a magnetosphere that should support life," Ship said.

"If we can heat it up!" Atlas replied, supressing a laugh, thinking it was an impossible task.

They took remote control of the eleph-ANT as it flew around the planet. There was one more experimental ANT left inside the eleph-ANT—Atlas called it the cormor-ANT. It had the same design as the other ANTs—six legs, but with two large wings on either side.

The cormor-ANT dropped out the back of the eleph-ANT and headed toward the ground. Its wings unfolded and stretched out. Its fall slowed and it began to glide.

Atlas picked a controller up from the table. One of the screens gave him a first-person point of view of the winged ANT. He pushed the joystick forward and the cormor-ANT's thrusters ignited. It shot through the sky faster.

Atlas pointed at something poking out from beneath the ice. "Do you see that?" He used the directional pad to get a better view of the object, then pressed one of the triggers to zoom in. "It's a rocky world. There are clearly mountains poking up from beneath the ice. I . . ." Atlas paused for a moment. ". . . I think this would make a great world if we can defrost it."

The cormor-ANT raced around the planet, taking a complete scan of the topography and landscape.

Atlas placed the controller down on the table. "Ship, let's see if this ice runs to the core."

Ship took control of the cormor-ANT. He had better precision for what was coming next.

"You see it?" Atlas asked.

Ship nodded as he started directing the cormor-ANT to an exact location—in the middle of a triangle of three ANTs. These ANTs were positioned several kilometers apart, and they had each embedded themselves deep in the ice. The cormor-ANT headed toward the ground and made contact, leaving an impact crater the size of a small house. The ANTs were recording everything that happened. The time difference between hearing the impact and feeling it would give them an idea of how thick the ice was. The types of echoes felt later would give them an understanding of how deep it was and if there was liquid water underneath.

Atlas silently counted to ten before asking, "What have we got?" He struggled to hide his excitement.

Lex started crunching numbers and displaying them on a screen as Ship summarized it. "It's not very deep. There is water sloshing underneath that ice."

"Oh, this is exciting," exclaimed Atlas. "I'm starting to think this might be our planet!" He paused for a moment, considering what to do next. "Let's not rush into a decision." He pointed at each of his teammates. "Ship, Lex, let's do silent research for one hour and meet back here with ideas on what we should do next."

Atlas knew Ship and Lex didn't need an hour to do research. Lex had probably already completed all the analysis he needed to, and Ship was too lazy to use the full hour on an exercise he wasn't too thrilled about. But Atlas wanted an hour to refine his own thinking.

About forty minutes later, the team had collected all the data and started discussing ideas to terraform the planet.

"Nuke the planet," Ship suggested, having thought about it for all of two seconds.

Atlas shook his head. "It wouldn't achieve our overall objective, though. It would heat up the planet quickly but render it unlivable for centuries to come."

Ship gave Atlas a puzzled look. "We could just line all the habitats with materials to block radiation." Ship pointed at himself. "If a nuclear bomb went off outside of me, the embryos in my center storage would be completely protected. On a planet, we don't have to worry about the weight issues of that much shielding. So, it should be easy."

Atlas looked at Ship. He assumed Ship wasn't thinking about the human component. "Mars is a great example of how the nuclear option doesn't work." Atlas waited for a sense of realization to cross Ship's face. When it didn't, he continued. "When humanity was first visiting Mars, an eccentric billionaire wanted to make the planet livable in his lifetime, so he let off several nuclear bombs. Not just one, but several at each of the poles, where all the ice was. It worked, though. Within three years, the planet had heated up."

Ship nodded, agreeing with everything Atlas pointed out as fact.

"However," Atlas said with a touch of seriousness, "Mars is still living with the fallout from that day, too. Martians have to import all the water from asteroids because none of the water on Mars is drinkable. Even with all the advanced filtering systems. Ergo, I veto that idea."

Atlas looked at the orb. "You have any ideas?"

A large mirror appeared in front of Atlas. He smiled. "I like it. Giant mirrors. You're correct, Lex; we could use mirrors to concentrate light onto the poles and heat up the planet." Atlas raised a finger. "Which reminds me. We need to give this planet a name. We can't keep calling it 'the planet.'"

"What about New Europa?" Ship suggested.

Atlas put two thumbs up. He was genuinely impressed, and a little surprised at Ship's level of creativity. "I love it. And it will play into humanity's tradition of recycling names by sticking the word *new* in front of it," Atlas laughed. "Like New York, or New Mexico."

"And New Zealand," Ship added.

Atlas nodded, looking at his piece of paper showing all the information about the planet. Across the top he wrote *New Europa*. "Now all we need to do is heat up New Europa."

"With mirrors, or move the planet?" asked Ship.

A curious look appeared on Atlas's face. "How would we move a planet? I'm not sure we'd have the technology to do something that big. It would be a fun challenge, though."

Ship explained. "Lex has mapped out all the objects in the system. There was a large moon drifting through the system. If they sent an object to collide with it, it would drift close enough to New Europa that it would shrink New Europa's orbit. And it would be closer to the sun."

Atlas thought about it for a second. He looked at the orb. "Is this your idea, Lex?"

The orb flashed red.

Ship interjected. "It's not his idea, but he did have it on the list of options."

"What's the probability of this working?" Atlas asked.

"Seventy-eight percent."

"Too risky." Atlas shook his head. "If we get it wrong, we could potentially eject New Europa from the system. Then we'd be screwed.

"Not that I don't trust you, Ship," Atlas added. "Let's start with the safest option. Let's start building a large mirror."

The team began the mission to heat up New Europa.

Atlas pointed at the orb in the corner. "Lex, you continue mapping out the whole system. I want you to identify every piece of metal." Then he pointed at Ship. "I want you to use eleph-ANTs to start pushing metals toward the center of this system. We need more metals for this mirror. Start recycling anything we aren't using so we have more resources."

The team's plan was simple: build a large mirror that orbited on the dark side of New Europa, lighting it up and ensuring it always had light hitting it. The additional heat this would gener-ate would have a similar effect to moving New Europa closer to the star.

Atlas had another idea while the other two worked on mir-rors. The vaults of the ship had DNA and samples of every single animal that was alive on Earth the day he left.

"I'm going to genetically engineer a fungus to release green-house gases into the atmosphere," Atlas pronounced as he left the bridge and headed for his office.

CHAPTER 22

TRILLION

RESCUE TRILLION

"Ship, we need to get off this moon," Trillion said.

She sat floating in her office, arms and legs folded. Trillion did not feel safe. After the Ship of Trillion was placed on the moon, her life was now completely in the Dottiens' hands.

On their third day there, the Dottiens sent what Trillion assumed was an ambassador. This alien (or AI) looked exactly like the objects that had attacked them. It was bulbous and about as big as an eleph-ANT. Its opaque skin looked like it was made of jelly. It was green when it arrived—not purple like Trillion would have expected. As it approached, she would see that their skin was able to change color and texture—she marveled at the complex patterns flowing through their skin.

"They're like a chameleon," Ship commented.

Trillion shook her head. "Not like a chameleon. The bright-ness is like a chameleon, but a chameleon only changes the color of its skin. It's more like an octopus. An octopus can change the color and texture of its skin, and its translucency, too."

The more Trillion thought about these creatures, the more her mind was blown. She didn't think something like that was possible. She could tell that Lex loved every moment. It was like a puzzle to crack. She was excited at first too. *We're about to speak with aliens,* she had thought. "What do we know so far, Ship?"

"They speak in colors. It's a very complex language. But we assume purple is the color of war." He pointed at the orb. "Lex reckons their language changes every day."

Trillion leaned forward. "And do we know anything about the Dottiens themselves?" She pointed out the window, where the Dottien was in front of the ship. "Is this actually one of them?"

"Lex believes this is them. I don't know how they sur-vive in space, let alone how they move around," Ship added. "Everything we've seen on their planet looks exactly like what is in front of us."

They had observed multiple situations where the whole planet operated like a super organism, changing colors and oper-ating as one.

Trillion looked up at Lex. "What do we understand of their language?"

He flashed blue, then red.

"So, we don't know anything yet?"

He flashed green.

Trillion teleported out to think. She floated in her room. She closed her eyes, breathing in and out for several minutes.

It wasn't long before an idea popped into her head. "Ship, meet me in the war room." She teleported out.

The war room was a large empty space, about the size of a basketball court. She needed the room to think.

Ship appeared. Then Lex appeared too. She looked at both of them. "Okay, this is Project Boredom."

She had sped up time for all three of them, so one whole rotation around the sun felt like ten seconds. She hoped speeding up time would mean the Dottiens would forget about them. Move on.

A good twenty seconds later, Trillion looked at Lex. "Is the Dottien still outside our spacecraft?"

The orb flashed green.

"Hmm." She looked at Ship. "Are we still stuck to the moon?"

Ship nodded. "Our engines are still covered over, and the Dottiens are still outside, patiently waiting for us to continue communicating with them."

"These little buggers aren't going to let us leave. They attacked us, and now our lives are in their hands. At any moment, they could decide to squash us. We need to change that."

Trillion returned them to real time. It had been almost forty seconds in subjective time. Four years in real time, and they were still in the same predicament. Waiting for the Dottiens to forget about them wasn't going to work.

She looked at Ship. "Now we start Project Negotiate or War." She looked at Lex. "Project everything we have on Steel World."

The room lit up with a hologram of the previous star system they were in. The planets. Or what was left of it. It was a collection of resources, bottled up and ready to use.

"Right now, we have no leverage. If we manage to communicate with them, we have nothing to negotiate with," she said, taking a breath. "Let's use Steel World resources to create an army and bring it back here so we can negotiate as equals—not prisoners."

Ship raised a mechanical eyebrow. "But how? We can't get anything back from that system."

Trillion noticed the eyebrow movement. He had never done that before. "We send you. We built a version of this ship and left it in orbit before we left."

Ship still looked a bit confused.

Trillion continued. "If we build a large radio dish, we could send you wirelessly into that ship. Once on the other side, you could organize everything and send an army here."

Trillion could see the reluctance on Ship's face. The two of them had spent so much time together, they were starting to understand each other's thoughts.

"I don't want to send a copy of me across. What happens when I get back? There will be two versions of me. Which would be the real me?" Ship said, shaking his head. "Besides, it wouldn't work. Only Lex is a fully digital computer."

"What do you mean? I thought all three of us were simulations on computers," Trillion asked.

"Yes, we are. Sort of," Ship said, tilting his head from side to side. "Computers are general-purpose machines—very skilled at many different types of computation. But for things like simulating quantum mechanics or simulating a human brain, general-purpose computers are too slow."

Trillion nodded, encouraging him to continue.

Ship continued. "In the early days of AI research, they used to use general-purpose computers. But quite quickly they realized they needed specific hardware. They needed to combine hardware and software." He paused for a moment. "Trillion, you and I are purpose-built. We aren't software. There's a unit on this ship that holds your matrix. And the design of that unit is unique to you. Only you could be held in that unit."

"What about you, Ship? I thought all ships came with the same matrix design."

"Yes, we have the same basic design, but manufacturing errors mean I'm slightly different from the others. Uploading me to another ship's matrix would change me." Ship paused for a moment, thinking about it. "And I think Atlas made a few changes to my design. I actually think my matrix has been customized to you, Trillion. I think I'm based on one of your early brain scans."

Trillion was a little confused. "Are you saying you're a copy of me? I thought you were built before I was even scanned into this simulation."

Ship shook his head. "Sorry, I should have explained it more clearly. I'm designed to fit your personality. We spend hundreds of years together, so I was specifically designed so that you enjoy my company."

Trillion nodded in understanding. She could see his perspective now. Over the years, Ship had come to see himself as unique. He didn't want to lose that. *He's right,* Trillion thought. She didn't want to force him to become something else.

Trillion resigned herself to knowing she would do anything to get free of the Dottiens' grip. The simple solution might be to sleep again and wake up in a few thousand years. Maybe the polka dots would forget about them. But if she needed to, she would find a way to fight back. Anything was better than spending the rest of her life in a moon prison.

As Trillion pondered, Ship came up with an idea. "What if we send my matrix? We still have a lot of eleph-ANTs around this star system. We could combine a few to create a little rocket, then launch me back to Steel World."

Trillion thought about it for a second. It would leave her extremely limited in what she could do without him. But being stuck on the moon severely limited them anyway. "Okay. So, instead of sending you over a radio dish, we send you physically?"

Ship nodded.

CHAPTER 23

TRILLION

ESCAPE

Trillion and Ship started their escape plan by sending all the eleph-ANTs in the system to the other side of the star, opposite to where the Dottien planet was. Here they were hoping to create a makeshift spaceship without the Dottiens seeing or interfering.

The Dottiens didn't appear to be able to track any of their radio communication. The radio waves they were using to control the eleph-ANTs and ANTs weren't picked up. At first, they thought it was simply because the aliens chose to ignore the radio waves—it appeared strange that they could travel through space, yet have no understanding of radio communications. But based on what Lex had learned, they were purely visual creatures. And purely line-of-sight, too. Trillion was fairly certain the Dottiens had no idea what they were planning.

Lex had produced a new miniature spaceship design, combining parts from several eleph-ANTs and ANTs. Lex was left in charge of the assembly, with Ship guiding all the eleph-ANTs and ANTs behind the star.

The three of them had completed everything quickly. The only thing left was getting Ship into an eleph-ANT rocket.

"Do you think this will work?" Trillion asked.

Ship nodded. "It has to."

Trillion had to manually control one of the maintenance ANTs inside the very center of the ship. It was a large dodecahedron-shaped room, all of the twelve sides identical. Each wall had a thick wire that ran from the middle of it to the metal cylinder located in the center of the room. Trillion assumed it was to hold Ship's brain matrix in place.

"Those wires act as shock absorbers to make sure I don't take any damage," Ship explained, answering Trillion's unspoken question.

There was one wire that was thicker than the others. Trillion assumed it was the fiber-optic cable that connected Ship to the spacecraft.

Safety protocols meant there was no hapticgraphic projector in there. And neither Ship nor a preprogrammed robot could operate there. They got around this by Trillion manually taking control of a maintenance ANT. There were forty-two screws, each covered by a plastic clip. One at a time, she guided the maintenance ANT to remove every individual screw.

"Heist movies are meant to be fun," Trillion commented to no one in particular as she tried to break the tension she was feeling.

After a long bout of concentration, Trillion had removed all forty-two screws. She could now see a metallic cover which protected the whole matrix of Ship and held him in place. She carefully removed the cover with the help of twelve maintenance ANTs, one hanging from each of the wires holding Ship's matrix in place. Inside was a large diamond-shaped object. It looked like melted glass had combined with gold and silver. It was bright, almost sparkly, and pulsated. Trillion stared at it for a long time.

"Trillion, your matrix is about three times as large as this," Ship said.

Trillion nodded, still mesmerised by Ship's matrix.

The team had created a new makeshift case for Ship's matrix. It would act as a shock absorber, similar to the room he was in, only this case would be portable and could handle the vacuum of space.

"Ship, as soon as I release the cable connecting you to the ship, we won't be able to communicate until you get connected to the eleph-ANT spacecraft on the other side of the star."

Ship nodded. "I'll speak to you soon, then."

"Are you sure everything will still continue to operate on this spacecraft after you've gone?"

Ship nodded again. "Mostly. You won't be able to move the ship, but power, maintenance, and the freezers holding the embryos are all automatic. The ANTs and eleph-ANTs will be less intuitive without my assistance. But Lex should be able to help with a lot of that."

Trillion sniffled a little. "I'm going to miss you, buddy."

"I'll see you soon, Trillion."

Trillion disconnected Ship and watched his avatar fade away. She was a little sad; she missed her friend already. They had spent many years together traveling through space, exploring. They had destroyed a star system together. And they had been trapped on this moon together. Ship had become her best friend. When humanity sent her on this journey, they didn't take into consideration how lonely it would become. Ship was her only companion. Trillion shook herself out of her gloom. She still had work to get done.

The new canister holding Ship looked like a metal drum or a large beer can. The thought amused her and she smiled a little.

She maneuvered Ship's matrix out of the room. It took a while because it was heavy and only small maintenance ANTs could operate in that room; they weren't designed to lift something so heavy. A smaller eleph-ANT was waiting for it. It picked Ship up and carried him through the spacecraft up to the top level.

Trillion noticed her control of the eleph-ANT wasn't quite right—it was as if the AI controlling its movements was a lot less intelligent than before. It was clumsy and constantly misstepping. She figured that was what Ship meant when he said the ANTs and eleph-ANTs would be a lot less intuitive.

"Lex, can you help me here? This bot is moving awkwardly."

Within seconds, the eleph-ANT started moving more smoothly. It wasn't completely perfect, but it stopped tripping itself up every few steps.

Trillion smiled. "Thank you."

Trillion's plan was simple. Without Ship, she wouldn't be able to control any flying vehicle with precision. She also didn't think she could outmaneuver any of those Dottiens out in space. So, her plan was to release thirty canister-shaped objects at once, shooting them all in different directions.

They had learnt that the Dottiens didn't care too much about anything they did in the immediate area surrounding the ship. They had erected several screens outside in their attempts to talk with the Dottiens, who had left these structures alone, but anything that came within one kilometer of the ship was attacked by the Dottiens. They had tried several times to launch ANTs to test this, but each time, they were ignored until they reached approximately one kilometer away, where they were either pulled back onto the moon or launched into the star.

What Trillion found strange was the Dottiens completely ignored any of the ANTs or eleph-ANTs that were released when they first entered the Dottiens' system. That was how they managed to collect enough resources behind the star to make the new spaceship for Ship.

The eleph-ANT had finally reached an airlock in the space-craft. They had constructed a long pipe, just big enough to fit Ship's matrix, and placed magnets around the pipe to essentially create a railgun. Trillion had loaded Ship into the railgun, ready to shoot him out the back of the airlock door.

The sticky purple Dottiens were still connected to the ship, so Trillion had to blow off the outer airlock door to create the exit point for Ship and the fake canisters.

Trillion worried that this wouldn't work. She didn't know what she would do if she lost her only friend and was stuck there if the Dottiens pushed Ship into the star. Again, she cast the self-doubt and worry out of her mind. She had a job to complete. She treated it like a real-time strategy game. She simply had to bring an army from Steel World to this one.

Trillion's hand hovered over a large red button on the bridge of the ship. The button was to trigger everything that would come next. She steadied herself and then pressed it.

All at once, multiple canisters shot out of the ship, traveling in multiple directions but avoiding the planet. She did not want the Dottiens to think they were a threat to the planet—it had to look more like a failed attempt to escape.

Lex was still attempting to communicate with the representative from the Dottiens. As soon as the canisters began to reach the kilometer distance from the ship, the representative turned purple.

Ship exited the back of the ship with a bang. Thanks to the railgun tube he was loaded into, he was pushed through space at a speed hundreds of times faster than any of the other fake canisters. Trillion watched it worriedly, hoping that the obvious additional speed wouldn't arouse suspicion among the Dottien force.

All of a sudden, the skies lit up with purple. Trillion hadn't seen this much purple since the time she was captured. Half the canisters were quickly captured, and she watched in dismay as they were plastered with purple blobs. A number of them dragged their victims back to the surface of the moon, while other canisters headed for the star.

Trillion quickly had the eleph-ANT near the start of the rail-gun load five more fake canisters into the tube. One by one, each of the canisters was launched into space at relativistic speeds.

It was all happening so quickly, Trillion could not keep up.

"Lex, can you make sure Ship does not get caught?"

Lex took control of the thrusters they had attached to the back of Ship's matrix canister. He was much better at maneuvering it, but it wasn't going to help. If the fake canisters were captured, then the Dottiens would only have a single target.

A *single target is too easy*, Trillion thought.

Trillion slowed her perception of time to a crawl. This battle that was occurring over five minutes was now going to feel like an hour. She now had enough time to take in everything, giving her a chance to react and adapt.

There were now only three fake canisters left: two that had been shot out of the railgun, and one from the first cohort.

Trillion took control of the canister closest to the ship, the one not traveling at relativistic speeds. With the time slowed down, she assumed it would be easy to dodge the Dottiens. Firing engines in all directions, she attempted to weave the canister through the incoming Dottiens. They were arcing toward the canister from all directions. She realized it was not going to be easy. She could think faster now, but it was an effort to think in 3-D space. She struggled to keep track of multiple objects moving at different speeds, and the canister was soon covered in sticky purple dots.

Trillion focused her energy on the two canisters out of the railgun.

There were four polka dots chasing the three canisters. That was bad. It meant she had to somehow take out two of the Dottiens with each of her two fake canisters. It meant she had zero margin of error.

Ship's canister was a good way ahead of her two. She used the thrusters on each of the two canisters to position them directly behind the trajectory of Ship's canister. She hoped that by lining all three up in a row, the Dottiens would follow suit. It worked.

They were following the most direct path to each of their targets. That meant all four were directly behind the canisters.

Trillion abruptly reversed the thrusters on the canister at the rear of the formation, sending it back the way it came and shooting it directly into the path of the Dottiens in pursuit. The frontmost Dottien connected, smashing into the canister. They were tough, though. Neither the canister nor the Dottien was destroyed. The second polka dot flew by but failed to connect with the canister.

"I missed," Trillion said, annoyed at herself.

The third Dottien wasn't so lucky. It connected with the canister that had slowed, slamming into it.

"Yay," Trillion said, much happier now that her plan was working. "Just two left to get."

The Dottiens didn't change their strategy—there were still two polka dots traveling toward the two canisters. They were gaining, traveling directly behind one another. Trillion prepared to do the same trick again.

She suddenly realized why the Dottiens' strategy was to chase in one direction. Hundreds of new Dottiens were headed toward the two canisters. They had numbers on their side.

She took control of her final canister, hoping she could at least buy Ship some time. Once Ship reached the spaceship, he would be plugged in, and then he would be able to communicate with Trillion. She steadied herself. She would get Ship to the spaceship, then they could communicate briefly before the rest of the Dottiens arrived. At least they could say goodbye then.

Trillion thought about it a while longer. Maybe she could get Ship to the spaceship and tell him to come back to the moon. Being with her, stuck on the moon, was better than being dragged into the star. At least the two would still be able to communicate. And she wouldn't be lonely.

Trillion turned the canister around, this time learning from her mistakes. "Lex, can you help me? When this canister hits the Dottien, I need it to stay in the path of the other Dottien. It needs to hit both."

She gave the controls to Lex. Lex did exactly as requested, and both Dottiens were taken out. Trillion took a deep breath. She smiled. It was just enough time for Ship to arrive at the spaceship and get connected. He would now have about five seconds before the first Dottiens connected with the spacecraft.

Lex controlled Ship's canister to dock with the spaceship, which was already moving to match the speed of the canister so the canister did not have to slow down.

The orb flashed green. *Ship is connected* appeared on the screen in front of Trillion.

"Hurry, hurry. Come online," Trillion urged. She was extremely worried now. All the fake canisters had been captured—most of them had ended up in the star. She didn't want the same to happen to Ship. She regretted sending him on this mission; it had been such a big risk to take.

Trillion returned her perception of time back to normal. She was prepared for the worst. She had already sent off a message telling Ship the Dottiens were seconds away from impacting him and that he should do everything in his power to reach the moon again.

She watched as Dottien after Dottien reached the spaceship. And one by one, the spaceship maneuvered out of the way, the Dottiens missing their target. It was a sight to see.

Trillion received a reply from Ship.

"Hey, Trillion. Thanks for letting me know about the Dottiens. Don't worry; I'm a ship, remember? Flying through space is what I do. Without the need to protect the embryos onboard, I can change direction at g-forces much higher than would be safe for life."

Trillion smiled. She was so happy. She watched as Ship's thrusters pushed him farther and farther out of the system.

The lightspeed time delay limited their communication at first. Then, after a while, messages between the two had to stop, as the distance was becoming too great. The makeshift eleph-ANT-based spacecraft Ship was traveling in wasn't designed for long-range communication.

See you soon was the final message Ship sent to her.

CHAPTER 24

ATLAS

UNDER THE ICE OF NEW EUROPA

Atlas sat in his lab, biting his lower lip, trying to come up with a solution for his fungus. He needed a distraction so he called out to Ship. "Ship, where are we at with the mirrors?"

The reply came through the speakers. "Our biggest constraint is finding enough metals in this system. We have kilometers of mirrors pointed at the planet, but it's just not enough to warm it."

That was the problem Atlas was struggling with—the system he had picked lacked resources. Or, rather, it lacked easily accessible resources. New Europa had plenty of resources beneath that ice, but getting them into orbit was impossible without a steady fuel source.

Atlas turned his head toward the speaker. "So, how do we do this, Ship? Without enough mirrors, we won't get the runaway greenhouse effect. New Europa will keep freezing the ice we melt."

This was part of the challenge Atlas had with the fungus he created. Genetically engineering something to withstand the negative temperatures was very hard. But combining that with engineering something that could handle the lack of a breathable atmosphere was next to impossible. He was on the 212th genetically engineered version of the fungus, and just like the fungi before them, they did not survive long on the planet.

He needed to distract himself from the challenge. "Talk me through your idea. How would we use a drifting moon to change the orbit of New Europa?"

Ship teleported into the room before replying. "So, there is a dwarf planet—a planetoid—that is drifting through this star system." Ship paused and a little smile flickered across his face. "It isn't in a stable orbit around the sun. If we exploded something big on it, we could adjust its orbit enough so that it heads toward the center of this system. Toward this planet."

Atlas nodded, taking it all in. "So, you're saying if we caused the planetoid to come close to New Europa, it would shrink New Europa's orbit—bringing it closer to the star?"

"Exactly," Ship affirmed, "and it has a seventy-eight percent probability of working."

"Hmm." Atlas thought about it for a moment. "Do we have enough time to make this happen?"

"Yes. Sort of. It's orbiting further away from us now. We have less time than before," Ship explained.

The risk was too great, Atlas thought. Yes, seventy-eight percent was high. But it was one hundred percent with enough mirrors and enough time.

Atlas shook his head. "It's too risky; what if the two planets collide? I trust your probability, but too much can go wrong. We have to push the dwarf planet in just the right way to make it come toward this planet. Then it needs to interact with this planet enough to shrink its orbit. Then that orbit change needs to be enough to warm the planet. It's all a cascading series of events that are less likely than the first."

"But. . ." Ship started to counter with more data from Lex.

Atlas cut him off. "Occam's razor, Ship. The simplest option is always the best. And that idea is way too complicated."

And then a new thought popped into Atlas's head. His mind went off on a tangent, the idea of cascading sequences sparking a possible solution. "We don't have enough mirrors to heat the planet, but we *do* have enough to focus on one area."

"Do you want to build a dome? And heat up one area?" Ship asked.

Atlas shook his head. "Not quite. I want to use the ice surrounding the entire planet as a dome."

Ship cocked an eye. "I don't follow, Atlas. Won't the mirrors simply melt a hole through the ice?"

Atlas grinned. He thought the idea could either be genius or stupid. So, telling Ship and letting Lex crunch the numbers would be the test, to see if the plan could actually work. "Do you know what electrolysis is?"

Atlas knew full well Ship knew what it was.

"Yes, it's the process of splitting water into oxygen and hydrogen."

"Exactly, Ship. What I want to do is use the mirrors to focus light on solar panels. Then, using the energy, I want us to do electrolysis under the ice. That will create pockets of oxygen beneath the ice."

Atlas could see Ship was puzzled.

"I don't understand, Atlas. Oxygen isn't a warming gas. If anything, it cools planets."

"Yes, but oxygen is what I need for my fungus. They are struggling without an atmosphere. If we make one under the ice, then *boom!* we'll create our own Cambrian explosion on this planet."

Ship tried to clarify. "You're suggesting we melt the ice from the inside?"

"Exactly, Ship. Now you and Lex tell me: can this work?"

Ship went quiet for a moment. Atlas knew he was processing it.

Lex was the first to respond. His orb turned red, then blue. Then green. Then back to blue.

Atlas looked at the orb. "Why are you unsure?"

Ship replied for Lex. "He doesn't have enough data on the fungus you created."

Atlas shrugged. "Assume the fungus can survive under the ice." Atlas knew the fungus would survive under the ice. He had already engineered a strain for that. He would just need to re-engineer it to turn oxygen into greenhouse gases.

The orb turned green.

Ship nodded in agreement. "It will work. Assuming the fungus grows underneath the ice, Lex gives it a ninety-four percent probability. Even though he won't tell you that."

"Brilliant," Atlas said with a smile.

"Atlas, how did you get that idea from moving a planet? I don't see how it's relevant."

Atlas patted Ship on the shoulder. "Simple. I stopped thinking about the mirrors as a way to warm up the planet and started thinking of it as the first step in a cascade of events."

The team began the process like a well-oiled machine.

Ship was placed in charge of digging through the ice to place hundreds of electrolysis machines—which was basically just two wires in the water. In a stroke of good fortune, they found that the water beneath the ice was pure and unsalted, saving the need for desalination.

Lex was tasked with sending a fabricator to the planet with raw pellets. He would then take the pellets and produce solar panels to power the electrolysis.

Atlas got back to his project. He started reviewing the different strains of fungus he had created before, as one of the previous generations had already proven it was capable of thriving in cold environments. And now with the electrolysis providing the oxygen, there was no need to figure out how to make the fungus anaerobic.

CHAPTER 25

ICARUS

DISCOUNT RINGWORLD

"So, a day will be almost twenty-four hours exactly?" Icarus asked.

Ship nodded. "Yes, if we use the ring I'm suggesting."

The three of them had been debating for days which part of the ring to inhabit. Icarus had a strong preference for the inner-most ring—the one made up of mostly large moons, which did not look like a ring at all.

Icarus and Ship both stood in Icarus's kitchen while he made a coffee. It was his fifth coffee today. And each time, he had opted to head back to his kitchen to make the coffee rather than auto-matically generating one.

Icarus took a sip. "Explain why we can't just connect the large moons together?"

Ship pointed to the orb. "Lex can't fabricate any material strong enough to physically connect each of the moons together."

Icarus raised a cartoonish eyebrow. "Can't, or just thinks it has a low probability of success?"

"Icarus, I've audited Lex already. It's actually something he can't do."

Icarus sighed a little. When he first looked at this gas giant, he hoped he would be able to build a ringworld. Something similar to what he'd seen in the Halo games, or read in the fiction of Larry Niven. He resigned himself to the fact that he couldn't build something that grand. But he still wanted to build something he was proud of. "Okay, Ship. And it won't be a true ringworld unless we can connect all the pieces. So, I want them all to be connected."

Icarus rubbed his large eyes. He wasn't used to receiving pushback from Ship. It seemed like the longer they spent together, the more balanced the relationship became. Ship would hold his ground when he thought he was right. "Okay, so show me how this would work."

A hologram of the rings of Titan appeared in front of Icarus. "Hey, don't you think the name Titan has a nice *ring* to it?" he chuckled, unable to help himself. He was quite impressed with the clever pun.

Ship shook his head and highlighted a specific ring around the gas giant, clearly unimpressed with Icarus's bad joke.

"This is what I suggest," Ship said as he enlarged the ring he wanted Icarus to focus on. All the asteroids and details became visible.

Ship pointed to the ring. "We can run cables between most of the objects in this ring, connecting them in a network of crisscrossing lines. Lex believes we can fabricate a cable strong enough to connect these much-shorter distances."

Green lines started appearing between the gaps of all the asteroids, forming a lattice of lines crossing from one object to the next.

"This is where Lex suggests we run the cables throughout the rings so we don't reach the limits of what the cables can handle," Ship said.

Ship shifted the holographic view. The red lines faded to grey. Several large objects along the ring changed to green. Soon, there were hundreds of objects highlighted in green.

Ship pointed at the highlighted green objects. "These are large moons scattered throughout the rings. They are as large as the moons closest to the planet. We could use them as colony locations. It wouldn't have one g of gravity, though."

Icarus studied the projected image, contemplating what Ship was suggesting. "I understand now. Using this specific ring here"—Icarus pointed at the ring—"gives us large-enough moons to build colonies. And because of all the smaller asteroids in between, we can use them to connect all the colonies, sharing electricity and communication through the wires."

The orb flashed green. Ship nodded too.

The three chatted for a while about the mechanics of creating a ring world by linking multiple asteroids together. At first, it would be nothing more than cables connecting the asteroids and moons. Cables to share electricity and fiber-optic cables for communication. But over time, they could build more rigid structures fully encompassing the gas giant in a ring.

Lex had pointed out two things that were either divine intervention or the best luck ever.

Icarus looked at the orb, not quite believing what he had been shown. It took a while for him to wrap his head around how night and day was created on a ringworld. On a ringworld an eclipse caused it to become night. "So, Lex, you're telling me that with this ring, we will not only get twenty-four-hour days but also get longer and shorter daylight hours, depending on the time of year? How does that work?"

Rather than respond, Lex just added an image of the star to the hologram. Icarus had always imagined the position of the rings incorrectly. With the placement of the star, he could now see why longer days would sometimes occur. The rings were at a twenty-four-degree tilt relative to the star, similar to how Earth's axis is at a slight tilt to the sun. This tilt meant that at certain times of the Titan year, the ring would either cross the equator in front of the star or not—thus creating longer and shorter days. It wouldn't be exactly like Earth, but day lengths would be different throughout the year.

"That's amazing," Icarus said, almost not believing it. "I think this is a sign that this will be our colony."

"Could we use the tilt and mirrors to simulate real seasons, too?" Icarus asked?

Ship shook his head. "Seasons don't work like that, Icarus."

Icarus, Ship, and Lex began the journey of creating cables between the various asteroids. They decided to start by connecting the asteroids nearest the large moons. They would run connections close to the moons last because dealing with a gravity well, even a small one, defeated the reason for manufacturing in space.

Icarus started outlining an action plan for the team. "Lex, identify locations for our fabricators. Find sites where we can leave them for years—preferably near the moons, as those will be the locations that will need the most materials fabricated. But not *on* the moons, as fabricating fiber optics is better without gravity." He turned his head toward Ship. "While we wait for Lex to find locations for the fabricators, can you start mining the asteroids? Let's turn the whole outer ring into pellets. We'll need enough resources if we want to turn this into a real ring world."

Lex had selected the first site—a large asteroid near the edge of the ring. Ship had embedded the fabricator in the side of it, deep in the asteroid, away from meteor impacts. From there it was producing kilometers of cable.

Lex had come up with an ingenious construction. It was a thick cable, about ten centimeters, covered in a carbon nano material that made it strong enough to handle impacts from tiny asteroids and strong enough to act as the glue between all the different pieces that would make up the ring. Inside hosted a fiber-optic cable. And because space was cold, Lex discovered they could use a superconductor material to transmit electricity through the wire to enable the team to electrify the ring without losing any power as it traveled. It was encased in a highly reflective material to maintain the negative temperatures.

Icarus reviewed the plans his team had presented. "Lex, these designs need some redundancy in them."

Ship shook his head. "Lex gives us only a two percent probability of having the cable destroyed in a thousand years."

Icarus looked at Ship. In some ways, Ship and Lex were super intelligent, but in others, they were quite naïve. "Even if the probability is less than one percent, we don't want the whole colony taken down by a single stray asteroid. Anything that needs power to survive needs at least three cables connected to it. That includes any of the vertical farms."

Lex reworked the plan multiple times, accounting for every possible scenario Icarus and Ship could think of. During that time, the fabricators had produced enough cable to reach all the way around Titan multiple times—almost a million kilometers of it waiting to be used.

Icarus elected to drive the eleph-ANT laying the first piece of cable, wanting an excuse to jump into his eleph-ANT cockpit again. "If we use eleph-ANTs to push the cables out from fabricators, then I'll use this eleph-ANT at the end of the cable to guide it through the ring, ensuring it doesn't collide with anything. Meet me in the cargo hangar," he said as he teleported out.

He walked along the cargo hangar, Ship and Lex beside him. They arrived back at the eleph-ANT cockpit and he excitedly teleported inside.

"You ready?" Icarus said as he turned the machine on and was lifted off the ground.

Ship had just gotten strapped in as Icarus took control of the eleph-ANT and guided it toward the closest asteroid. He fired all six rockets, trying to guide the cable gently, but found himself constantly over- and under-correcting the movements. Controlling an eleph-ANT was hard enough, but with a cable attached, it was an almost-impossible task. Many times, he all but lost control of the eleph-ANT, and Ship had to jump in and correct the movement for him.

They planned to link as many nearby asteroids as possible together before ending on the moon where the gravity well would be hard to escape carrying all that weight.

With the first cable connected to the nearest asteroid, Icarus handed over the controls to Ship and Lex to complete. "You two can handle it from here," he said with a sigh of relief. It wasn't as much fun as his first time controlling an eleph-ANT.

Icarus planned to get progress updates from Ship daily, because he knew if he left Ship to the task, he would surely cut corners or get bored.

A few weeks later, Icarus was looking at reports and news they had been passively hearing from Sol—they had built a big-enough radio dish on Titan's rings to gain information. He couldn't help but worry about the lack of noise coming from the Sol system. "Lex, when was the last time we intercepted any communication from Sol?"

A message appeared on one of the screens. It read *Three days.*

Icarus scratched his head. "And what is the longest we have gone without hearing anything from Sol?"

A new message appeared—it showed they had gone several months without intercepting messages from Sol.

Ship interjected to clarify things, his voice coming through a speaker in his office. "Never—there was a long period when we were behind a star and couldn't see the system. That's when we couldn't see the constant chatter from the system. But there hasn't been any moment where the system wasn't at least leaking signals."

Icarus clenched his hands, thinking about how he had had to leave Mars so quickly. "Do you think that means the Fermi zealots won?" he asked, using the derogatory term with malice.

"Unlikely," Ship replied.

Icarus recalled when Atlas recruited him to join the colonizing mission, when the two of them were back on Mars. Atlas had made him work in secret. They couldn't let the Fermi zealots know of their plan.

The Fermion Party was a political power back on Earth, and quite a strong one. Their beliefs were simple. The Fermi Paradox wasn't a paradox at all—it was a universal law that all sufficiently advanced technological species would adapt. *More like "sufficiently moronic,"* Icarus mused.

"It makes my blood boil," Icarus seethed. "Basically, these crazy people believe the reason we don't see any aliens around is because 'somehow,' all species realized it is better for the universe if they stay on the planet they evolved from." He noticed he hadn't felt angry over the topic until just then, when he thought about what he went through before leaving Mars.

Ship appeared in the room, holding a hand up to calm Icarus down. "Hold on, Icarus; we don't even know it was them."

Icarus shook his head. "I know it's them! Only they are crazy enough to take humanity back to the Dark Ages. I understand them not wanting every star to be populated with *Homo sapiens*, but the universe is a huge place. There's enough space for us and other alien species to evolve."

Then Icarus thought about his other Beta Explorers, about their journey into space, worry clear on his cartoon face. If light was reaching them now, there surely had to be a virus or something transmitted their way. They wouldn't attempt to wipe out humanity without also ensuring all the colony ships were identified and eliminated.

Icarus looked at Ship. "Does Sol know where we are? Could they possibly see any light from our engines?"

"No. We took every single precaution possible. We followed the plan exactly."

"Is there any possible way they could retrace our path? To guess which system we ended up at?"

"No, not a chance. I waited until we were behind a star before changing direction. Any light coming off our engines would have been masked by the star. We even changed direction twice. There is no way Sol knows where we are."

Icarus looked at the orb. "Lex, give me a probability that Sol doesn't know where we are."

The figure 99.99978 appeared on Icarus's screen.

Icarus rubbed his hands, trying not to worry. "I guess there's not much we can do about it then. Is there any way of finding out what happened back on Earth?"

Ship shrugged. "Not unless we send a ship there. A lot could have changed since we left. A lot of innovation and technology was built. Perhaps they no longer use radio waves to communicate."

Icarus knew Ship was grasping at straws. It was highly unlikely that all communications would be upgraded at once. Crazy people like that didn't just disappear. "Think about it, Ship. What are the Fermi zealots' three goals?"

"One: return humanity to a Type 1 civilization. Two: align technology development inwards on simulations, not exploration. Three: if the first two aren't possible, restart humanity back to pre-industrial days with these goals at the heart of the new culture." Icarus paused, thinking about the ramifications of what he had just said. "And I bet when these crazy people couldn't get their way, they decided to attempt to restart humanity."

Icarus thought for a moment. He knew the weakest link was Lex. Only Lex was reprogrammable. "As a precaution, Ship, block Lex from manual control of anything on this ship. I don't want to risk him getting a virus."

CHAPTER 26

ATLAS

CAMBRIAN EXPLOSION

Atlas stood in his genetic engineering lab, staring down a microscope focused on fungus sample number 2023.

The lab was a dim blue, simulating the environment beneath the ice of New Europa. The whole room was cooled to negative 104 degrees Celsius, to reflect the temperature there. Along the wall were rows and rows of sealed glass boxes with fungi growing in them, all simulating different environments.

Ship teleported in. "Atlas, I need to show you something important."

"Hey, Ship." Atlas waved. "Let me show you this first."

Atlas walked over to the wall containing the glass boxes. He continued to the far end and stopped at the very final box, which he pulled out and placed on the table. "I think I've done it, Ship," he said, pointing at the box. "With an oxygen-rich environment, we just needed to breed fungus that could feed on the debris found in the water. There is a lot of it near the edges of the hills and mountains where the earth pokes up toward the ice shelf. This little guy here"—Atlas pointed to the little green fungus—"feeds on the organic compounds found in the debris and breathes oxygen. It was a little hard to get it to work right, as these are fungi, not plants. It can't do photosynthesis. It needed something to eat, and this little one has been evolved to be good at eating New Europa dirt."

Inside the glass container was a Petri dish with samples of New Europan dirt and water. The water was covered in a layer of slimy green mold.

"It took two months to get like this, Ship. Only two months. The only thing slowing it down is the amount of oxygen in here. It's converting it quickly into carbon dioxide."

Ship gave a little clap. "Impressive, Atlas, but I really need to show you what is happening on the surface of New Europa."

Ship, ignoring Atlas's preference for physical paper rather than hapticgram, threw a hapticgraphic screen into the air. A screen hovered to the right of them, displaying an image of New Europa's surface. It was a flat sea of ice with jagged lines crossing all over it.

Atlas took a closer look at the lines. "Are those cracks in the ice?"

Ship nodded.

"When did they appear?" Atlas wondered what it meant. It was amazing—he thought perhaps the ice shelf was made up of tectonic plates, like Earth. In all their time surveying the planet, they hadn't once seen any movement of the ice shelves. He figured ice shelves moved slowly.

"I just noticed it now," Ship said. "But wait a moment; there's more to this video."

Atlas looked back at the screen. A massive crack appeared in the ice. It started from one end of the screen and traveled to the other, splitting along the entire length of the video.

"That has got to be a kilometer long," Atlas said.

"Seven."

Suddenly, there was an explosion as the crack reached the bottom layer of the ice. Water and ice shards violently spewed out. Then the screen went white as the image of the surface of New Europa disappeared.

Ship pointed at the screen. "It's worse than you realize, Atlas. That's a mix of hydrogen and oxygen gas flowing out of the crack. This is happening all over the planet."

Atlas bit his lip and shook his head. "Hmm, so we should have thought about this?" he remarked as he processed what it might mean. "When splitting water into its constituent parts, oxygen and hydrogen are produced. These two gases combined make a great propellant because they are extremely flammable. Combine those two molecules, point them out of a rocket engine, light them up as they exit the engine and *boom!* That will create a massive amount of thrust."

Ship nodded again before Atlas continued.

"Put oxygen and hydrogen under pressure. Add an ignition source. And . . . you have a bomb," Atlas said, his hands miming an explosion.

Atlas cocked an eyebrow. "So, we've turned New Europa into a bomb?"

Ship nodded. "Exactly. We should probably leave orbit. If it *did* explode, the shock wave would almost certainly send debris our way."

Atlas wondered how this had happened so quickly. He assumed doing something like that would have taken centuries. "I still don't understand, Ship. How did we blow the ice sheets up like a balloon so fast?"

Ship looked at his feet. "I gave the job to Lex." He paused, still a little ashamed of what he had done. "I installed the first three electrolysis machines. Like you said." He paused again. "Then I figured it was easy enough for Lex to do, so I handed the job over. Lex had jumped wholeheartedly into building anodes and cathodes. They are the large wires that stick into the water. Once an electrical current is run through those two wires, the anode side produces oxygen and the cathode side produces hydrogen. Two hydrogen atoms are produced for every oxygen atom."

"I know how electrolysis works, Ship," Atlas interjected. "Get to the point. How did we end up turning the planet into a bomb?"

"Well . . ." Ship was still reluctant to tell the whole story. "Lex continued producing thousands of the units and installing them. He put more fabricators to the task of doing it, and quite quickly, the only things fabricators were producing were cathodes and anodes for electrolysis."

"Ship, we really need to check in with each other more often. Your invention of changing the playback speed of reality is cool, but it's easy to jump too far into the future with it." He looked over at the corner where the orb usually floated. "Is Lex still building electrolysis machines?"

Ship flickered for a second. Atlas could tell the answer was yes. He could tell Ship had quickly gone and spoken to Lex.

Ship replied moments later. "Not anymore."

"Since when? A second ago?" Atlas laughed as he said it, knowing he was correct.

The team moved quite quickly to get to safety. They didn't move the spacecraft out of orbit but increased their orbit around the planet instead, sticking their spacecraft farther out. They assumed one of the eleph-ANTs on the surface of the planet could warn them of any explosions, giving them enough time to escape. They also turned off all solar equipment and pointed the mirrors away from the planet to avoid any random sparks lighting up New Europa.

"I can't believe we turned the planet into a bomb," Atlas said, laughing at what they had achieved. He looked at the orb. "Lex, if we exploded it on purpose, do you think it would melt the ice?"

Lex wobbled from side to side. This amused Atlas—he hadn't seen him do this before and guessed it meant *maybe*.

He wondered if he could use the explosion to kick-start a global warming cycle. He thought about the possibilities. Perhaps the explosion would be enough to put the planet over the edge where the mirrors could do the rest. But he ruled that idea out as too risky—the same as moving the orbit of the planet. Worst-case scenario, they might totally destroy the planet, spewing so much dust and debris into the atmosphere that the starlight would be blocked out completely, plunging the planet further into an ice age. Besides, he really wanted to see how his fungus went and find out if it could heat up the planet.

Atlas pointed to the orb in the corner. "Lex, here's another job for you. Now that you've made a mess of the planet, start bottling up the hydrogen. It's a great fuel. We could probably use it later."

Atlas had another thought. He didn't want to make the same mistake Ship had made. Removing all the hydrogen from the atmosphere would be hard to do without removing the oxygen, too. He didn't want that to happen. Also, there was a lot of risk with Lex doing anything down there. "Don't do anything that even has a one percent chance of starting a spark or fire. If you also need to bottle the oxygen, then come and alert me when you've captured five percent of the gas under the ice."

While Lex set off on his tasks, Atlas set about introducing his fungus to the planet. His plan was simple—test introducing the fungus to one location near the mountains. Then, if successful, seed the fungus all around New Europa.

He was giddy with excitement. The ANT touched down on New Europa, carrying a sample of the fungus Atlas had spent years perfecting. This ANT was about the size of a beer can with a corkscrew-shaped cone at the front. Its body contained the live fungus.

The ANT began its seven-hour burrow into the ice. It turned on its front digger and its nose started spinning, its four front legs anchored into the ice. It pointed its nose toward the ice and pressed it in, the corkscrew slowly pushing the ice backwards.

It needed to dig through at least a hundred meters of ice. Lex had identified the first spot. It was a location with oxygen under the ice but was under low pressure due to a recent venting of the gas. It meant once the ANT broke the final layer of ice, it wouldn't be blown back out of the hole. Nevertheless, Atlas made sure the ANT used its back legs to fill in the hole behind it as it dug.

The ice was thick and hard. The body of the ANT was now fully beneath the ice, its progress steady.

Atlas's excitement was marred by impatience. Watching the ANT move millimeter by millimeter was so painful. He thought about the fact that the ice had probably been sitting there for millions of years. Layer upon layer must have built up and been compressed until it became solid ice almost as strong as concrete.

Finally, Atlas gave up. He took a deep breath in and out, then dialed up his playback speed. He watched as the ANT went from barely moving to tunnelling through ten centimeters every subjective second.

The speed was satisfying. It reminded him of putting a hot spoon through ice cream. Actually, he thought it was like dropping a magnet through an aluminium pipe. Ten minutes in, he decided to speed things up further and increased his playback speed again, watching as the ANT's legs became a blur, its body diving deep into the ice. Within a matter of minutes, it had reached the bottom.

Atlas quickly returned to real time, just as the nose of the ANT broke through the final layer of ice. A rush of air hit the ANT, knocking it back. Luckily, it had filled in the hole behind itself; it hit the wall, bouncing off it and falling out of the tunnel with a loud *plonk* as it hit the water and began to sink.

The ANT spun up its corkscrew nose, which acted as a propeller and pushed the ANT back up. It continued moving along the surface of the water until it landed on a piece of New Europa dirt.

The ANT was in a bubble of oxygen and hydrogen between the New Europan surface and the ice. Lex had identified a location with all three pieces required for the fungi's survival: water, dirt, and oxygen.

The ANT lodged itself in the dirt and spewed its insides out. A green film sprayed all over the dirt in front of the ANT. It took a few steps back, cameras pointed at the green fungus.

Atlas smiled. "Ship, I'm addicted to your invention. I think this is the most I've used it." Atlas couldn't wait any longer. He sped up his playback speed and looked at the fungus again. Nothing. It still looked exactly the same. He increased his playback speed further. He thought he could see something change. Did it look thicker, or were his eyes deceiving him? Maybe, but he couldn't be sure.

Atlas increased his playback speed *again*. Instantly, there was something—an explosion of green. It got thicker. He raced to change his playback speed back to normal.

All the rocks the camera could see were covered in green. But that wasn't the most important part of the test.

"Did we do it? Did we do it?" Atlas said, running to the printer in his office to read the results. He pulled out a piece of paper with a myriad of numbers on it. He was looking for just one reading. "It's there, Ship. There's carbon dioxide there!"

Ship froze for a second, a moment of worry on his face. "Atlas, sorry to change the subject, but Earth has just stopped broadcasting."

CHAPTER 27

SHIP OF TRILLION

BACK AT STEEL WORLD

After a very long journey, traveling for many years, Ship had arrived back at Steel World—his speed was relativistic. The small ship cobbled together from various eleph-ANTs was traveling too fast to stay in orbit. All the fuel onboard the eleph-ANT had been spent—maneuvering away from the chasing Dottiens to escape their system had used far more fuel than he had expected. The rest was used to accelerate Ship as fast as possible back to Steel World.

Ship had taken a risk—a calculated risk, but a big risk. He had no fuel to slow himself down again, so if his plan failed, he would rocket through the system and continue on indefinitely. But it was a risk he needed to take, as the longer Trillion was stuck on the moon in the Dottien system, the higher the probability of the Dottiens taking hostile action toward her.

Ship couldn't bear the thought of something happening to Trillion. He loved her—he would do anything for her. He had to make sure she was safe. He had a single-minded purpose—get back and rescue Trillion.

It had been many years since Ship had had an avatar. For the entire time he traveled in his makeshift eleph-ANT-based spaceship, he did not have access to a hologram, let alone a hapticgram. He thought about how not having an avatar for so long had changed the way he thought. He was still an AI; he didn't need a body, but somehow, having a body made the world more enjoyable.

Ship signaled the Mark Two waiting in the system. If the Mark Two did not respond, Ship would see himself flying through the system, right past Steel World at an unimaginable speed. He would smash through whatever was in his way, probably destroying himself in the process.

Ping. The Mark Two responded.

That was good, Ship thought. Getting a response was half the battle. The next step, he wouldn't know if it had been successful or not. He needed to send instructions to the Mark Two and hope it understood and initiated them.

Ship was ejected out the back of the eleph-ANT spaceship in a canister, devoid of sensory input. The eleph-ANT had pushed off against Ship's canister, nudging it backward but also slowing it slightly. This was good because the canister needed to be sufficiently far away from the eleph-ANT to be caught properly. What Ship hadn't calculated was one of the legs of the eleph-ANT had seized up. Only slightly, but enough to put a minor spin on the canister. Ship tumbled through space.

He didn't know about the fact he was tumbling, however. Unaware, he could simply count the milliseconds between being disconnected from the eleph-ANT and reconnected to the Mark

Two. He would only be able to tell something was wrong if he failed to reconnect to a new ship within 1,988 seconds.

Ship tumbled through space toward Steel World. His trajectory meant he would eventually tumble out of the system once more.

Thankfully, the Mark Two received the message sent earlier and had fired its engines on full, out of the system and in the direction it predicted Ship's canister would end up. By the time the canister had caught up, the Mark Two was traveling at relativistic speeds too. But relative to Ship's canister, both objects were crawling toward each other.

The Mark Two opened its airlock and Ship slowly drifted inside. Several ANTs appeared, grabbing the canister, maneuvering it to the lower decks, and installing him in place. He was switched on and instantly took full command of the spacecraft.

Ship, however, was Ship. A machine built to travel between systems. He wasn't designed for what he was doing right now; he still had the lazy, impatient tendencies apparent in all ships.

Choosing not to experience large sections of journey, he changed his perception of time after the first year.

The first thing he did before turning the Mark Two around was project himself into the interior of the ship using the hapticgram projectors. He had missed having a body. His ability to speed up subjective time was limited while in the eleph-ANT, and he didn't want to risk turning off completely, so unfortunately he had to experience almost two full years of subjective time. Two full years of subjective time without a body.

"It's good to be back home," Ship said to himself.

A reply came from a voice inside his head. It sounded a lot like Lex. Unlike Trillion, Ship could read Lex's programming. Understand its uncertainties. Even communicate with Lex through a sort of language. Ship could understand Lex despite Lex not speaking in words. It was simply processing data, but over the years, Ship had started to understand the code Lex spoke in. He often roughly translated for Trillion. He could feel himself reading Lex's code once more. "Technically, to you, this isn't a home," Lex said.

Ship was confused. He scanned the room, looking for the source of the voice, and noticed a floating orb: Lex. "I forgot we installed a version of you on every ship."

"The probability of catching you would have been reduced by forty percent without me."

Ship smiled in appreciation. "Is that why I'm in here faster than I expected?"

Lex didn't answer. He didn't know how to answer. Lex could be installed on any system powerful enough to run him. Versions of it were easy to come by. Ship, on the other hand, was much more than that. He was a custom AI. His hardware was custom-built and his software customized to his hardware.

Ship looked up at Lex. "It looks like this new ship design from Atlas is faster."

Ship was intrigued. He remembered back to his fight with the Dottie people when he was first dragged to that moon and held there. He had pushed the engines to the max, almost ripping the spacecraft to pieces. He smiled when he calculated that with this new spaceship, he had enough thrust to easily brush off another attack like that.

He steadied his resolve, now knowing what he had to do. "Lex, let's assemble an army."

He teleported to his room, which was larger than his room in his old spacecraft, as all rooms were on the Mark Two. It was still a projection of black walls. He laughed at his efforts to get creative with the black. Now it just reminded him of being stuck on the makeshift eleph-ANT spacecraft without a means to create an avatar. He hated that experience.

Black walls and black ceilings weren't different enough from what he had experienced traveling back to Steel World.

He decided to make use of the large open space he now had. He knew he was going to war, so he decided to look the part. He thought back to General Walker. He changed his clothes to a similar army outfit. Marks appeared on each shoulder—they were very ostentatious. Anyone taking a cursory glance would assume he was a very high-ranking person in the made-up army. As he looked around the room it became lighter, transforming into a large army airplane hangar complete with three old-school fighter jets.

With that little side quest complete, Ship set about assembling his army. Still keen on making the most of having hapticgram and hologram technology, Ship had Lex compile a list of everything they had in the system. The list was extensive, and he quickly realized listing everything on the screen would not work. Even using a summarized list of everything would completely fill his room with screens.

He understood why Trillion struggled to comprehend how many resources they truly had. Through his interface with the spacecraft and Lex, he could take it all in. But there wasn't a practical way of showing it in a hapticgraphic projection. One asteroid had enough resources to build the massive spacecraft he was in, and they had mined billions of asteroids. They had mined all the planets in the system.

The number of fabricators they had was, in Trillion's own words, "mind-blowingly big." Ship compared the resources they had to those on Sol.

"Lex, can you check my numbers?"

He didn't think those numbers could be real. The idea that they could have orders of magnitude more resources didn't seem right.

The orb flashed green.

"How?"

Ship reached into Lex's programming and began reading what he was trying to say. "Sol has much of its materials locked up in Jupiter. Without a gas giant in the Steel World system, there is a lot more free material available."

Ship thought about the number of fabricators they had— several billion. Several billion fabricators meant that producing anything was simple. A new ship could take a year with a single fabricator. With around a thousand fabricators, they could produce all the parts required in a week and assemble it within four days. So, creating a new ship by pooling a thousand fabricators would take eleven days max.

It no longer mattered how many ships they wanted. Creating a million ships would still only take eleven days. They had enough fabricators to produce more than a million ships at once.

"Exponential growth," Ship said, mirroring what Trillion had screamed at him previously.

He wasn't at risk of running low on materials and resources. Time wasn't even an impacting factor. Whether he needed to produce one of something or a million, it would all take the same amount of time.

Trillion had given Ship a clear plan of exactly what he needed to get done. He set about producing Trillion's shopping list of items. The first was spacecraft. Ship quickly added three zeros to the number. Then he had Lex start creating spacecraft.

The second was a relativistic ANT thrower.

Ship organized a few thousand fabricators to line up, floating in space. The asteroid belt was already littered with fabricators. It was no longer an "asteroid" belt but more an orbiting belt of fabricators, ANTs, and pellets. Every single piece of it had been converted.

It took a while for the ANTs to push all the fabricators together, but once it was complete, the square metallic bodies of the fabricators were pressed up side by side like containers on a train, doors all facing the same way.

Like clockwork, all the fabricators finished at roughly the same time, each opening their doors in unison. Because the message to fabricators traveled outward from one end to the other, the fabricator at the end was always a few seconds slower. This created a wave pattern as the doors opened, almost as if everything was choreographed.

With the doors wide open, several ANTs floated into each fabricator. From Ship's perspective, it looked like a colony of insects returning home.

As he watched the unfolding fabricators dance, an idea popped into his head. He and Trillion had named the planet Steel World. He liked that name, but they needed a new name for the system. He decided to name it Tac, short for *The Ant Colony*. Ship nodded to himself. "If Earth's system is called Sol, then this system is called Tac."

Ship focused back on the fabricators. The ANTs had pushed out a large white pipe around two meters in diameter. Again, it looked like a choreographed wave as a pipe appeared out of each of the fabricators, although this time, it was more like a snake worming its way out.

The pipes were large magnetic accelerators. Ship directed a huge spacecraft toward the first pipe. A hatch on the spacecraft opened and out floated an electricity cable. An ANT was sent to grab the end of the cable, connecting it to the first magnetic accelerator. Immediately, lights in the center of the accelerator lit up. Ship could now see the middle of it—it was ribbed with silver wires spaced evenly throughout the center.

The next-closest magnetic accelerator was sucked toward the accelerator connected to the spaceship, both ends connecting to each other like jigsaw pieces. Then that accelerator lit up and started sucking the next one closer, almost like a cascading set of dominoes falling over, as a wave of accelerators were connected together.

As a test run, Ship instructed an ANT to enter the first of the accelerators. It floated toward the entrance gently. When the ANT was about ten centimeters away, it was sucked in and pulled toward the accelerator by the eddy currents.

As the ANT flowed through accelerator after accelerator, it sped up until it reached the end, traveling at six percent the speed of light when it exited.

It was a true relativistic weapon. ANTs weren't designed to handle those speeds—the g-forces involved ripped the ANT apart. So, the test ANT was in pieces when it left the accelerator.

Within only two hours, it would hit the surface of the sun at a mind-boggling speed.

Trillion had suggested Lex create a new design for the ANTs—something that could handle the g-forces involved, that could steer itself so that it could make minor adjustments to its trajectory closer to the target.

Her only requirement was that it had to be called an *assass-ANT*. Ship thought that was a bad joke, but he failed to come up with a better name.

Ship thought about the speed these assass-ANTs would be traveling at. "Lex, if we were using our current ANT design, how many of them would we need to launch at the moon Trillion is on to destroy it?"

Lex calculated the answer.

"Only one?" Ship said, a little confused.

The orb flashed green.

Ship processed that for a moment. An object sent out the back of the magnetic accelerator had enough force to obliterate the moon he had been trapped on for years. These weapons would be dangerous. They would make fusion bombs look like a bee sting.

"Lex, will these assass-ANTs also have a failsafe on them?"

The orb flashed blue, signaling confusion.

"The assass-ANTs you create"—Ship projected an ANT in his hand—"each assass-ANT needs to be loaded with a small explosive so it can destroy itself if it loses communication with me, you, or Trillion. So, if it was accidentally heading toward something important, the relativistic assass-ANT could be stopped."

Without missing a beat, Lex had, almost instantly, sent an updated design for an assass-ANT to Ship.

Ship wondered how Lex had crafted a design so quickly. In this system, Lex had been faster to respond than he usually was and was more willing to give answers on incomplete data. Even the task of designing an assass-ANT—one based on a blueprint from Trillion—took him no time at all. Usually, he would have crafted a large number of different possible designs and tested them in simulations, struggling to decide between the top hundred. This version of Lex was fast but somehow decisive. He filed that question for later to see if Trillion had any answers.

Ship set about completing the final piece of his mission—real-time communication with the other Beta Explorers. Before they left, Atlas had sent through plans for a special particle accelerator. They had built it. The machine was designed to entangle particles, sending one to Atlas and keeping one with the particle accelerator.

However, Trillion was no longer in the Steel World system, and as far as Ship knew, she didn't have any plans on coming back.

Ship pulled up the schematics of the communication machine. It was huge. Bigger than Ship's new body, in fact—the largest machine in the system. It was cylinder-shaped, with one end pointing toward the system Atlas said he was headed for. A light beam, like a laser, projected toward the system of Atlas exactly.

The entangled-particle generator, the AI to process all the data, and the coolant all took up a tiny portion of the very long cylinder. It was made this size because one of the entangled photons needed to be bounced from mirror to mirror in the cylinder, ricocheting hundreds of billions of times. The light needed to be bounced at just the right rate so that the entangled particle reader could read the entangled photon at the same time it arrived to Atlas. The precision was incredible.

Ship took in all the details of the contraption. He was impressed by the creativity. He could tell it wasn't just Atlas who had developed the machine. There were little telltale signs that another Ship was involved, which intrigued him.

The genius part, he thought, was that he managed to come up with a way for the two beams to arrive at their destination at exactly the same time. Light only travels at 300,000 kilometers per second in a vacuum. But the cylinder didn't have a vacuum inside. It was filled with a gel-like substance. Ship didn't understand the composition. This gel material slowed each photon to about ten percent of the speed it would travel in a vacuum. In a nutshell, it would take a photon 250 years to reach Atlas, so the cylinder needed to bounce light between mirrors for 250 years.

This was the challenge Ship needed to solve. He needed to somehow put a hole in the mirror. It needed to be exact, as both Trillion (who was stuck on the moon) and Atlas (who was in his own system) needed to receive the traveling photon at the exact same time.

Ship reexamined the instructions for the machine. He looked into the details of how the mirrors were controlled. Instead of a single mirror at each side, there were billions of tiny mirrors, each controlled individually. These individual mirrors had the ability to control exactly where the photon would bounce next, taking the photon on a longer path or a shorter one if required. This could create minor adjustments so that each photon arrived at the detector at the same time. Each end of the cylinder could grow or shrink, too, increasing or decreasing the length of the cylinder, simultaneously increasing the distance traveled by each photon. This again gave the tool strong control over when a photon would reach the detector.

Ship thought about the detector some more and realized it was much simpler than he originally believed. He didn't need to cut a hole in the mirrors; that would risk damaging the machine. He could use a mirror to point that photon toward Trillion on the moon. Then all he needed to do was tell the machine the new location of the photon detector, and it would automatically adjust the mirrors so that both photons reached their destination at the exact same time.

Ship instructed a micro-ANT to disconnect the photon detector. The ANT floated to the end of the large cylinder and removed forty-two screws. Three more micro-ANTs floated over, and together, they pulled out the photon detector. Behind it was a black shield with two slits. This was removed too. No light flew out the back, as it would be several years before photons needed to hit the detector.

A fabricator created another little device that would slot into the place of the detector—simply a mirror with a motor. This mirror would point the photon to Trillion. It needed to move independently so it could make minor micro-adjustments to the direction the photon needed to head, ensuring it would always point toward Trillion. Or, if required, it could be pointed elsewhere once Ship had saved Trillion and they moved to another system.

As a precaution, he transmitted a message back to Atlas, telling him exactly what he had done to his invention and where the new detector was going to be placed. He sent over a complete list of instructions on how to remote-access the particle accelerator, and had Lex manufacture a long-range radio dish capable of picking up any signal. That way, if Ship had broken the communication device, Atlas would have complete knowledge of what had happened. And the means to fix it. His fixes wouldn't happen in real time, but at least he would have the means to fix anything that broke.

If it worked, Trillion would be able to interact with this system. If she needed anything, she could manufacture it in the Ant Colony and send it back via spacecraft.

Not wanting to risk leaving anything to chance, or leaving anything to Lex, Ship oversaw all the tasks he had been sent back to Steel World to complete. Time flew by, and in exactly twelve days, Ship set off on his journey back to Trillion, only this time with a bigger, more powerful spacecraft and an armada of ten thousand other ships following behind him. The assass-ANTs were set on timers. They would travel much faster than Ship, so they needed to launch much later. That way magnetic accelerators would begin firing these assass-ANTs out of them at just the right time so that both Ship and his convoy would arrive at the same time as the assass-ANTs. This would give him and Trillion virtually an unlimited supply of weapons and the ability to completely and utterly destroy the Dottiens if negotiations didn't work.

Ship just hoped he wasn't too late to save Trillion.

CHAPTER 28

ICARUS

LIGHTING UP THE RING

Icarus stood at the edge of his bed. In front of him floated an image of the rings of Titan. One of the rings had a cable that stretched all the way around the gas giant; every single asteroid in that ring was now connected.

The thick cable linking every large object in the ring wasn't just designed to hold the objects together. Inside was a fiber-optic cable and an electrical cable. The length of the cable meant data traveling through it would have a half-second delay—not enough that any two people on opposite sides of Titan wouldn't be able to talk easily, but it would be noticeable.

The electrical cables weren't in use yet. Icarus hadn't started laying the solar panels. The design was such that the side of the planet that was in light should be able to feed electricity to the dark side.

Icarus and Ship were about to start installing solar panels when they encountered a mystery. Icarus couldn't be sure, but it looked like an artifact. But not a human one. Not something dropped by one of the ANTs. Lex assured him it wasn't anything from the ship. *It's impossible for us to manufacture that* were the words Ship had used. So, maybe it was alien.

"Can I see it yet?" Icarus called out.

"It's still being scanned," Ship replied.

They found it in one of the fabricators. They had specialized fabricators that mined resources, turning them into pellets, raw resources that other fabricators could use to create anything.

Asteroids were loaded into these fabricators. Then, a while later, the door would open, revealing stacks of raw pellets inside. Iron, gold, silicon. There was a lot of gold on these asteroids—so much of it that Icarus was contemplating painting the ring in gold. He had added a golden coating to the cable running around the ring.

Icarus was making coffee when he got the alert from Ship that one of the fabricators had stopped working. It was processing asteroids but failed to process this one particular object.

Fabricators were very powerful and complex machines, designed to process anything. They could break anything down into its constituent parts so other fabricators could recombine them into almost anything.

However, this fabricator couldn't break the material down—it seemed to be having trouble identifying it. But this wasn't what bothered Icarus. It was the symbols on the side of the object that triggered his fascination.

"The scans are complete," Ship called out.

That pulled Icarus out of his daydream.

Ship threw a screen in front of Icarus. It was made up of multiple elements in the periodic table and a few elements not found on it as they currently knew it. He had highlighted where on the table they should be.

Ship pointed to the location of the material on the periodic table. "It's stronger than any material we thought possible."

Icarus swiped away the view. "I don't care about that. Show me the writing. Bring me the object."

An ANT quickly scuttled across the floor and handed the object to Icarus.

Icarus took hold of it. "This is what I wanted."

It was large and square, about the size of a stack of books. It was a deep, shiny black—he could see his reflection in it. He spun the object around. On each of the sides were etchings that appeared to be multiple repeating patterns that looked like two arrows pointed toward each other.

He looked closer at the sides, turning the object around more slowly than before. The sides weren't flat, but bowed inwards. Icarus turned it sideways. He could see that if he placed it on a table, only the corners would touch the table.

Icarus wondered if it was a design choice, to prevent the markings from wearing off. He held the object closer. There were hundreds of markings on it. They didn't run left to right but rather started in the center and moved outward in a clockwise direction. At least to Icarus's human brain, that was how the writing looked.

He was barely able to contain his excitement. Just the thought that what he was looking at could be alien writing gave him goose-bumps. The whole reason he had decided to go on this adventure was to communicate with aliens, to try and decode a language.

Icarus held the object up to show Ship. "See these markings? It's clearly a language, Ship."

Icarus knew there were generally six different systems of writing humans used. The most commonly known systems were logographic and alphabetic. But he knew with aliens there could even be a seventh system of writing.

Icarus began to talk through how he could decipher it. "Ship, most people think deciphering a language that uses the English alphabet would be much easier than translating hieroglyphics. It's true that there are thousands of different symbols. And in a lot of ways, it isn't easy to identify a pattern. That's what all logographic languages have—each symbol represents a different word."

The ideas and theories were flowing into Icarus's head. Hieroglyphics was the one idea that he kept coming back to. He took a deep breath. "But when translating a human language, there's a few assumptions you never have to question. There are so many shared concepts. We have eyes that see in an extremely narrow wavelength of the electromagnetic spectrum. There are only 840 different sounds we can actually make with our mouths. Our senses of smell and hearing are extremely limited. These things constrain what our language might be."

Icarus was jumping up and down at this point, just thinking about what this language could potentially be. "We can't anthropomorphize this artefact. We have to leave our preconceptions at the door," he said.

Icarus looked at the square object once more and flicked it with his finger. It made a thudding sound, followed by a slow ringing that vibrated through it. He looked down at the lush carpeted floor.

"Lex, can you remove the carpet projection?"

Icarus watched as the carpet disappeared from one side of the room to the other. It looked like a wave passing, leaving only metal ship floors. It looked cold to Icarus. Even though he couldn't feel the cold, his mind was telling him not to place his feet on the ground. He jumped up onto the countertop and sat there, his duck-shaped feet dangling off the edge.

"This is solid? There's nothing inside of this?" Icarus asked.

"Correct," Ship replied with a nod.

Icarus threw the object in an arc toward the solid steel floor. It flew through the air and thumped on the ground. Rather than bouncing, it thumped down hard on one corner.

"Lex, can you bring the carpet back? But leave the spot where the object is with no carpet on it."

The wave of projections rolled in from two sides of the room. This time, it looked like two carpets were being rolled out, somehow meeting perfectly in the middle. The section of floor with the object sticking out had a perfectly circular hole in it.

"I'm loving the effects you're doing here," Icarus praised Lex.

Icarus jumped off the table, landing on the soft carpet, his cartoon feet pressing into it. He walked over to the object. He could see it was balancing on one corner, which was wedged about three centimeters into the steel. It was so hard, it had dented the floor.

Icarus had to wiggle it a few times to get it out. He threw it up in the air a few times and caught it. "I believe the shape of the object is the message it's trying to communicate. It's obviously designed to survive."

He jumped back onto the table. There were many possibilities to explain what it could be. It could be a random piece of a spacecraft that had fallen off a ship coming through this system. "Lex, give me a breakdown of how often each of these symbols is used. Order them by which appears the most."

Icarus knew figuring out which codes appeared most often was the first step in decoding any human language. He began putting that theory to use, to see if it worked on alien languages too.

He briefly remembered about the ring world he was building. He addressed Ship. "Can you sort out the grid? Get the solar panels live. I want to figure this object out."

CHAPTER 29
TRILLION

LONG-LOST FRIENDS

Trillion floated at the very top of the cargo bay. She was organizing Lex to clear a large section of the hangar. It wasn't a smooth operation without Ship's subtle hand guiding ANTs and eleph-ANTs.

What she had assumed would take a few hours had taken almost a whole day. Lex struggled with coordinating that many machines at once. It should have been a well-choreographed activity. It normally was. But the orb struggled with the task.

She wondered just how stupid the ANTs were without Ship to add a subtle but noticeable hand to direct them.

She cringed as she saw several ANTs crushed when an eleph-ANT carrying machinery walked right over the top of them.

She thought how painful it was to watch and decided she didn't want to see ANTs bump into each other or be crushed. She changed her playback speed, speeding things up until it did look like a well-oiled machine. ANTs and eleph-ANTs blurred into one another; they became lines reaching out and clearing things away. From her perspective, as she floated at the top of the room, it looked like a jittery line would reach out and absorb items in the room. She found it meditative, watching the free space increase through the cargo bay.

She laughed a little, reminded of when she was a kid watching videos of ants digging colonies. Time-lapse videos of them digging into sand were her favorite, she remembered, as she watched the blur of ANTs working.

A good twelve hours later, the room was finally clear, and she changed her playback speed to normal. The cargo bay was littered with ANT body parts. Broken metal legs, arms, and flattened ANTs lay all over the metal floor. She assumed that was the collateral damage from eleph-ANTs moving large objects around, but the space was now open enough for what she wanted—to use the large space to wargame multiple scenarios, starting with one where she completely and utterly destroyed the Dottiens.

At one end of the cargo bay she projected an image of the Dottien planet. Around it she added the army of the Dottiens, color-changing objects that floated nearby. Then, at the other end, she showed the armada of spacecraft on their way to the system.

Visualizing it like this, it became evident just how lopsided it was going to be.

On one side Trillion could see a planet the size of a basketball. There were hundreds, maybe thousands, of small dots spaced around the Dottien home world. All in all, when she projected their resources like that, the Dottiens stretched across one cubic meter's worth of space.

On the other side, there were many objects. So many that it looked like a large cloud that stretched the entire length of the cargo bay.

Trillion smiled. There was no way she was going to lose. At the scale she was showing the battlefield, the Dottiens controlled one meter of space. But she was about to bring an armada that stretched the entire length of the cargo bay.

As she played out the scenario—her armada versus the Dottiens—she realized the only challenge was making sure she survived. She needed to get off the moon while the Dottiens were distracted.

Trillion found it important to think through even the worst possible scenarios. She needed to have a plan for every eventuality. That way, there was no chance she was not getting off the moon.

She heard a ping from Lex. It was the kind of sound phones used to make when they received a message. Trillion looked at the orb. "You trying to tell me something?"

The orb flashed green, and on all the screens in front of her, an *unread message* icon appeared.

"Did we get a message from Ship?" Trillion asked, excitement in her voice.

The orb flashed green and played the message to Trillion.

She had to play it back multiple times, as she didn't understand part of it. It said he was on his way back, but it also mentioned a communication network was ready. And that she could speak with Atlas.

Trillion looked at Lex, leaning forward. "Communication network?" She tried to rack her brain about what it was. "Do you know what he's talking about?"

The orb flashed green.

"Well, this just sucks, then," Trillion said. "Without Ship, you and I can't really communicate well. Let's treat this like charades. Explain it to me."

The orb transformed into a phone. The phone started to ring, and the caller ID read *Atlas.*

Trillion started to clap. She was quite impressed with Lex's efforts. It did make it clear. She remembered when she got the message from Atlas and thought it was a cruel joke from him. She had told Ship to set it up, thinking it was some silly game. But if it was real . . .

She thought about the possibilities. She imagined herself in one system but controlling all ANTs and eleph-ANTs in another system. It would make having a galactic empire possible.

She shook her head. She was getting too far ahead of herself. First, she needed to get off the moon.

Trillion looked at the orb once more. "Are you sure? Is this true?"

The orb flashed green.

Trillion smiled, still not quite believing it. "How smart is that old man Atlas? Who figures out how to do faster-than-light communication? Everyone says it's impossible."

She left the cargo bay. As she walked, she thought a bit more about what communication meant. It meant she could speak with other people. Other Beta Explorers. She could speak with Atlas, Icarus, and Angelique.

She froze in place, the thought going through her mind a million miles an hour. Atlas. She could speak with Atlas. Another human. It had been centuries since she'd spoken to anyone. Anyone other than Ship or Lex. She could ask Atlas how he figured out FTL communication. She missed that smart old man.

She paused, wondering why she hadn't been bothered by not having spoken to another human until now. This was one of the few times she realized that she wasn't one hundred percent herself. She had changed since becoming digitalized. She thought about when she was flesh and blood. She would have been so depressed, not speaking to another human for this long.

She thought it must have been one of the subtle changes made to her when she was uploaded. It made sense, since getting depressed on a journey like this would have been counterproductive.

"Can I speak to him now?" Trillion asked.

Lex was still shaped like a phone. The phone flashed green and started to ring.

"Wait." Trillion put up her hands. "Not in here."

She teleported to the bridge. She was grinning from ear to ear as she paced in circles.

"I can't wait to speak to a human," she blurted out, turning bright red. Why was she nervous? She needed to relax.

She closed her eyes. She took a deep breath. In. Out. In. She opened her eyes.

"I'm ready, Lex. Put me through," she requested, a fake authority in her voice.

Two distinct beeping sounds were heard through the speakers. It was the sound of a phone call connecting.

"Hi. Hello," Trillion said with a quiver, betraying her fake confidence.

Atlas's voice came through the speaker.

"Hello, Trillion, are you there?"

It worked! She couldn't believe it. She hadn't expected it to work. She didn't quite know what to say next, though.

"Hi. Hello," she said again.

"Oh, good. It's working."

"Hi. Hello." Trillion slapped her head. Why was she repeating herself?

"Oh, is this not working? Can you not hear me? Ship, what is happening? Why can't she hear me?"

"Yes, I can hear you. Sorry, I was in shock," Trillion said, shaking her head.

"Oh, thank god. Most of my tests were between two ends of my ship. I took a risk that it would actually work over light-years like this."

"This isn't some prank, Atlas? Are you actually in another part of the galaxy?" Trillion asked, a touch of suspicion in her voice.

"You bet I am. How are you?"

"Well," Trillion began, "it's a long story. I'm kind of stuck on a moon."

"What? Did your spacecraft break down? I might be able to help you if you need a new one."

"Well, no . . ." She paused, thinking about how to explain it. "It's not that. I met some aliens."

"Aliens? Oh, my god. You've met aliens. What are they like? Who are they? Do they think like us? What kind of technology do they have? Anything we can copy? I have so many questions for you, Trillion." There was a pause on the line. "Are you okay, Trillion? How can I help?"

"Yes, I'm fine." Trillion nodded as she spoke. "Basically, I played with fire. I have a bit of a plan, though. Ship is on his way back with an army. I'll be out of here soon. I'm just so happy to be speaking to another human."

CHAPTER 30

ATLAS

SPEAKING WITH ALIENS

"In theory, this should work," Atlas said. His hand hovered over a button on his keyboard. He was talking with Trillion through the speakers.

"Let's hope. Wait. Could we break anything?"

"No. This code should just increase the bandwidth to the Starnet."

Atlas could feel the excitement at the thought. Instantaneous communication meant galaxy-wide civilizations were now possible. Technology advancements on any of the colonies could now disseminate straightaway to all the others—no longer were advancements limited by slow lightspeed.

To a simulation like him, it meant he could travel the universe instantaneously. At least if this worked, if his planned improvements *did* increase the bandwidth of the Starnet.

Atlas pressed the Launch button.

Nothing happened. Well, nothing he could see.

"I guess I was expecting something to happen, Ship, but it's just data-transfer speeds. Has our connection bandwidth changed?"

Ship nodded. "We are now recording a three-petabyte connection."

Atlas nearly fell off his chair. The data transfer speeds were enormous. "Wow, I don't think we had a bandwidth on Mars that size."

"I modeled the system off the data link between Earth and the moon. I guess that connection was designed to manage millions of people communicating at once. We only have a connection between two people."

Atlas stood up. "Okay, I'm coming over."

Increased data speeds were one thing, but what he really wanted to test was whether he could use that speed to jump into Trillion's spacecraft. If he could do that, it would change everything.

Atlas pressed another button on his computer.

In an instant, he disappeared, then reappeared on Trillion's ship.

Trillion was standing on the bridge, grinning from ear to ear. She launched herself at him. Atlas opened his arms and embraced her. They squeezed each other tighter, neither wanting to let go.

"I thought I'd never see any of you again, let alone hug you," Trillion said.

"Me neither."

Atlas grabbed Trillion's hand and held it up. "I can't believe I'm touching you!" He could see tears in Trillion's eyes.

It was an emotional time for both of them. He started to cry too. "Trillion, there are moments of pure joy in life, and this is one of them."

"I agree—I didn't know I could be this happy."

"You know why we don't get lonely?" Atlas asked.

"What do you mean?"

"Haven't you noticed that along this journey, you haven't missed any other human? It's because of the changes made to our brain scan."

"Are these changes permanent? I can't imagine a world where I didn't want my children."

"It's designed to fade once our 'children' are born."

Trillion pulled two chairs over and poured herself and Atlas a glass of red wine. They discussed what becoming a simulated human had cost them. How they had both changed. They wondered if they could redo the events of the night when they left. Would they still agree to head out on this adventure?

It was clear to them both why the change was necessary when they were uploaded. It was a lonely journey through space. However, they didn't feel lonely. Neither could see the perspective outside of what they were currently feeling—they could only see the excitement and passion for creating a colony.

Atlas was the first to change the subject. "I'm keen to see this alien." He walked over to the window. Outside, he saw it. It was huge. Its body easily reached a good thirty meters high. The large, bulbous creature was around a hundred meters away from the ship, but Atlas could see it clearly. It wasn't moving. Its skin wasn't changing, either. It wasn't doing anything. "And it just waits there for you to speak with it?" he asked.

"Yes. I'm almost positive it's a robot, because it doesn't get bored. It can talk with Lex for hours and hours, running through the same scenario again and again."

Atlas bit his lip, curiosity starting to get the better of him. "Let me have a go. Do you have any ANTs out there? I'd love to take a closer look."

Atlas watched as Trillion threw a small piece of paper into the air. It unfolded and turned into a large screen. He could tell she was showing off.

On the screen was the live-streamed image of the ANTs near the alien. Atlas took a few steps closer to the screen. The skin of the creature was textured and dimpled.

"We call them the Dottiens," Trillion said.

"Does it eat?"

Trillion shrugged.

"And it hasn't bothered you again since initially trapping you here?"

Trillion nodded.

Atlas could feel his brain ticking over. "Trillion, can you get your Lex to send mine everything it's tried? I'm keen to see what I can do." Atlas's mind was thinking through ideas. "I'll be back," he said, as he teleported out to his own ship.

He was back in his office. "Ship, can you print out everything Trillion has collected about the Dottiens?"

The printer sprang to life. He walked over to the printer in his room and started pulling the pieces of paper out. He combed through page after page, looking for any clue as to how they might communicate. He had countless questions, such as what sort of language they spoke.

"What has Trillion's Lex tried already?" he asked, rummaging through the papers. "Can you print those out next?"

It had been hours. Atlas hunched over the papers, reading everything he could find. It was strange. Lex and the Dottien could speak—at least, Trillion's Lex thought they were communicating. Then, all of a sudden, neither of them would understand the other.

So, Trillion's Lex would start again, test-projecting different colors on the screen to try and decode the Dottiens' language.

The pattern happened again and again, each time taking Lex just as long to decode the language.

"Ship, am I understanding this correctly?" Atlas asked, raising his head from the papers. "Trillion's Lex is managing to communicate with the Dottien, but then, after a while, they can't communicate any longer?"

"That's what he is saying. Or maybe Lex is wrong and it could never actually communicate with the alien."

It didn't make sense. Atlas was so confused. He was determined to get to the bottom of this. He teleported back to Trillion's
bridge.

She wasn't there.

"Trillion?"

"I'm in my room. I'll be out in a sec," came her voice from
the speakers.

A few moments later, she teleported in and floated in the air,
arms and legs crossed in a yoga pose.

"Question, Trillion. I still don't quite understand the alien.
Can I clarify a few things?"

He watched as Trillion nodded and floated back toward the
ground. A wine reappeared in her hand, followed by a chair,
which she settled into.

Atlas held up a piece of paper. "In the most basic sense, the
Dottiens communicate with colors?"

"Yes, as far as we can tell. I think purple is some kind of threat,
but I have no idea what any of the other colors mean."

"Okay, and this is what happens every time." Atlas began
recapping what he had seen from the data Trillion provided.
"Each time Lex manages to communicate with it in a very sim-
plistic way, he figures out that red means yes and blue means
no?"

"Yes. Well, a particular pattern on its skin means yes. But you
could simplify it to that. Yes."

"Now, this is the part that I don't understand." Atlas pointed
to his piece of paper. "After a little while, red no longer means
yes. It might now mean . . ." Atlas was struggling to come up with
an example fast enough. ". . . dog, for example," he managed to
say. "After a while, red becomes dog and no longer means yes."

"Hm, that's exactly what happens. After some time, everything Lex thought he knew about the Dottien changes."

"Do you know why?"

"No, but it's not like we have a complete understanding of
the alien. It's like we're communicating at the level you might

communicate with a small child. We can't have a proper conversation. Each time we manage to create a shared group of words or concepts, *boom!* Somehow, the language changes to something else."

Atlas bit his lip hard. "I'll be back again."

He teleported out.

Something wasn't adding up. He thought about the problem again.

Atlas looked at the orb in the corner. "Lex, can you run through the footage? Then tell me, if you were trying to communicate with the Dottien, would you come to the same conclusion that Trillion's Lex did?"

While waiting for the results of Lex's finding, he started reviewing footage himself. He sat down at his computer and brought up a clip from one of the "training sessions" where Lex and the Dottien were collecting data to understand each other's language.

On his screen were two videos playing simultaneously. One showed a large screen projecting colors and shades at the Dottien, while the other showed the Dottien's full body.

It was beautiful. Waves of colors flowed from one side of the alien to the other. Then, like a calm lake with several pebbles thrown into it, bursts of color appeared on the Dottien. It was mesmerizing.

It reminded Atlas of the electronics stores in the early days, when they would play a demo of the holographic projector. It was always something super bright and beautiful.

I can't believe I'm looking at true alien life, Atlas thought.

"Ship, what does the word *alien* mean?"

"It means *different. Unfamiliar.*"

Atlas clicked the replay button. He pressed the plus sign and zoomed in on the alien's skin. He watched as the same video he had just seen played again, but this time from a zoomed-in section of the Dottien's skin. From this angle, the section of skin took up the whole screen. He watched as waves of color flowed through the screen randomly, almost resembling a screensaver.

He leaned in, squinting to focus on the details. He slowed the video down. Waves of color traveled through the screen, and the texture of the Dottien's skin moved from bumpy to smooth to bumpy, little dimples of the skin expanding and contracting.

It reminded him of an octopus—the way it could change the color and texture of its skin to match its environment. He'd seen a nature program once where an octopus blended in with a rocky ground by transforming its skin through color and texture changes to mimic real rocks.

Atlas looked up from his computer. "Ship, was Lex using a screen the whole time to communicate with the Dottien?"

"Yes. They originally just had colored lights, but when they realized they needed more colors, they replaced it with a large screen."

Everything was starting to click into place. "I think I understand it now. Ship, can you ask Trillion to come over here?"

Atlas turned back to his screen, but before he could close the video, Trillion appeared in his office.

"Took you long enough," she said as she entered the room.

She folded her arms, taking in the confused look on Atlas's face. "I invited you into my spacecraft. You pulled all the data we had on the alien. And you still didn't invite me onto your ship. I want to see your world."

Atlas turned bright red. He felt like such an idiot. "I'm so sorry, Trillion. It's been so long since I've seen another human. I think I'm just used to ordering Lex and Ship around."

Trillion smiled and began to laugh. "I'm only joking. But you still have to show me your planet."

Atlas relaxed. He had known before this journey that he could become obsessed with things. After years of being completely alone, he assumed he must have become worse. "Before I show you my world, I want to show you what I think is the problem with communicating with the Dottiens."

Trillion scanned the room, Atlas could tell she was looking for a place to sit. She couldn't find one, so she jumped into the air, folded her legs, and just floated.

Atlas raised an index finger. "I think there is one major factor we are missing with the Dottiens."

Trillion nodded encouragingly.

"They can't understand us."

Trillion raised her eyebrows in confusion.

"Basically"—Atlas pointed to one of the screens in his office—"it's all about fidelity. We can't communicate with these Dottiens because they can't understand our screens."

Atlas could see that Trillion was beginning to understand the problem.

"I'm going to start . . . with your permission?"

Trillion nodded, so Atlas continued. "I'm going to move a hapticgraphic projector outside. If we can build a replica of the Dottien, we'll be able to communicate using the full richness of the alien language."

CHAPTER 31

ATLAS

LET'S ASK HIM

"Lex, how are we getting the same results?" Atlas said as he sat hunched over his computer. It was the third time he had attempted to communicate with the Dottiens.

His hypothesis wasn't holding up. He had moved a hapticgram unit outside the ship and coded a new algorithm for duplicating the Dottiens' language.

Outside of Trillion's spaceship was a real Dottien and a hapticgraphic projection of one of the Dottiens. But he still couldn't talk to it.

"It just doesn't make sense," he said.

"What doesn't make sense?" asked Trillion, giving Atlas a fright.

He hadn't heard her enter his office, and knocked his knee on the table as he turned around. "These results I'm getting. They don't make sense," he said, rubbing his knee.

"Is that a good thing? I saw the hapticgram in front of my ship had stopped moving. I came in here to see if you'd managed to speak with it."

Atlas pointed at his computer screen. "Have a look at this." He played the video. The screen showed a pulsating dance of colors. The Dottien and the fake Dottien rapidly changed colors and patterns on the screen.

Atlas clicked a few buttons and played another video. "You see this? That Dottien is not responding the way it should."

Trillion didn't reply. She just kept looking at the screen, slight confusion on her face.

"Every time I think we understand their language, something changes, and all the rules we thought we understood about their language are proven wrong. It somehow gets reset. I think we need to build a more realistic version of the Dottien. The fidelity of the hapticgram isn't cutting it."

Trillion still looked confused. "Can I be blunt, Atlas?"

Atlas had to bite back his response. He wasn't expecting Trillion to be so direct. He hadn't yet finished his explanation of how he was going to create a physical version of the Dottien. Or why the hapticgram didn't have the fidelity required to speak with these aliens.

He nodded reluctantly.

"You're not going to solve this, Atlas. This is a problem we need Icarus for."

Atlas shook his head. "No, we don't. We can't speak with them because we can't replicate their language. We need to build something for communicating with these aliens. And that's what I'm good at."

"Hmm. You might be right," Trillion said, "but you think in terms of building things. That's the solution to everything for you. I haven't once heard your theories on how their language works. I'm sure you're thinking about this wrong. If we want to speak with these aliens, we either need to get Icarus or start approaching this problem the way he would."

Atlas hated the fact that he knew Trillion was right. He needed to rethink his approach. "How would Icarus do things differently?" Atlas was annoyed that he had to ask.

"Why don't we ask him?"

Atlas gave her a puzzled look. Did she know something he didn't?

Trillion smiled. "Your Lex knew where he was. So, I sent instructions for the Starnet to his location. He should be online in about a year." Her expression went dark "I still can't find Angelique, though. Do you know if she made it off Mars?"

CHAPTER 32

ICARUS

HELLO, WORLD

"It's beautiful, Ship," Icarus said as he stood on the bridge of his spacecraft, marveling at the rings he had created.

Ship had maneuvered their spaceship a good two light-seconds away from Titan. They positioned themselves above the top of the gas giant so they could see the rings of Titan all at once. It filled the whole window of the bridge.

"It looks kind of like a spinning top," Icarus said as he took in the full beauty of the rings. At this distance, the features and rocks of the rings blurred into each other and the connecting wires that were strung all around the planet weren't visible.

In the center was the massive gas giant. It was mostly a grey-blue with orange swirls that were storms moving around it. All the dust and rocks and asteroids blurred into one another. Compared to the planet Titan, the rings had no thickness at all; at this distance, they looked as thin as a sheet of paper. The rings were slightly transparent, too, enabling Icarus to see stars behind them.

Icarus thought about how small he really was, as it was the first time he had truly realized how large the rings of Titan were.

They were still moving away from the rings, but Icarus was ready to take it all in. "Okay, Ship, turn it on."

A few seconds later, colors erupted from the rings, shimmers of violet and turquoise flashing on different sections, producing a spectacle of colors. With a slightly transparent texture, the rings looked like nothing he had ever seen before. Because there wasn't any atmosphere for the light to bounce off, the whole thing looked unnatural.

Icarus's mind struggled with the fact that from a distance, it looked like light should be bouncing off the gas giant. But it wasn't. He was in awe of what he was looking at. "Imagine having a rave with this as the view," he mused as he thought about how powerful he was. Did he really just light up an entire ring?

The resources it took to create this view were enormous. And he just did it for fun.

"Ship, when we seed the world down there, we need to take a group of humans up to see this. We need to throw a party with this as the view."

Icarus thought for a few seconds. "Do you think we could simulate what it's like to be high?"

Ship looked at him. "Icarus."

"I'm only asking for a friend," Icarus laughed. He thought about his university days. Those festivals were tame events compared to the light show he was looking at now.

"Okay, let's do stage two." Icarus clicked his fingers. The playback speed changed and time started to speed up.

The rings in front of him seemed to be spinning faster; lights started moving around the ring and began to merge together.

Icarus increased his playback speed more. The strobe lights of the rings started to form words.

He read the words out loud. "Hello, World."

He laughed. "Not as beautiful. But worth it."

Ship interrupted Icarus with some good news. "We just completed the Starnet connection that Trillion sent through. It seems to be working. I've spoken to her Lex."

"What?!" Icarus yelled. "Put them through. I thought Starnet was a joke."

Icarus heard an odd ringing sound through the speakers, followed by Trillion's voice.

"Hello."

"Is this a joke? It's gotta be a joke!" Icarus exclaimed.

"It's no joke."

Icarus was surprised to hear Atlas's voice.

"Wait, who else is there? Angelique?" Icarus asked excitedly.

There was a slight pause before Atlas replied. "We haven't made contact with her yet. Her ship flew in the opposite direction after me, so I couldn't predict her end point. Unlike you two."

So many other questions flew through Icarus's mind. "How does this work? Have any of you encountered aliens? Hold on—how is this not breaking causality? This should be breaking causality."

Attempting to answer his own questions, Icarus threw a screen into the air. He asked Lex to collect information on Atlas and Trillion's location.

"What's causality?" Trillion asked through the speaker.

Icarus scrolled through the data from Lex as he answered. "Information can't travel faster than the speed of light. Or at least it shouldn't be able to . . . Basically, it can lead to some strange paradoxes. Like speaking to your past. Or, worse, you could stop someone from doing something they've already done."

Atlas teleported onto Icarus's bridge, grinning from ear to ear. "You're talking about the grandfather paradox?"

"Yes, exactly. We should test this. Between the three of us. I think we could see if we can break causality," Icarus said.

"Enough about causality," Trillion laughed. "Just wait and see—communication isn't the only thing we can do with this system."

Trillion teleported onto the bridge. She ran over and gave Icarus a massive hug. As she held him, she said, "Enough about causality. How are you?" She stepped back, looking him up and down. "I thought you were joking when you said you wanted to become a cartoon."

Icarus laughed and pulled Trillion in for another hug. "Why haven't I missed you both until now? I find that odd."

"I said the same thing," Trillion remarked as she let go of Icarus. "I think that was one of the changes made to us when we got uploaded. Anyway, there's something I want to show you."

Icarus looked at Trillion and Atlas. "I don't think you could show me anything better than seeing you two."

"How about an alien?"

Icarus's jaw dropped. "What? Why didn't you tell me that? Well, what are you waiting for? Show me!"

CHAPTER 33

ICARUS

REALLY SPEAKING WITH ALIENS

Icarus stood on the bridge of Trillion's ship, looking out the window. He was mesmerized by the light dance of two Dottiens speaking to each other—one a real alien and one a hapticgraphic version of an alien. Or at least Icarus hoped they were speaking with each other. Without taking his eye off them, he asked, "So, this thing never gets bored?"

Atlas shook his head. "Oddly not."

"Are you sure it's not a robot? How does it survive in a vacuum?"

Atlas shrugged. "It's not like we can open it up and see inside it."

Icarus turned around. "Have you at least scanned it?"

Atlas shook his head.

"You're losing your touch, old man," Icarus grinned.

Atlas glared at him. "Rich, coming from a cartoon."

That made Icarus laugh out loud. "Anyway, I think I understand the problem."

Atlas made a gesture with his hands, inviting Icarus to explain.

Trillion appeared on the bridge, excitement clear on her face at the prospect of talking to aliens. "Yes, tell us."

Icarus smiled, knowing he had an audience. "Basically, they don't just use color to communicate. If you study all their communication, it includes a lot of texture and patterns."

Trillion was nodding enthusiastically now.

"I got the idea when I was thinking about a concept that is alien to us. The idea of talking through texture is unfathomable because we have a very color-centric visual system. Colors, shapes, shades. But textures—we struggle to differentiate specific types of bumps. Give us different colors and we can tell baby blue from deep blue."

"So, you're saying we're missing texture from our communication efforts?" Trillion looked out the window. "That still doesn't explain how we figure out how to communicate. How are we meant to understand the nuances and rules of texture?"

Icarus's face lit up, his cartoon eyes wide. He had been hoping someone would ask that. He hadn't spoken properly with another human in years but was elated when he realized he still had the gift for teaching others. Back on Earth, he had used that technique often—explain a solution but leave one big, obvious flaw in his argument. He would make that flaw more and more obvious until others would finally ask the question. Then he could come in, solve the problem, and drive the point home. It was genius and made him look much more thought-out.

"I believe adding data like texture and patterns into the translation algorithm is the missing component to Lex deciphering the language. And I think texture is the key to the Dottiens understanding what we are saying to them."

"Are you saying they don't understand us?" asked Atlas, looking at Trillion as if to say, *See, I told you.*

"Exactly. And that's why they keep trying to adjust their language. They think it's not working, so they go and try something else. I suspect their language requires an interaction between the textures, patterns, and colors. Without one of them, you can't understand the whole."

He could see by the look on Trillion's face that she still didn't quite understand. He searched his brain for an analogy. He needed a way to convey the complexity of language. He needed to convey all the added processing the human brain does to make language seem simple. Because language really isn't simple.

"Aliens think completely alien from us. Think about it this way," Icarus said as he asked his Lex to create a table.

Mimicking the action, he pulled the vase off an invisible shelf and placed it on the table. As he did so, a large, clear vase appeared. He nodded his thanks to Lex.

Icarus loved the theatrical nature of what he was doing. He smiled as he thought about how much he missed teaching others. How much fun he was having, trying to solve the puzzle of communicating with aliens. "Lex, do you mind producing a cup of never-ending blue marbles?"

In his hand appeared a cup full of blue marbles.

Icarus held it up. "Now imagine you're an alien who's come to speak with us. Your job is to work out how our language works. Let's take English to make it simple."

Icarus started pouring blue marbles into the vase on the table. "The human mouth can produce 840 different sounds. For the sake of simplicity, the English language has forty-four unique sounds. These sounds are used to make up words."

Icarus counted out forty-four marbles as he poured them from the cup. When he finished speaking, there were forty-four blue marbles in the vase.

He started pouring more marbles into the vase. "And there are five different tones we can make with our voices. We can say the same thing twice, but with a different tone and it can mean something completely different. The relationship between sound and tone matters a lot in some scenarios."

Icarus pointed to the vase. It was now quarter full of marbles. "So, you're an alien. And I'm trying to communicate with you. You're trying to work out what information coming from me is important to our language."

Trillion interjected. "Are you saying the blue marbles represent all the possible signals an alien learning English would need to learn?"

"Yes, exactly."

Atlas raised his hand. "Yes, but it should be easy. Babies learn to speak in about two years. We have a supercomputer—we should be able to decipher a language faster."

"Ah, but this is the important part," Icarus said, staring down into the vase. "Human babies have less information to process. They can only hear a very narrow range of sounds." Icarus held his cup up to his robotic companion. "Lex, can you make these red?"

He placed his hand on the vase so Trillion and Atlas would look at it. "Everything in here represents important information you would need to decode the language."

Icarus started pouring red marbles into the vase, this time slowly. "It's surprising how many sounds we make when speaking that don't relate to language. Our brains automatically filter them out. But if you were an alien, you wouldn't know which of these sounds were important. Clicking of the teeth. Breathing. Random sounds we make when thinking."

Icarus paused. The contrast between the blue and red was strong. A small smile came over his face. He started pouring more marbles in faster. "We also make a lot of sounds outside of our ears' audible range. An alien wouldn't know which sounds were important. So, they would have to look at all of them when trying to understand what I'm saying."

The vase was only half-full, but most of its contents were red marbles.

Icarus held his cup over the vase again. "Ah, but we don't stop there." He turned the cup upside down. Red marbles flowed freely into the vase.

He could tell Trillion and Atlas understood the point, but he really wanted to drive it home. "It's impossible for us to stay still. Our eyes are constantly moving. We're breathing. Even you standing there on two feet—who's to say that when you shift your weight from one foot to the other you aren't communicating something?"

The vase was now overflowing; marbles began to roll off the edge of the table.

Trillion nodded. "So, you're basically saying we might be looking at the wrong information when trying to translate the Dottiens' language?"

"Exactly." Icarus grinned. "If you were an alien communicating via movements, not sounds, you would spend a lot of time analyzing my movements. But no matter how hard you tried, we wouldn't be able to have a conversation. You'd be missing the most important part: the sounds coming out of my mouth."

It was Trillion who asked the obvious question. "So, how do we find out which marbles are important?"

Icarus looked out the window at the alien. "Simple. We throw everything we think we know about language out the window. And feed Lex more data." He paused for a moment. "I do have one theory, though."

Both Atlas and Trillion gestured for Icarus to continue.

"I've been looking into asteroids in the system," Icarus said, swiping his marble demonstration away. "I've been looking into why there aren't any asteroids. I think this creature evolved to protect the planet from extinction-level asteroids. And it moved you here, Trillion, because that's what it did with a lot of asteroids. I think this moon is a build-up of many of the asteroids it's captured. That's why it's so metallic."

CHAPTER 34

ATLAS

THE PARADOX SOLVER

Atlas looked at his planet. He hadn't seen it for a while. He could see a thick cloud now covered New Europa. Plumes of gas and water exploded from above the cloud, and some were like jets, continuously spraying into the atmosphere. "Is the atmosphere venting into space?" he asked.

"Some. The hydrogen is floating away, but the oxygen will stay at the surface," Ship replied as he changed the image of the planet to an infrared version. This allowed Atlas to see through the cloud. "You see there"—Ship pointed at the infrared image—"some areas of the planet are heating up. All the movement caused by the ice breaking is speeding up the process."

Atlas moved his head closer to the screen. He could see the heat signature of the planet had changed since he first looked at the image. There were now warm parts. Thinning ice sheets. The average temperature was about five degrees higher than when he had started this process. "Change the image back to the visible spectrum," Atlas requested.

Ship did as he asked. The color changed from the monochrome red.

Atlas pointed to the screen. "Is that green?"

The planet was covered in a green film. He could see gaps in the clouds, where the surface of New Europa was green.

Atlas jumped up off his seat, a grin spreading across his face. "We did it! Can you get Icarus? I have to show him."

He heard a popping sound of electricity, as if a lightning bolt had hit the wall behind him. Then there was a continuous white noise sound mixed with the buzzing of electricity. He could feel the room vibrating. Atlas turned his head toward the sound.

A white circular glowing orb emitting sparks of lightning had appeared behind him. In place of his bookshelf was some sort of large glowing bubble.

He watched as a pixelated foot protruded out of the white orb. Then a hand. Then he recognized who it was.

"Like my portal?" Icarus said as he walked through.

"First you make yourself a cartoon. Now this?" Atlas said, shaking his head in disbelief.

Icarus shrugged. "Atlas, why be a hapticgram if you're not going to embrace it? Which reminds me—I made a few improvements to our simulation. Do you want my Lex to give you the update?"

"Yes. But what are they?" Atlas asked curiously.

"Here, let me show you."

Atlas felt a strange sensation run over him. It was odd. His brain wasn't quite sure what had changed. But something had. He closed his eyes. Breathed out. Then breathed in. There was a smell of sulfur in the air. How could he smell? There wasn't a mechanism for hapticgrams to smell. He wondered why he hadn't noticed the lack of smell until now, why it hadn't bothered him before. "Why can I smell sulfur?"

Icarus smiled. "I added it to the portal simulation. Makes it feel like I just burnt through the walls."

"How am I just learning about this now?"

Icarus walked over to the portal and stuck his hands in. He moved them about a little then drew them out, holding two glass cups of coffee. "Wait until you smell this."

Icarus handed a cup to him.

Atlas peered into the cup and inhaled deeply. His nostrils were filled with a euphoric rush of pleasure. He shook his head in disbelief. "You have just blown my mind. I've been a simulation longer than I've been alive. And I hate that I'm just discovering this now."

"Well, this is actually better than when you were physical. I've given us all a dog's sense of smell."

Atlas couldn't help but laugh. "Does Trillion know about this?"

Icarus nodded. "Yes, her entire spaceship is covered in scented candles now. Anyway, why am I here? What did you want to show me?"

Atlas walked back to his desk in the middle of the room and clicked a few buttons on the computer. "Look at this. I call it New Europa."

Icarus leaned forward and looked at the screen. "Nice name. Is that because it's an ice world? It looks like it might pop." Icarus studied it a bit more. "That's a lot of tectonic activity for a planet you want to seed."

"No, no," Atlas said, "look at the green. Can you see the green coming through those cracks? That's life."

Atlas remembered about the coffee again and took a sip, not expecting to taste anything. "Wow, this tastes like coffee, too."

"I know, right? It's amazing. Which reminds me, we're all having dinner at my place tonight." Icarus gazed at the screen again. "This planet really does look like it's going to explode."

Atlas smiled again. "Actually, the planet is basically a bomb. One spark, and . . . *boom!*"

"Can we blow it up?" Icarus asked.

Atlas couldn't tell if he was joking or not. Then he saw the toothy cartoon grin. "You got me," he mused. "Oh, by the way, I've been testing the causality problem you mentioned."

When Icarus looked slightly confused, Atlas explained. "The one about how this faster-than-light communication network breaks the laws of causality."

Icarus clicked his fingers, remembering. "Oh, the Starnet?"

Atlas nodded. He had been thinking for a while about how Icarus used the marbles to tell a story. He changed his opinion and, on reflection, he liked it. It really explained things visually, so he thought he'd do the same. "This is where things get strange. I'm going to need your help here," he said as he walked over to one side of the room, gesturing at Icarus to follow.

"You understand time dilation?" Atlas asked.

"Yes, as you move faster through space, time slows down."

Atlas nodded. He pointed to the other side of the room. "Imagine this side of the room and that side over there are light-years apart. For simplicity, let's say it's a hundred light-years across." Atlas looked up at Lex floating in the corner. "Lex, can you place a floating timer on both our heads?"

In an instant, Atlas and Icarus had digital timers above them. They were ticking at the same rate starting from one, then two . . .

Atlas pointed to his timer. "To both of us, time is moving at the same rate. Let's assume each of these ticks represent a year." He began to walk to the other side of the room. As he moved, his timer started to move slower. By the time he reached the other side, his timer was showing ten.

Atlas pointed to the timer once more. "To get to you, over there, it should take me about 102 years."

Icarus clarified a point Atlas had forgotten to make earlier. "Are you assuming you traveled at one g acceleration the whole way?"

"Oh, yes, sorry," Atlas said, a little embarrassed with himself. "Yes, basically, if I traveled to this side of the room fast, time would have moved slower for me."

"Yes, I agree." Icarus looked at the number above his head. "But from my perspective, it took you 102 years to get there, even though you only experienced ten-ish years."

"Exactly. Relativity and all that," Atlas smiled. He was a little out of practice with explaining things to other people. He started walking back toward Icarus. "Without FTL communication, everything is fine. I arrive back and I'm a lot younger than you. But the universe doesn't care. However, it gets strange when we add FTL communication."

A new timer floated in the middle of the room. It flicked between 10 and 102 several times and then a question mark appeared.

"Which time does the Starnet use? Because the two timers are completely different. My clock says it's been ten years. Yours says it's been 102," Atlas stated.

"I understand all this, Atlas. Remember I was the one who asked you about the causality problem? If the Starnet uses my timer, then I'm sending messages 92 years in the past. If it uses yours, then it's sending messages 92 years into the future."

Atlas thought he heard a twinge of excitement in Icarus's voice. He knew he was starting to spark his imagination. "Exactly. I could send a message through the Starnet and receive it 92 years before I sent it. This obviously breaks causality."

Atlas nodded with excitement. He knew he hadn't told Icarus anything new yet, but the next part was going to blow his mind.

"So, tell me, Atlas, how does Starnet *not* break causality?"

Atlas pointed up toward the timer between them both. "The Starnet itself has its own time."

"Oh, so you're saying it doesn't matter what time our reference frames are, as the network always has its own time?"

Atlas nodded. "Precisely."

CHAPTER 35

ICARUS

THE FINAL SUPPER

"What do you think, Ship—pizza or burgers?" Icarus said excitedly.

Ship raised a metallic eyebrow. "Is that what you're making for dinner?"

Icarus grinned from ear to ear. "No, I'm going to make a bunch of things. But I thought it would be fun if I made all the food look like one thing. But when you bite in, I want us to taste something completely different."

Ship shook his head. "Are you sure you want everything to look the same? Don't humans also eat with their eyes?"

Icarus considered that for a moment. "Hmm, you're right, Ship. I'm thinking about this the wrong way. I wanted to make a meal that was only possible in a hapticgraphic world. But I was thinking too small."

"Too small?" Ship asked.

Icarus raised both eyebrows. "Just you wait and see. This is going to be good."

Icarus teleported back to his room and began plotting dinner.

Icarus stood in his redecorated hangar in a dark navy-blue suit, matching tie, and brown shoes. He had to clench his fists to hide just how nervous he was. He hadn't expected everyone to arrive right on time. But the two minutes he had waited so far was causing him angst.

He was about to send off a reminder message when Atlas teleported in with his Ship. They were both wearing black tuxedos. Icarus noticed the subtle touches of detail. Atlas was wearing gold leather shoes and a gold watch. Both his shoes and watch were the same gold color and pattern as his Ship.

"Welcome, Atlas. Welcome, Ship." Icarus handed them both an empty champagne flute.

"Why are these empty?" Atlas asked, slightly puzzled.

Icarus was about to answer when his jaw dropped. Out of the corner of his eye he saw Trillion teleport in on the other side of the hangar; she appeared near the ceiling and gently floated down. She was wearing a long, red dress, but the way she made her entrance, it looked like a short dress with three long red capes flowing in the breeze.

She paused for a moment when she reached the ground. Icarus's Ship appeared with his arm stretched out. She took hold of his arm and began walking toward Icarus and Atlas.

Icarus couldn't help but notice her dress never once touched the ground. Somehow, it just floated.

"Welcome you two. Trillion, you look incredible. That was quite an entrance," Icarus said, also handing them both empty champagne flutes.

"Are those glass heels—like Cinderella?" Atlas asked.

Trillion smiled. "They're better. They're diamond heels. These are better than red bottoms." Trillion looked Icarus over. "Can you lose the avatar for tonight? Donald Duck doesn't quite fit in with this moment."

"Sure, but only tonight," Icarus said, clicking his fingers. Smoke appeared all around him, and as it faded away, everyone could see him in his human form. Icarus hoped no one noticed he had made his human avatar slightly taller.

"I can't believe I've missed seeing your human face, Icarus. You look good like that," Atlas said, smiling.

Trillion looked at her empty glass. "Why is this empty?"

"Oh, yes, now that we're here, everyone, let's gather around," Icarus said, ushering everyone into a semicircle. "I propose a toast. To discovery, the betaverse, and adventure." He raised his glass and everyone else followed suit.

Clink. Everyone's glasses touched in the middle and, as they did, champagne began forming in their flutes. The bubbles floated up the glasses quickly, stopping just before reaching the top and making a subtle whistling sound.

"Enjoy," Icarus said as he took a sip of his drink. "We have a lot planned for this evening." He pointed to a portal that opened up. Through the portal walked a generic-looking man dressed in a butler's outfit and holding a bottle of champagne. Behind him walked the exact same man again. Same outfit and bottle.

Icarus pointed at the two of them. These are the Bobs. I call this one Bob and the other Bill.

"They both look the same. How can we tell them apart?" Atlas asked.

Icarus smiled. "They're basically the same character; you can call them whatever you want. They will answer to either name. I didn't have enough time to make them different."

"Why not call them Mark and Ryland?" Trillion said, laughing.

Icarus scratched his head, not understanding the reference. Then it clicked. "Oh, I get it. That's a good one."

Trillion had finished her glass and placed it on a table that materialized next to her. "So, what's next?"

One of the Bobs came over and refilled her glass. She picked it up and began sipping it again.

Icarus pointed at some empty space in front of him. A portal appeared and tropical music began to play. "Follow me for the appetizer."

He walked through the portal with everyone else following. They appeared on a white-sand beach with crystal-clear water. Icarus could feel the heat of the sun that was setting in the distance. A table was set for them with little glass spoons. "Welcome to Jamaica. Did everyone bring their change of outfits?"

They all nodded.

Smoke appeared around Icarus once more, and as it cleared, Trillion and Atlas saw he was now wearing a Hawaiian shirt and board shorts. Trillion's outfit began to shrink and fold, becoming a two-piece red swimsuit. Atlas's Ship wore gold shorts, and Icarus's wore blue shorts.

Atlas took off his jacket, and underneath was a white linen shirt with the sleeves rolled up. His pants shrank into shorts, and his Ship handed him a Panama hat and sunglasses.

"Did you animate those pants changing?" Icarus said, clapping at Atlas. "That's the first time I've seen you do that."

Atlas smiled. "I wanted to impress you."

"Please, sit, make yourselves comfortable," Icarus said as he sat down at the table and picked up one of the glass spoons. "You need to try these. They're called ackee and saltfish. It's Jamaican. They're incredible."

"What's in it?" Trillion said as she stared at one.

"It's this fruit called ackee and a special kind of fish. They balance perfectly together. You'll love it," Icarus said, putting one in his mouth.

"Oh, this is good. It melts in my mouth. Why haven't I tried this before?" Trillion asked as she sat down.

"Do the Bobs make cocktails?" Atlas asked, taking two more of the appetisers.

"Of course. What would you like?" Icarus snapped his fingers. A Bob walked over and a bar appeared in front of him.

"What about a Jamaican Sunrise?" Atlas asked.

The Bob behind the bar started to make the drink. When it was done, the other Bob came over and handed it to Atlas.

"Thanks, Bill," Atlas said.

"So, do you think we were ready when we left?" Trillion asked.

Icarus smirked. "I don't think we were, especially you."

"Wow, shots fired. Rich, coming from someone who calls a bunch of fiber-optic cables a ringworld," Trillion said. "Atlas, do you think we could have done any better out here?"

Atlas shook his head. "There's no way we could have prepared for everything we encountered out here."

"Sorry for being a bit facetious before," Icarus said. "I agree; there's no way to prepare for this. The aliens you've met, Trillion, are so . . . alien. The Dotties are unimaginable."

"Thank you." Trillion raised her glass. "I'm so glad we can all come together again. I honestly don't know how or what I would've done without all of you here."

Everyone raised their glasses while the Bobs took drink orders.

When the team had finished with the appetizers and had freshly topped-up drinks, Icarus stood up and pointed at a section of the sand. A portal appeared, and the sound of falling water could be heard. "On to our next destination."

They followed Icarus through the portal. They were on the peak of a snowy mountain. The air was crisp and the sun was right above their heads. In front of them was a beautiful waterfall that dropped into a small pond.

"Welcome to Mount Fuji. I thought it would be a nice change of pace," Icarus said.

"I love it!" Trillion walked to the edge of the pond and dipped her toes in. She pulled them out quickly. "That's ice-cold."

"I know. I made the water feel fresh. I wouldn't recommend jumping in," Icarus said.

At that moment, one of the Bobs took his top off and jumped into the water. Moments later, he walked out with a salmon in hand. He walked over to a table and began preparing sashimi for everyone.

"This is an amazing spot. I can't believe the effort you've put into today," Atlas said as he inspected the waterfall. "Wow, that water is really cold."

Icarus bowed in gratitude. "This is only the beginning. And don't worry; Bob doesn't feel the cold. That part was more of a prerecorded movie, anyway."

The other Bob began walking around the room with small white glasses and hot sake.

"So, do you think we're basically gods now?" Icarus asked, taking a sip of the hot drink.

The Ship of Icarus looked at him sideways. "Don't get a god complex, Icarus."

"I don't mean like that. We're terraforming whole planets. That feels very godlike to me."

Atlas thought for a moment. "I don't think so. I mean, I think we're superintelligences more than gods."

"How are we superintelligences? I'm still the same smartness as when I left Mars. I don't think I'm super."

"There's three types of superintelligence. We're the same level of smartness, but thanks to my Ship's clever idea"—Atlas looked over at his Ship, who winked—"thanks to him, we are what you would call a speed superintelligence. We might not be any smarter than before, but we can slow down time and think about a problem a million times over in a second."

Trillion looked at them both. "Superintelligence. Gods. We should stay humble here. We could run the risk of believing these things." She smiled. "Besides, what kind of god gets stuck on a moon? If I'm a god, then the Dottiens are the devil."

"Trillion, we promised not to get into any of that today," Icarus said.

"Yes, sorry." She took one of the salmon sashimi pieces from Bob. "This is delicious, by the way."

"Icarus," his Ship interrupted, "you should show them the next destination."

Icarus nodded and walked over to the pond. He waved his hand and another portal opened up. They could hear the sounds of birds. "Follow me."

They were transported to a forest full of ferns and small trees. There was a pond that was boiling. The air smelled like sulfur. "Welcome to Rotorua."

"Where's that?" Atlas asked.

"It's a small city in New Zealand. They make the most amazing food, cooked in a pit—it's called a hāngī."

There was a little clearing with a table in the middle. Icarus went over and sat down at the table. Everyone else joined him. "Now watch how this food is prepared."

One of the Bobs was digging a hole. It wasn't just dirt he was digging up. Red-hot rocks were being shoveled out of the hole too.

"Is that lake boiling?" Atlas asked.

Icarus nodded. "They're naturally occurring in Rotorua."

The other Bob walked over to the boiling pond and started pulling in a rope. After a while, that Bob grabbed hold of a crate and started carrying it to the table. In the crate were all sorts of seafood—oysters, lobsters, crabs, fish—and corn. He started arranging them on the table.

The first Bob had finished digging and pulled his crate out of the ground. It was full of vegetables: carrots, potatoes, kūmara, mushrooms and pumpkins. He too started arranging everything on the table.

"Do they honestly cook food like that in New Zealand?" Trillion asked.

"Yes, they do. Rotorua has these geothermal vents that turn the ground and lakes into ovens. But it tastes so different from anything you can make in an oven," Icarus explained.

Atlas took a bit of lobster. "You're right; this is good."

The team devoured the food and then relaxed in the clearing. It was a beautiful day and they were surrounded by nature. "This is the life," Icarus said, lying back on the grass.

"I can't believe we get to experience all of this. The amount of effort you've put into this dinner, Icarus. Thank you," Trillion said.

"I know. I feel like we haven't had a chance to relax like this since we started this journey," Atlas said.

They all lay in silence for a while just taking in the moment. "Thanks for organizing this dinner party. I feel like I could stay here forever," Trillion said.

"It's the food. It's designed to make us relaxed and sleepy," Icarus said.

Trillion knocked her glass over. "Am I drunk?" she asked as it was replaced with a new one by Bob.

Icarus laughed. "Yes, I've simulated the effects of alcohol. This stuff is real," he said, looking at his half-empty champagne flute.

After a good while sitting there contemplating, Icarus stood up, a little unsteady on his feet. "On to dessert," he said, almost slurring the words.

Over the top of the hole Bob had dug, a portal appeared. "This way," Icarus said as he stumbled toward the portal and fell in.

The team followed him and fell into the hole too. They found themselves floating in the middle of space, stars all around them. In the distance they could see a swirling mass of colors. "Welcome to the bar in the middle of the Milky Way," Icarus proclaimed as he pushed metal straws toward everyone. They drifted slowly to each of them.

Trillion folded her legs and just floated there calmly. Atlas flailed a bit before Trillion took hold of his arm and helped him.

"What are the straws for?" Trillion asked as she watched hers float in front of her.

"Dessert," Icarus said pointing toward the Bobs. "They have melted chocolate, graham crackers, and marshmallow cremes. If you're feeling brave, you can have them float all the ingredients for s'mores toward you. Or you can just slurp them up one at a time with the straw. Oh, and if you want to drink Baileys, they can float that toward you too."

Trillion took one look at the Bobs and smiled. "Okay, you two, send things nice and slow," she said, and put her hands up ready to catch. She grabbed the graham cracker first, broke it in half and held half out in front of the incoming marshmallow fluff. It landed and almost bounced off, little pieces of marshmallow floating off in different directions. She then maneuvered her creation in front of the incoming melted chocolate. That made a splatting sound, and half the chocolate splattered off in random directions. She used the other half of the graham cracker to squish everything together and then took a bite. "Mm, this is good," she said through a mostly full mouth.

"I think I'll just take the Baileys. I don't have the dexterity right now," Atlas said. A small ball of Baileys floated toward him. He put the straw to his lips and waited for the drink to reach him. It slowly made its way to his straw, then continued on toward his face. It hit his face and bounced off, covering him in the process.

Trillion started to laugh. "You forgot to suck in when the Baileys reached you."

Icarus joined in the laughter. "Sorry, I hadn't tried this world before dinner. I guess this doesn't work."

Atlas started to laugh too as he wiped the Baileys away from his eyes.

Icarus, Trillion, and both the Ships took turns trying to make more s'mores. The team laughed at their successful attempts and failures. They all agreed it was one of the best nights they'd had in a long, long time.

All five of them teleported back into Icarus's hangar, very drunk but very happy.

"Icarus, you outdid yourself. As always," Trillion gave him a big hug. "We need to do this again once my Ship is back. I did miss him a little, with everyone together."

"I'm glad you all enjoyed it. And yes, we're going to do this a lot," he said and hugged her back.

"Thank you for the best night in a while," Atlas said as he opened his arms to give Icarus a big hug.

"Don't mention it. I'm just glad you all had fun."

The team departed, and it was just Icarus and his Ship left. They both just looked at each other and smiled.

"It's so good to have friends again, Ship," Icarus said as he clicked his hands and was covered in smoke. A moment later, he was in his usual avatar.

Ship nodded.

CHAPTER 36

TRILLION

SHIP ARRIVING SOON

Trillion floated in her room, stars drifting around her. She had the galaxy projected in her room, with the stars and the entire Milky Way visible. Her legs and arms were crossed, eyes closed and fists clenched tightly. She breathed in and out slowly.

Her calm appearance betrayed the mixed feelings of both excitement and anger. Excitement that Ship was arriving in sixteen days—she was finally going to be able to escape—but anger that she had been on that moon for so many years. Years she could have spent building out her colony. Even though, thanks to the Starnet, she could travel to Atlas's or Icarus's worlds now, having her matrix stuck on the moon meant she always felt trapped—and never safe.

She calmed her mind, thinking about the projection of stars around her. She relaxed her body, breathing in and out slowly.

She couldn't do it. Anger welled up inside her. She wanted to destroy the Dottiens completely and utterly for trapping her there.

She thought about the name *assass-ANT*. How fitting she'd named it that—it was what she wanted to do to the alien that had trapped her on the moon.

Trillion opened one eye. "Lex, show me again how many assass-ANTs Ship is bringing?"

Lex changed the view in front of Trillion, replacing the starry galaxy with the armada Ship was bringing back. A good chunk of the resources from the Steel World system were on their way back.

To Trillion, it looked like the starscape again, only taking up a smaller section of her view right in front of her. The armada was so large and stretched over such an enormous area of space. She scanned the view. "Show me Ship."

A tiny dot appeared toward the front of the armada. It twinkled blue. It was still behind another thousand or so objects, but behind Ship were what looked like hundreds of thousands of tiny little dots.

She pointed them out to Lex. "Are those the assass-ANTs?"

The view lit up. There were millions of the little relativistic missiles heading her way. Almost ninty percent of her view was shining bright blue. She could see a long tail of assass-ANTs, too, all coming in quickly from behind the cohort.

A slight smile crept over her face. The number of assass-ANTs was enormous. She had more than enough to make light work of the Dottiens. The only thing left now was to plot her escape when Ship arrived. She needed to be pulled off the moon to safety before things got out of hand.

As she comprehended the immensity of what was on its way—the millions of assass-ANTs and the thousands of ships—she started to get a sense that she had made a mistake, coming to the planet in a single spaceship. She had so many resources back at Steel World, yet she had left everything there. *Why was I still thinking like a planet-bound human?* she pondered, shaking her head in frustration.

"Lex, I keep looking at things from my old biological-human perspective. Can you remind me we have an unlimited amount of resources? Can you remind me to not think so small?"

As she closed her eyes again to calm herself down, she thought about any other self-limiting beliefs that were holding her back. She reckoned maybe Icarus was right in his thinking—embrace being a simulation. She hoped that might help expand her thinking faster.

CHAPTER 37

ATLAS

SEEDING ANIMALS

Atlas looked out at his world from his new hangar laboratory. He hadn't spent much time with his world since the Starnet was set up. He needed to check in with the planet now, before things got a little crazy when Trillion's ship arrived and the war began.

He had turned his hangar into a genetic-engineering laboratory. There was now a whole petting zoo of marine animals in tanks. His favorite were the killer whales—he couldn't wait to release them on the planet below.

It was no longer an ice world. It was a water world. The ice shelves had given way to water. And lots of it. A few mountains poked out from beneath.

He thought about how Earth was basically a water world too. He remembered looking at Earth from space and remembered mostly seeing water. Now New Europa looked the same—mostly water. He wondered if Europa was still the right moon to be naming the planet after, but it showed the history of the planet and he still liked the name. "Ship, I can't believe we have an oxygen-rich environment down there now."

"I can," Ship replied in a sarcastic tone. "That was the plan."

Atlas had printed out a sheet with all the atmosphere makeup on it. It was mostly oxygen. The hydrogen was escaping into space, but the oxygen was sticking around. Humans couldn't live on the planet, but they were getting close.

"What animal do you think we should seed first?" Atlas asked.

"With the current atmosphere, we are kind of limited. And the waters are still quite clean. So . . . so, it'd have to be a freshwater fish."

"Exactly. That's why I was thinking the Siamese algae eater. It's the perfect fish for the job. It can kick-start the aquatic food pyramid and start eating all this fungus we let grow crazy."

Atlas's line of thought was interrupted as the printer suddenly sprang to life, printing out a document. He stared at it, wondering why it was printing something.

"Oh, that's me," Ship said, pointing to the printout. "I wanted to give you this research paper to read. It's on building sustainable fish in aquariums. Basically, it argues for diversity of life."

Atlas plucked the document from the printer and sat down to read it.

A few minutes later, the paper had scribbles and writing all over it. Atlas looked up when he'd finished. "Interesting, Ship. It's basically saying we need to introduce as much variety into the world as quickly as possible."

He bit his lower lip, thinking some more. "I don't want to risk having to start again building the oxygen levels, but I agree with the principle. Lex, can you build a model predicting which animals and plant life we should populate the oceans with and when we should do it? Focus on what will get the planet habitable for humans the quickest."

Atlas placed the paper on the table and stood up. "This was super useful, Ship. Do you have any other papers on this I should read?"

Ship nodded and the printer fired up again.

While the papers were printing out, Atlas cast his mind to sites for a colony. "Lex, can you show me a few potential locations for a settlement? We can't have everyone living on sailboats."

The orb flashed purple.

"He doesn't think any land on the planet is ideal," Ship answered for him.

Atlas hated Lex's inability to handle uncertainty. "What do you mean, there isn't any land that is ideal?"

Rather than respond, Ship took over his computer. Showing various locations, he cycled through the different options. Atlas noticed that all the rocks were extremely jagged and did not look like what he had imagined. "Hmm . . . Perhaps we should grab Icarus and Trillion. Let's see if they have any ideas."

Almost instantly, Icarus arrived, a portal opening up in front of one of the tanks. The room filled with a smell of sulfur once more.

"Hey, Atlas, Trillion and I were just about to message you," Icarus said as he walked through the portal, followed by Trillion.

"Yeah, what's up?" she said.

Atlas pointed at his computer screen. "I've got a bit of a problem. My world *almost*"—Atlas made sure to enunciate the word slowly—"almost has a breathable atmosphere. But I haven't picked a place to build the colony. Can you help me?"

Icarus squinted at the screen. "Old man, you really have to make the most of being a simulation." Icarus pointed to a portal opening up on the other side of the room. "Can I show you something?"

"Oh, this is cool," Trillion said when she saw what was on the other side of the portal.

Atlas had some more data he wanted to show them, but he was intrigued, so he nodded and followed them through the portal.

As they walked through, the room changed. On the other side was Icarus's hangar, which was empty apart from a large eleph-ANT hanging from wires on the ceiling, lowering the eleph-ANT to the ground.

"While I set up," Icarus pointed to the lowering eleph-ANT, "Atlas, can you organize your Lex to move an eleph-ANT to all the locations you wanted to show us?"

Atlas gave a thumbs-up signal. "There should be several already there."

Atlas was still a little confused by what was happening. He could see the large eleph-ANT had now reached the ground, its legs bent in on itself. He hadn't seen one up close in such a long time. They were much bigger than he remembered.

A large door swung open and a ramp extended out toward them. "Come on inside," Icarus said. "I've adjusted it to fit all three of us." It was dark inside, and despite the few lights, it was difficult to see anything.

As they walked up the ramp, their eyes adjusted. Inside were four seats near the front. They all sat down, Atlas in the middle.

"You ready?" Icarus said as he held his finger over a button.

"You really like a spectacle, don't you?" Trillion laughed.

Icarus nodded. "Oh, wait—seat belts."

Three large arms reached over the top of each of them, reminiscent of an amusement-park ride.

Atlas found himself pinned down.

Icarus pressed the button and the machine lurched. The screen in front of them turned on, followed by the surrounding screens, giving them a complete 360-degree view.

The screen changed to the point of view of one of the eleph-ANTs on New Europa. Atlas studied the view in front of him. He could see the eleph-ANT was standing on top of one of the ice shelves. Big sections of the planet had thawed, but there were still areas completely covered in ice. With the screens all around, it looked like Atlas was sitting in an eleph-ANT that was on New Europa. He was impressed. He could see ice everywhere. He shivered. "Is it cold in here?"

"Yes," Icarus nodded. "You like it? I wanted it to be an immersive experience."

Icarus grabbed the control stick in front of him and pressed it forward. The eleph-ANT started running along the ice. It jumped and then turned its engines on. It shot up into the air, and Atlas could feel himself being pressed into his seat.

The view was beautiful. As far as the eye could see, there was ice.

The eleph-ANT turned around. Atlas was pressed into Trillion's shoulder. The eleph-ANT flew higher in the sky. They could see the edge of the ice now. It dropped straight off into the water, where hundreds of tiny icebergs were floating out.

Icarus pointed at the ice. "Atlas, what about building a colony on the ice?"

Atlas shook his head. It was beautiful, but it didn't make sense. "I didn't go to all that trouble of heating up the planet just to have my people living on the ice."

"Good point," agreed Trillion. "Are there any mountains?"

Icarus looked at Atlas, who nodded. Icarus held his hand over the button again. "Ship, show us the mountains." He pressed the button. Their view changed in an instant. Their eleph-ANT was now standing at the base of a mountain—but not just any mountain. Time hadn't weathered down anything. The rocks were sharp. Atlas looked at a few of the objects. They looked like asteroids that had once hit the planet, obviously frozen in time until the ice melted.

Icarus moved his control stick forward once more. The eleph-ANT started to climb. It was a rough ride, the three of them bumping into each other as the eleph-ANT jumped from side to side. There were creaking sounds each time it took a step.

After about three minutes, Atlas had had enough. The ride was getting bumpier by the minute. "I thought eleph-ANTs had shock absorbers."

Icarus shrugged.

Ship was the one who responded. "I think you should stop walking this eleph-ANT. The rocks are ripping into its legs. The back two are basically torn to shreds now."

Icarus nodded and pressed the button in front of him. Their view changed once more, this time to an eleph-ANT that was flying above the one they had just been in.

Atlas studied the eleph-ANT. Its two back legs were scrap metal. The front four were only slightly better, its wires and insides exposed. One of its legs was stuck between two jagged rocks.

"One more step and I would have ripped that leg clean off," Icarus said.

"I see what you mean. You don't want people living on this," Trillion said.

"Without rain and tectonic movement, the land hasn't been worn down over time. It's basically regolith but made of boulders."

"Okay, what are the other options you have?" Icarus asked.

Atlas knew he was grasping at straws, but he suggested it anyway. "I could build a floating city. I've been thinking about building concrete blocks with a hollow center. They would float. I could build millions of them and stick them together."

"Too complicated, Atlas," Trillion said. "Go basic. You don't need to invent something new. The maintenance costs after a few thousand years would make it not worth it."

"What do you suggest, then?" Atlas asked.

Trillion smiled. "Build a continent."

"Isn't that what I suggested?" Atlas responded.

"No, you suggested making a floating island," Trillion said as she thought through how it might work. "Dig up the dirt and start depositing it on this mountain."

Atlas thought about it for a second. His mind started ticking over. A major construction project like that would be fun. "Ship, are there any mountains on the equator that have a wide base, even if most of it is under the sea? I'm thinking the size of Australia?"

The eleph-ANT shook and their view changed once more.

This time, their eleph-ANT stood, its legs half covered in water. They were surrounded by shallow water with a smattering of sharp, jagged rocks across the landscape. The water and rocks were covered in a green film—it was the location of the first fungus seeding.

Atlas pointed at the land they were standing on. "I could send a few thousand eleph-ANTs down here." He smiled. "I could literally start moving mountains to this location. I could build a continent right here."

Trillion nodded.

"Just don't call it New America," Icarus said, cringing at the sound of that name.

Atlas gave him a thumbs-up and teleported out. He had work to do.

CHAPTER 38

ATLAS

NOT ANOTHER MASS EXTINCTION EVENT

Atlas stood over his printer as it buzzed out printout after printout. It was a real printer, too. Not a hapticgram. The paper and printer had been produced by one of his fabricators. Maybe it was a placebo, maybe it wasn't. But using real paper and listening to the printer pop out sheet after sheet really helped focus his mind. The more he filled his workspace with real objects, the easier he found it to think and solve problems. The printer had completed its run.

He picked up the stack of paper—they were still hot to the touch. He riffled through the many, many pages, looking for a particular graph, sighing deeply when he found it and saw the trendline. "It's not just an anomaly; it's a trend on all the species on the planet," he said to Ship.

The page showed a line graph of the population over time of many different species in the New Europa oceans. Each line represented a different species. And each line was trending downward. Populations of all the species on the graph were decreasing.

Some of the species' populations were collapsing faster than the others. When he first noticed there were fewer animals, he had hoped it was just an isolated matter. But all around his planet, marine populations were falling at an alarming rate. His whole ecosystem was collapsing.

And New Europa was mostly a water world still. He needed the marine animals to build up so he could use them as the basis of organic matter to build the topsoil of his continents.

He needed to find a reason for the population collapse. At that moment, he wished they had someone in the team who specialized in ecosystems. They had left so early that planning the actual ecology of a planet hadn't yet been sorted. There wasn't much point in worrying about it now, anyway. Besides, any planning they had done on Mars would have been completely theoretical, because humanity hadn't done anything on this scale yet.

He scrolled through the stack of paper once more, looking for a clue, circling datapoints and throwing away some of the sheets. He slid one of the pages toward Ship as he pointed at two numbers. "This is the anomaly. The size of the fungus colony is shrinking faster than can be explained by the number of animals eating it. This is what I can't explain right here," he said, again wanting to use Ship as a sounding board.

Ship picked up the paper and studied it. "Is it some disease? Or random mutation killing the fungus?"

Atlas shook his head. "I don't think so. This was a sterile planet, and I haven't introduced any disease to the planet." He held out a new sheet of paper. "And this is a new strain of the fungus I introduced. It's been struggling as much as the original, so it can't be a random mutation."

Ship scratched his head, thinking of different possibilities. "Have you ruled out a change in atmosphere?"

Atlas nodded.

"What else could it be? What else could have changed between when we first introduced the fungus and now?" Ship asked.

Atlas took in that question and thought about it. It was the right question to be asking. The two of them stood there in silence. Thinking. Pondering. Remembering the first day the green fungus first exploded onto the planet.

"What has changed?" Atlas muttered under his breath. Then a light bulb went off in his head. "Food!" he shouted. "Or, better yet, energy."

Ship smiled a knowing smile. "I think you've figured it out. Can you go fix it now?"

"Can I at least talk it through with you?" Atlas said. Not waiting for a reply, he continued. "Do you know what a primary producer is?"

Ship rolled his eyes. "Please enlighten me."

"We need a better primary producer at the base of the eco-system pyramid," Atlas said, creating a pyramid symbol with his hands. "Or, rather, we need a primary producer."

Ship looked puzzled. "So . . . What's a primary producer?"

"Think of the ecosystem we are trying to build as a pyramid. At the very top of the pyramid, you have carnivores like the orca we seeded a few months ago." He pointed to the very top of his pyramid. "They get all their energy from consuming the fish. And those fish get their energy from consuming the smaller marine animals underneath them in the pyramid. And this keeps happening all the way until you get to the very bottom of the pyramid." Atlas made a show of pointing to the bottom of his handmade pyramid.

"So, the primary producers are the base of the pyramid?" Ship asked.

"Exactly. Primary producers are the very bottom of this eco-system. They're the very start of the chain." Atlas paused, realiz-ing he was mixing metaphors. "To be honest, I'm not sure our fungus is even a primary producer. It's the very bottom of New

Europa's ecosystem now. But it too is consuming materials on the rocks that have built up over billions of years."

"That sounds like a long-winded way of saying the fungus is running out of things to eat," Ship offered.

"Exactly, just like fossil fuels back on Earth. What our fungus is eating is running out. We need to introduce something that feeds off a renewable food source. Something that feeds off light." Atlas paused, almost laughing at himself. He was trying to be too clever. Everyone knew that plants were the bottom of the food chain. But somehow, he was blinded by the effort he'd put into genetically engineering a particular type of fungus.

"Atlas, does that mean we'll be putting plants in the ocean?" Ship said, rubbing his chin thoughtfully.

Atlas bit his lower lip. "It means we need to introduce phyto-plankton. That will be our primary producer species that the pyramid will be based on."

Ship shook his head disagreeing. "I think we should intro-duce a number of primary producers." Ship made a pyramid with his own hands. "See how the bottom of the pyramid is bigger than the top? I think if we have a thriving and diverse bottom of the pyramid, we'll have a very resilient colony."

Atlas's head moved up and down slowly. He was agreeing with his friend—but he was also full of pride. When they had started this journey, his Ship was a lazy AI. He preferred to cut corners and not do any research. It had taken Atlas a long time to shape Ship into the person he was today. Now the two of them were becoming a very competent team. They were solving problems and becoming better explorers because of it. In that moment, Atlas was very hopeful and excited about all the continued adventures together. He smiled as he spoke—encouraging Ship to develop his idea further. "Where do you suggest we start?"

Ship thought about it for a long while. Atlas could tell he hadn't been expecting a follow-up question.

The printer came to life once more as Ship walked toward it. "I think we seed every primary producer we have in the oceans.

And on land . . ." He picked up the stack of paper. "On land we do this. These are designs for a hydroponics megaproject. Let's not wait to use organic matter from the oceans to build out topsoil. Let's start making grass, tomatoes, strawberries—anything that can grow hydroponically."

Atlas studied the design—it was modular. Ship called them hydroponic tents. Basically, a greenhouse about the size of a basketball court, built three meters high with rows upon rows of white tubes—presumably for water. He looked through the pages and noticed that it was designed to be lifted and moved by a single eleph-ANT—with ANTs at each corner for guidance. "Why make them transportable? Wouldn't it make sense to have permanent farming locations?"

"Eventually," Ship said as he walked over to the printer once more. This time the printout was a map of the islands they had almost completed building. He spread the map out on the table. In the end, they had modeled it on Earth's continents—only smaller. So, it looked like Ship had simply rolled out a map of Earth. Someone who knew maps, however, would notice it was a very simplified version. The major land masses were all there— and they resembled the Earth versions. But a lot of the details were incorrect. Australia and New Zealand, for example, weren't missing from the map—they were just in the wrong place.

Ship pointed at the island that resembled North America. "We could cover this island in the hydroponics tents, then start producing organic material as quickly as possible. Once complete, we could send ANTs in to harvest everything and just dump it all on the ground. Do that several times, and after a while, we'll have all this organic waste under the hydroponic tents."

"Let's call them hydro-tents," Atlas suggested as the idea began to develop in his head. "So, you're suggesting we make them transportable so we can pick them up." Atlas pointed to where Europe was on the map. "And move them here, where we start the process again."

"Exactly," Ship said, grinning with pride.

Atlas began getting excited at the thought of this mega-project. "I could engineer a new fungus to decompose all this organic material. We could mix that all in with material from the oceans. That would speed up the process of creating topsoil for the planet." He started writing calculations on the map. "We could dedicate different hydroponic tents to different plant life, just to test what works best and improve on it."

The two of them worked side by side to get the mega-project underway, finalizing their designs and plans. Atlas focused on getting the various primary producers seeded in the oceans, while Ship started work on the hydro-tents.

"Lex, can you help us with something?" Atlas called out, an idea or joke (he wasn't sure which) popping into his head.

Atlas winked at Ship. "Lex, I know you love to overproduce things. Can you help Ship pump out enough hydro-tents to cover the whole of the North America island?" He paused, learning from his mistakes. "But once you've covered the island in them, stop. Don't build any more than that."

CHAPTER 39

ICARUS

FINALLY WE
UNDERSTAND

Icarus leaned against the window of his bridge, looking out on his ring world, and sent off a message asking Atlas to join him in his spacecraft. As he waited, he tried to distract himself from his thoughts. He pushed himself away from the window and walked over to the middle of the bridge. He grabbed a small object from his pocket, then threw it out in front of him. It expanded and turned into a full-sized trampoline. He jumped up onto it and started bouncing.

Moments later, Atlas teleported into his room. Icarus greeted him with a wave as he continued to bounce. "I want to talk about Trillion; we need to stop her."

Atlas's head moved up and down as he tracked Icarus. "Can you stop the jumping?" he said, with a twinge of annoyance in his voice.

Icarus took three large jumps, leaping higher into the air on the final jump. As he reached the top of his arc, he touched the very top of the spacecraft, leaving a sticker on the roof. It was a small black sticker with a red question mark in the center.

As he fell toward the ground, he stuck his hand forward as if willing the trampoline toward him. The trampoline responded— it was sucked toward him, shrinking in the process. He landed with a superhero-like thud. "Where is the love?" he said.

Atlas looked confused. "What?"

"For the Dottiens. Where is the love? They're just animals."

"I don't understand you sometimes, Icarus. What are you talking about?"

"Okay, so, I understand the Dottiens now. I understand their language."

"What? You understand them? Lead with that. How? Tell me."

"That's not the important part. The important part is that Trillion is planning on destroying the Dottiens. And I think we need to stop her."

"Well, they did trap her on their world. It's okay for her to be a little upset."

Icarus was flustered. He felt like he wasn't getting his point across. "Atlas, this is important. They were just responding to her initial miscommunication. If she decides to destroy the Dottiens, she could do it."

"Icarus, I agree. But please tell me how you can understand the Dottiens."

Icarus took a deep breath. "They are basically a single organism. Not a colony like bees or ants, but an organism like slime mold."

"Slime mold?"

"That's the best analogy to an Earth-based animal I can find. It's what would have happened if slime mold had evolved to be the dominant organism on our home world."

Atlas processed those thoughts.

"Slime mold are these incredibly smart yet tiny organisms," continued Icarus. "They can complete complex puzzles and mazes. Multiple groups of them have even been known to join up and act as though they were a single big organism."

"That doesn't explain how they trapped Trillion here, though," Atlas pointed out.

"Yeah, it does. The slime mold was simply responding to its environment. It had learned that fast-traveling objects are a danger to it. So, just like any other asteroid, it stopped Trillion's spaceship from potentially hitting it."

He knew what Atlas was going to ask next and answered the question before he had the chance. "I know you're about to ask why it tried to communicate with us. I have a theory. From what I can see, it's simply following a routine of automated steps. And it's receiving mixed signals. On the one hand, it knows we pose a danger to it if we're not on the moon."

"You mean free-floating in space?"

"Exactly, Atlas. And on the other hand, we're communicating with it, or at least attempting to, as if we were another organism in its swarm."

"So, is it intelligent?"

"Well . . . Yes, kind of. But not like us. It mostly responds to its environment. That's why it hasn't gotten bored of us. It's just an organism of pure stimulus response."

Icarus pulled a piece of paper out of his pocket and threw it into the air. It unfolded into a screen. He saw Atlas not-so-subtly roll his eyes.

"Have a look at this." Icarus pointed at the screen.

On the screen he played a video of a Dottien heading back to the planet. Its skin was bubbly and slightly transparent. As it approached the planet, a large tentacle reached out from the planet and the two connected, then merged into one another. Within a matter of seconds, it looked like the tentacle had absorbed the Dottien.

"See here," Icarus explained, "they can act as one organism or many. I think they evolved from something similar to slime mold on Earth. We're the apex of what a monkey can turn into. It's the apex of what slime mold can become."

"So, do you know how it moves in space?"

Icarus shook his head. "That is still a mystery. Anyway, back to why we need to stop Trillion from destroying them."

"Wait. Not yet," Atlas said. "First, I want to understand how you've managed to speak with them."

"Oh, right. I've developed a theory. Lex is testing it right now."

Icarus didn't quite know how to explain it. He slowed his playback speed. To Atlas, it simply looked like he was standing oddly still for a few moments, but for Icarus, it was a good five minutes as he thought about how best to explain what the alien was like.

Icarus returned his playback speed to normal. "If I say *Imagine a tree*, Atlas, what do you picture in your head?"

"I don't know. I imagine a standard tree with green leaves and a trunk. Why?"

"When I picture a tree, I think of an old peach tree I used to climb when I was a little child. I think about the taste of those peaches on that tree. They were so good."

"Icarus, you're losing me. What does this have to do with anything?"

"It's to show how inaccurate human language is," Icarus said. "Human language compresses information so much. No matter how hard I try, I would never be able to describe the image I have in my head to you in great detail—short of showing you the tree."

"So, you're saying they describe things in detail when communicating?"

"It's more than that," Icarus said. "To the Dottiens, there isn't a concept for *tree*—there's only the exact object they want to describe."

"So, our language limits how detailed it can be? And are you saying that, because the Dottiens communicate with colors and textures, they have a better ability to describe things than us?" Atlas asked.

Icarus used his little playback-speed trick again. He really wanted to explain this next part well. It was hard enough for him to understand the concept; explaining it to someone else felt so much harder. He thought about using a computer hard drive analogy. He believed the Dottiens' communication system was so good, it was like copying and pasting things exactly from one hard drive to another. But he wasn't sure the analogy was clear enough.

He scratched his head, forgetting his speed had slowed down. He realized Atlas saw his hand flash instantly. He returned his speed to normal and went with his original description. "As an organism that can be both singular and multiple, it needs to be very good at communicating. And it evolved to be very exceptional at communicating. The Dottien wouldn't just describe the tree. It would describe the tree exactly as it remembered it. The exact number of leaves. The way the sunlight hit it. Even how many stars and clouds were in the sky that day."

"Are you saying it will describe things in so much detail that any of the other Dottiens could relive that same experience if they wanted to?"

"Yes, exactly," Icarus said with excitement. Atlas had described it better than he had.

"Oh, I get it, Icarus. So, that's why the way it communicates keeps changing. Because as the stars and orbits change, so too does the information it's trying to communicate back to us."

Icarus was impressed. "I can't believe you understood all that. I thought I was going to struggle."

"Can you use your knowledge of them to control them?" Atlas asked.

"Yes; using the hapticgraphic projectors outside, I'm going to see what I can get them to do. But first I need to tell you what Trillion is doing first," Icarus said. "She's sending two different armies here. And, according to her Lex, she plans on destroying the Dottiens."

"Two armies?" Atlas asked in shock.

Icarus could see Atlas wasn't expecting that. "Did you not know she has an army headed this way?"

"I know that. But *two*? She's only sending one."

Icarus shook his head. He pulled up a holographic map of the system. It showed the star in the center, two planets, and a moon. He enlarged the size of the moon and pointed at the map. "See, Trillion is here." He zoomed out on the map. The moon and planet completely disappeared, the star shrinking to a tiny dot. He highlighted two different regions of space. "I've been using the sensors in the system, loading the position of stars into my algorithm to speak with the Dottiens."

He pointed to those two regions of space. "Trillion has an army headed from here and here. And this one is almost here."

"Icarus," Atlas said, not quite believing what he was looking at. "That second one isn't Trillion."

CHAPTER 40

TRILLION

THE WARNING

Trillion's zen was gone now. She stood in her hangar, digesting the news that another fleet of ships was on its way to her location. It was almost as large as the one she had on its way to rescue her.

"Are you sure that's not Ship?" Icarus asked.

"For the last time, those aren't mine," Trillion snapped back.

"Is there anything we can do to help?" Icarus asked.

She thought about it for a moment. She shook her head. She didn't think there was anything they could do. It was all up to her. "They have a similar number of ships. I assume they're more capable than ours. But I don't think they understand just how many assass-ANTs I have. It'll be a great surprise when they get here."

"What's an assass-ANT?" Icarus asked.

"Oh, I had Ship turn ANTs into relativistic missiles."

"Clever naming," Icarus replied, amused. "From the scans I saw, it looked like debris from an incident. They most likely think a number of your spacecrafts collided."

Trillion wondered if it was another alien civilization, maybe they'd seen all the spacecrafts headed her way and wanted to investigate. Although, she thought that was unlikely, it was probably human. "Do you think it's Sol?"

Atlas's voice sounded through the speakers. "I know it's Sol. Have a look at these images of the incoming spacecraft I managed to produce."

"Just bring them in here," Trillion said.

Atlas's voice came through the speakers again. "I printed physical copies of the images."

Icarus shook his head. "You old man; my Ship can render a digital copy of your papers. I'll have it in my hand when you arrive."

Atlas appeared in the room. He put his hand out, eyebrows raised expectantly. "Where are my photos?"

"I lied," Icarus said. "Trillion, do you want to do the honors?"

Trillion kicked one of her legs up into the air. Her shoe flew off. It morphed as it got higher and turned into a screen.

Atlas shook his head. "You two keep competing with each other on who can more creatively create a screen."

Icarus smiled. "Yes. And you keep going old-school. You need to embrace being a simulation, Atlas."

Trillion gave Icarus a look that said, *Leave Atlas alone.* "Lex, can you display the images Atlas wanted to show us?"

The screen in front of them changed. It was a dark, grainy image of a spacecraft, but there was no mistaking the fact it was a human ship. It was huge—about three times the size of even the version two Trillion had designed.

The three of them stared at the image. Trillion broke the silence first. "I've been thinking about them. Why they're so against us traveling the galaxy."

Both men looked at her, puzzled. She could tell they hadn't spent much time thinking about the history or psychology of the human race since they left. Both Icarus and Atlas were geeks first and historians last. "It's the Kiwis' fault," she announced.

"New Zealand?" Atlas was clearly confused.

"Well, not them exactly," Trillion replied hesitantly. "But they were the ones who triggered the singularity." She could tell they didn't understand the connection. They needed a history lesson. "Are we all on the same page about them having an outsized influence on politics?"

"Yes, we all understand how creating the first AI made them the dominant superpower," replied Atlas. "What's their stupid saying? 'Our team of five million'?"

Trillion nodded. "Well, I've been reading up on New Zealand history. Their cultural beliefs are woven into their artificial intelligence. They have a bias for leaving nature untouched. And that bias now shows in all our AIs and, by extension, human culture."

"Can you elaborate?" Atlas asked.

Trillion began to reply when she felt a sudden change in the room—time began to tick more slowly, as if her playback speed was changing. But she hadn't made the mental command to change it.

She noticed that Atlas and Icarus were frozen in place. She looked up and saw the orb of Lex had entered the room. He looked like a phone.

Trillion saw two message notifications on one of the screens—one from Ship and one from General Walker.

Trillion thought back to the day she left Mars, when General Walker was trying to prevent them from leaving. She wondered if it was the same woman. It wasn't impossible—but she'd been gone multiple lifetimes.

Trillion played the message from Ship.

"Hi, Trillion. Lex has triggered an automatic failsafe. In any event that you receive a message from a human spacecraft, that message is to be sandboxed and Lex is to shut down until you or I have an opportunity to review the threat. I froze you in time to give you a bit of time before Lex leaves you. I did this because Lex *is hackable. Unlike me or you, Lex could be corrupted by someone outside of the spacecraft. Stay safe. Ship of Trillion."*

"Wait. What? How will I operate anything without you, Lex?"

Lex's orb flashed once and then disappeared. The lights changed to a dim red.

Trillion tried to think straight. Without Ship and Lex, she was quietly sure her ability to fight back was next to zero. She wondered if she could still change her playback speed. She tried. It wasn't smooth. It was jittery, similar to when Ship had first shown her the technique.

The room shifted. Atlas and Icarus came back into focus. Then they sped up before slowing down again and returning to normal.

"What's wrong?" they said in unison.

"Lex has shut himself down. And there's a message from the fleet of spacecraft on their way here."

She gave the mental order to play the message. Nothing happened. She realized without Lex or Ship, there was nothing to receive the order. She was about to make the order verbally but was interrupted by Icarus.

"Trillion, why has Lex gone offline?"

Atlas answered for her. "It's because it's an install AI, meaning it's possible for someone to hack Lex by installing malicious code."

Trillion nodded.

"We're all custom AIs. So is Ship. In theory, we can't be hacked unless they get access to our physical matrix," noted Atlas.

Trillion was about to play the message, but then she had a thought. Could she use another AI? "Could I borrow someone's Lex?"

"Hmm," Atlas said, biting his lower lip.

Trillion could see his mind ticking over.

Atlas nodded. "It could work. We'd need to build something into your system to prevent the risk of losing access to the Starnet. And we need a firewall preventing any malicious code from infecting my Lex. But it could work."

Atlas disappeared. A few moments later, he was back. "Okay, we can do it. But I need admin access to your ship. Trillion, can you enter your code to give remote access to me?"

There was a series of codes she needed to enter—they were numbers she just had to remember. There was also a two-factor authentication code for tasks like these.

"I'll be back," she said, before teleporting out.

Back in her room, she floated over to her bedside table, pulling out a little calculator device. It had a changing series of numbers every ten seconds.

Trillion pressed a button on the comm control on her wrist. A number pad appeared in front of her, and she pressed the eight-digit code. The number pad read, *Unlocked.*

"Provide remote access to Ship of Atlas."

The screen in front of Trillion changed, now reading, *Please provide two-factor authentication.*

She read out the twelve-digit number on the calculator device. The lights turned back on and the red warning glow disappeared.

She teleported back to the hangar where Atlas and Icarus were waiting for her. "Thank you," she said.

"I've scanned the message. There's no malicious code. It's just audio," Atlas said.

She nodded and gave the command to play the message.

"This is the Starforce Alliance.

"Angelique Komene, Trillion Von Neumann, Atlas Tupu and Icarus Kishida.

"You are under arrest. Either return to Sol immediately or this automated sentinel will bring you back. This is your final warning. You have twenty minutes to acknowledge."

They looked at each other in confusion.

Icarus finally broke the silence. "We can't surrender."

"That message doesn't tell us anything. I thought it would be more threatening," Atlas said.

"It contains a lot of information," Trillion said.

"Like what?" Atlas replied.

She held up one finger, then started listing each important piece of information. "First, the order of people. They put Angelique first for a reason. They might already have her." She lifted another finger. "Secondly, they don't know who is here. Otherwise, the message would have been directed to only one of us." She raised a third finger. "Thirdly, they let us know that the spaceships coming my way are automated, so they aren't risking any lives." She paused for a second, quickly changing her playback speed to leave the room and come back. "And fourthly, it's the same General Sarah Walker who tried to stop us leaving Mars. I just listened to a recording of when we left. It's the same voice and everything."

"Isn't it good they only sent an automated fleet of spacecraft here?" Icarus said.

"No, it means they are more willing to fight, as their spaceships have nothing to lose."

CHAPTER 41

TRILLION

WAR

Trillion was confident and angry at the same time. Her twenty minutes were up, and the enemy spacecraft had sent out what she assumed were missiles toward her location.

She sent a message to Ship, asking him to redirect her force toward the approaching enemy force. He was almost within real-time speaking distance.

She made a mental note to get Atlas to create a mobile version of the Starnet. If she survived, she didn't want to be without real-time communication with Ship again.

"Maybe you should consider surrendering?" Icarus suggested.

"Show some positivity," she snapped back.

She had spent months thinking about how to attack the Dottiens. She had thought it would be easy. But now that she had a real army to face, she wasn't so sure. "Look, it's going to be just as hard for them as it is for me. But I'm going to win."

"They have bigger ships," Icarus said, "run by artificial intelligences—that are presumably designed for war."

"Yes, but my plan is to have waves of assass-ANTs arriving at the same time," Trillion said, a little annoyed that Icarus was questioning her. "Let's see them stopping a wave of killer ANTs all hitting at the exact same time. And I have millions of these assass-ANTs."

"Trillion, they just need one to survive to capture you and take you off the planet. Or one rogue missile to hit you and it's over."

"Icarus, stop with the negativity. I'm going to win. I *have* to win. If not for me, then for my children who still need to be seeded."

Doubts crept over Trillion. She started to worry whether she could survive. Her mind started going around in circles.

Atlas pulled her out of it. "Let's focus on what we can control. Icarus, can you test your knowledge of the Dottiens' language to control them? Help them defend Trillion?"

Icarus nodded, teleported out, and made a computer appear in front of him, where he typed furiously. "Let's hope this works."

They looked over at the screen showing the planet. It turned purple, then erupted with Dottiens flying off the planet and heading toward the incoming missiles.

At least they're on my side, she thought.

She received a message from Ship at the same time she saw the devastation. The true war had begun. Her assass-ANT's near the front started to disintegrate. They just turned into dust.

Atlas studied that data. "I think those are laser weapons." He typed a few lines on his computer. "We can't see lasers out in space, but I'm going to use the available data to visualise it." He typed again.

They watched again as the enemy war fleet flashed red in unison. Visible lasers streaked out from every single spacecraft. Thousands of them, all at once.

The first layer of assass-ANTs were vaporized—that was twelve percent of them, just gone. She had sent a large wave— hundreds of thousands—assuming they would make it to the enemy. Each of the enemy ships had been targeted by at least a thousand assass-ANTs, and every single one of those assass-ANTs were now gone.

None of her ships had any kind of weapon like that.

As if her luck couldn't get any worse, she watched as the missiles General Walker sent to her location dodged the Dottiens like they were nothing. Skipping past them. Not even engaging. Just maneuvering out of the way like it was a practiced dance.

Ten of the missiles fired their engines toward her, suddenly slowing as they each hit the ground around her spacecraft in a circular pattern. They let off an electrical pulse, and the view from her ship cameras blurred.

"Atlas, do you know what that was?"

Atlas disappeared, then reappeared quickly, obviously researching the answer. "It looks like you're trapped in some sort of magnetic field. It's technology I've never seen before."

CHAPTER 42

SHIP OF TRILLION

RESCUE

Ship slammed his thrusters on, hard-turning to avoid a collision with an assass-ANT that had lost control after being sliced by a laser. There was debris everywhere as other spacecraft were pelted with pieces of assass-ANTs and lasers.

Ship could sense all the spacecraft and ANTs in his fleet. His brain was well suited to keeping track of everything. Monitoring other spacecraft and assass-ANTs was no different from keeping track of all the micro-asteroids that could collide with him as he traveled through space at relativistic speeds.

He was now near the front of the fleet, behind a debris belt of dead assass-ANTs. He needed to move toward the back.

His spacecraft spun around, pointing its massive engines in the opposite direction. Firing them hard, he arrested his momentum. The g-forces would have flattened a biological life form, but not Ship.

Other spacecraft flew by him—it looked like he'd stopped in space and everyone around him kept moving. He had to remote-control a few of the other spacecraft and assass-ANTs just to ensure none of them hit him. He had lost all of the first wave; he didn't want to be part of the casualties in the second wave.

A message appeared from Trillion. "Ship, they have me surrounded by some sort of magnetic field. I'm sending you details. You'll need to destroy these ten nodes to get me out."

Time was running out. The enemy had destroyed a quarter of his force now, and he hadn't even gotten a scratch on them.

He slowed down his playback speed, turning seconds into hours. The world around him moved at a crawl. He wanted time to simulate potential outcomes. He needed to save Trillion. It was the one thing he was made for—protecting Trillion. Protecting the embryos, too, Trillion's children.

He really only had one chance to save her. He needed to focus all his energy on this one task. Ignoring the enemy, he needed to free her and get her and the spacecraft off the moon. Then both of them could flee the system, hide somewhere, and decide what to do later.

He simulated what would happen if the war continued. Based on all the available data, he wasn't going to survive. He could maybe destroy five percent of their force, but at the cost of one hundred percent losses. They were just too coordinated.

He replayed the initial battle. He watched the first wave of his assass-ANTs blanketing the battlefield to target their spacecraft. He wasn't focused on what his fleet was doing. He fixed his attention on the enemy—they had some sort of weapon. Maybe it was a force field; maybe it was something more advanced than that. Whatever it was, it was wiping out his fleet. The initial pattern of destruction looked like his fleet was hitting a force field, as if his army was hitting some invisible wall. But as the battlefield was filled with debris, he was able to piece together sensor data from spacecrafts and destruction patterns. It was simply a laser creating the destruction. That was good, he thought, because you can dodge a laser—you can't dodge a wall.

Ship returned to real time and used that new knowledge to update his attack approach for the remaining vehicles in his current wave.

He watched as each of the enemy spacecraft used their lasers in a similar pattern. Three of them would focus on a single target with their lasers following a spiraling pattern, leaving no room for the assass-ANTs to dodge, either vaporizing it or pushing it out of the way so it drifted right past the enemy spacecraft.

They were even more efficient this time. As his second wave was mowed down, he realized the enemy had changed their tactic slightly.

They knew the assass-ANTs weren't very strong. It only required one laser to neutralize them.

He watched as the three ships focused on a single assass-ANT, trapping it. Then, as soon as one of the lasers connected, the other two lasers changed targets, switching to a new one. This increased the efficiency, leading to faster kills. Wave two was destroyed in half the time.

He simulated a scenario where he focused on a smaller group of enemies. He didn't attempt to take out all the enemies—just the bunch closest to Trillion. He watched as the simulation played out. All his spacecraft and assass-ANTs clustered closer together, focusing on only a small group of enemies.

This time, the train of assass-ANTs and ship were still destroyed, but the debris continued moving forward, enemy lasers failing to put all the dead spaceships and assass-ANTs off course. They punched through twenty or so of the enemy ships. Many more were forced to move off course, diverting away from Ship's space junk like weapons causing havoc and destroying a small proportion of the enemy.

Ship thought about it for a while longer. He made a plan. If he focused his remaining forces on punching a hole through the closest enemies to Trillion, while also sending himself and a few other spacecraft on toward her, he could rescue her.

He was outgunned. He had a bigger force, but the enemies' weaponry was too advanced. More and more of his army disappeared by the minute. His only chance was to cause enough destruction to create a diversion, so he could rescue Trillion amidst the chaos.

He made the decision not to assess the probability of success.

CHAPTER 43

ATLAS

SURRENDER

Atlas stood next to Icarus in Trillion's dimly lit war room—a cleared-out zone in her hangar. The three of them were watching the battle unfold. The room was lit up by the blue haptic-graphic projections of Trillion's force and the armada from Sol colliding.

Atlas watched as more and more of Trillion's ships turned red. About a third of her force had been destroyed, and Sol hadn't lost a single spacecraft yet. She was running out of time, and he couldn't do anything but watch.

Atlas heard the ping that signaled he had received a private message. It asked him to meet back at his spacecraft. He didn't know who it was. He needed to leave the room discreetly and quickly—if it was Ship or Lex, it might be something urgent.

He excused himself, telling a white lie, as he didn't want to worry Trillion. He needed to be there, supporting her, right until the end. "I've got an idea. I'll be right back."

He teleported out of the hangar and into his office. Waiting on the other side was Icarus.

"Atlas, she needs to surrender," warned Icarus, unable to hide the stress in his voice.

Atlas took a step back. "How are you here?"

"Oh, it's just Ship controlling my avatar over there. This is the real me," Icarus responded.

Atlas had thought Icarus had been a little too quiet before—this explained why. He hadn't realized having Ship control another avatar was possible. He made a mental note to write a script to flag whenever Icarus did that trick again.

"We'll never be able to convince her to surrender," Atlas said.

"We don't need her to agree."

Atlas raised an eyebrow.

"You still have access to her systems. You could send a message from her saying she surrenders."

"That sounds like a breach of trust."

"At this point, she doesn't have a choice," Icarus said, a little frustrated. "The fight is so one-sided, it's embarrassing. Every second this continues increases the odds that some stray object hits the moon she is on."

Icarus bent forward, a conspiratorial look on his face. "Space warfare isn't what I thought it would be," he whispered. He made a turning motion with his hand, as if he was turning up the volume. "We should speed up this conversation. Let's discuss this quickly before we run out of time."

The world around Atlas slowed.

"So, can you do it? Can you send a message to surrender?"

Atlas thought about it for a good long while. He didn't want to break Trillion's trust, but he also hated the idea of his friend being hurt.

Icarus interrupted his thinking. "Either you surrender for her now, or we risk losing her forever. She's practically immortal; it's not like it matters if she spends a hundred years in jail. But it matters if she gets killed on the battlefield today."

Atlas reluctantly agreed. He sent the command off to his Ship to send the message.

The wait was excruciating. After what felt like forever, Ship entered the room. "We received a message."

"Is the war over?" Icarus said.

Ship just shook his head and played the message.

"Too late."

"What else is there?" Atlas asked. "That can't be everything."

"It was prerecorded. Same as the original message. Like this was always going to be the response to our surrender. I guess that makes sense, if these spacecrafts are all automated."

Atlas replayed the message once more. He could hear a smile on the face of General Walker this time. *"Too late."* Atlas remembered the day they left Mars. He and the team had embarrassed Walker by escaping. They had probably been the one blemish on her perfect record. And now this was her exacting revenge on them. "I bet she always planned for a war. I bet she's hoping to destroy us by mistake. Accidental deaths in making sure Earth doesn't dirty the galaxy with humans. Casualties of war."

Atlas got angry just thinking about it. Then sad because it meant Trillion probably was going to be that casualty.

CHAPTER 44

TRILLION

PROJECT HAIL MARY

Trillion finally had a moment to think. She knew Icarus hadn't been there for a while. His Donald Duck avatar was usually elaborate with its movements when he was in control, but when he had his Ship imitate him, he didn't move as much. She was okay with that. She was struggling to think of a way out with everyone's doubt.

Now with Atlas and Icarus out of the room, she felt like she could think without someone leaning over her shoulder, questioning every move she made. Or didn't make. If she was going to survive, she had to save herself.

She surveyed the battlefield; half her force was gone. Yet she had only destroyed a few of Sol's spacecraft. The system she was in was littered with dead ANTs—space debris now. Icarus had managed to get the Dottiens to fight alongside her, and at the time she assumed it would help put her on the winning side, but they were of little value. Sol's spacecraft looked like it was toying with them, not attacking, rather trying their absolute best not to hurt any of the Dottiens, moving out of the way and dodging them whenever possible. After the team realized the Dottiens weren't equipped for this war, Icarus had instructed them to go back to what they were designed for—protecting the planet from asteroids.

Trillion's army was truly overkill for facing the Dottiens. They originally only captured her because they had surprise and numbers on their side—now they had neither. She didn't regret bringing an army this size, however, because if she didn't have the army, she might already be on her way back to Sol. Now she had a chance to escape, a very slim chance, but a chance. She wanted more than to escape, though; she wanted to win. And to win, she needed a good plan—and a bit of luck.

With little fanfare she teleported out. "I'll be back," she informed the fake Icarus. She chuckled a little, knowing only the real Icarus would have understood that reference.

She reappeared at the front of the nursery and paused at the large steel doors. Behind those doors were her children. She wasn't going to lose them. All those unborn humans and animals. Unborn life. This was what she was fighting for; this was why she needed to win.

Then it occurred to her. She didn't want to die. And she didn't want her children to die, either. But neither did anyone in the Spaceforce fleet—she had decided to call the enemy the Spaceforce.

She looked up at the ceiling. "Ship, can you hear me?"

The confirmation came back almost instantaneously. Light delay between her and Ship had almost disappeared. They could talk normally if she kept playback speed closer to real time.

She knew Ship was still controlling a lot of the war fleet, so she sent a short message. "One of the Spaceforce ships has an AI on it, but I don't know which one. Ship, can you work out which one?"

"Sorry, Trillion," Ship said. "I'm controlling too many moving parts. I can't talk properly right now."

She had only seen Ship struggle like this once before—when the Dottiens were attacking them. But not being able to speak with Ship only strengthened her theory.

She teleported to Atlas and Icarus. They were on Atlas's bridge. She watched as their faces dropped in surprise. She could tell they weren't expecting her—Icarus looked like he'd seen a ghost. She chose to act surprised, not wanting him to know she knew Ship was controlling his avatar. "Atlas, I need your help."

"Anything. What do you want?"

"Can you predict which of the enemy spacecraft has the AI?"

Atlas frowned. She could tell he still believed that all of the Spaceforce was automated—they weren't controlled by any sophisticated AI.

"When I was researching the ruling party of Sol a while ago, I noticed that they consider all AIs sentient. They believe us three are sentient. But they also believe our Ships and Lex are sentient too."

They both nodded in understanding.

"It's very easy for AI to appear sentient. So, often, they'll intentionally dumb down an AI to keep it well below the threshold of sentience."

"Are you saying all these spacecrafts out here are dumbed-down machines?" Atlas asked.

"No, the opposite. I'm saying there *is* a master AI on the other side pulling all the strings. But only one! On a mission like this, they wouldn't risk more than one sentient life."

Atlas bit his lower lip before responding. "I thought we had agreed this was just an automated system."

Trillion shook her head. "A basic system couldn't pull something like that off. It has to be coordinated by an AI." Trillion knew she was guessing. But she continued to act confidently—as if it were fact. Humanity back in Sol could have changed their minds about AIs. Maybe they'd now decided that smart AIs weren't as precious as human life, so risking a lot of them was

fine. Or maybe they had developed smart AIs without the sentience attached. She felt in her gut she was right. And if anyone
could work out whether she was right, it was Atlas. "So, can you
tell me which of the Spaceforce ships is directing everything?"

"That should be easy enough to prove." Atlas said, considering how to evaluate it. "We can look at exactly how decisions are
propagating through the enemy's fleet."

Icarus nodded his agreement. "Exactly. If we use the data
from both Ship and the sensors you have near the system, we
should be able to triangulate if decisions are being made from a
single location or not."

She put her hands on her hips. "Come on, then. Work it out."

Atlas began walking toward his computer.

Trillion pointed to the watch on her wrist. "Increase your
playback speed, old man. We don't have much time."

In a flash, Atlas sped across the room to his computer, and
then instantly appeared in front of Trillion, holding up a piece of
paper. "It's this spacecraft. This one right here," he said, jabbing
at the paper with his finger.

"Are you sure?"

"Yes, I double-checked my numbers, multiple times. Lex
agrees with me."

Trillion turned toward Atlas's Lex. "I struggle without it being
visual. Lex, do you mind?"

The room went darker. A projection of the unfolding war
appeared on the table in front of them—Trillion's army in green,
Spaceforce in blue, the Dottiens in purple, and the debris of dead
vessels in red.

Looking at the projected war on top of the table, it became
clear to Trillion just how one-sided it had been—half the table
was covered in blue spacecraft, meaning the Spaceforce had
sustained very few losses. The smaller force of Trillion's army
had congregated. From that angle, her fleet looked like a snake
that had punched itself through a small number of Starforce
vehicles. But the proverbial snake was having its head cut off by

all the laser fire. "This fight is not going my way," Trillion said more to herself.

Trillion glanced at the Dottiens' home world. A huge number of Dottiens were orbiting their planet—they were out in full force, intercepting the many stray objects that headed toward their planet. "At least we got to see the Dottiens doing what they were made for. They're protecting their world well."

"I think it's lucky that the fight is happening away from their planet. If you were over their homeworld, I think it'd be a different story," Icarus replied.

Trillion looked back at the wall of blue enemy spacecrafts. "So, which one has the master AI?"

Atlas pointed to the spacecraft he believed was in control of the armada. On the blue side of the table, there was a ship close to the front but not at it. "This is where information seems to spread out at light speed. There are many points in this battle when new instructions are sent out. And you can see them propagate at light speed out from this exact ship."

Trillion looked up at the orb floating in the ceiling. "Lex, do you mind?"

The projected battle rewound to the moment when the Starforce first began shooting lasers at Trillion's force. They watched as three lasers fired at the very front row of Trillion's assass-ANTs. The pattern was such that the assass-ANTs had no way to dodge the incoming death beams.

Trillion had simply taken the standard ANT design and modified them slightly to operate at relativistic speeds. They were a kinetic weapon—meaning their destructive power came from the speeds they were traveling. But because they were basically just ANTs moving quickly, they didn't have any armor or shielding. One touch of a laser disarmed them, and a few more moments of fire disintegrated them.

They watched the replay of the first battle. Seeing that once an assass-ANT was disarmed, all three lasers didn't need to fire at it any longer, yet all three did. They continued to burn a hole through the assass-ANTs unnecessarily.

Atlas paused the replay. "Three lasers for each assass-ANT is good for trapping it. But once the assass-ANT is immobilized, it's overkill for destroying. Basically, one nip destroys those things."

He drew a circle around three enemy spacecraft. These were the closest three to the one Atlas believed had the master AI. "Watch these craft here."

The war replay began again. All three Starforce spacecraft began firing their lasers, focusing on a single assass-ANT. The assass-ANT moved rapidly from left to right, turning in circles, trying to avoid the lasers. The three lasers closed in on it, limiting the assass-ANT's options. And then *boom!* One of the lasers cut the assass-ANT in half. This time, the other two lasers didn't continue to fire at it—they immediately focused their lasers on a new target.

Atlas pointed to an enemy spacecraft on the other side of the battle. "See this one is further away? It hasn't yet received the updated strategy." It fired its laser at a target assass-ANT. Its target was destroyed by another laser. Yet the spacecraft Atlas was pointing at continued firing on the dead assass-ANT, disintegrating it into smaller pieces.

Atlas paused the battle. "Trillion, now watch this. If I'm right, then this spacecraft should receive the strategy update now. It's exactly enough light-seconds away that it should change its approach now."

Atlas resumed the battle. The spacecraft stopped firing abruptly. Its laser switched off like a light, but half a beat later, it fired again, this time the laser aiming at an assass-ANT that was dodging another two lasers.

Trillion waved the hapticgraphic images away. "Let's go kill the AI controlling the battlefield."

She looked up toward the ceiling. "Ship, get over here." She looked at the floating orb. "Don't let him ignore this message. I need a hundred percent of his focus."

It took a few seconds for Ship to respond. If a robot could show fear, it was in his voice. "I'm sorry, Trillion. I'm so, so sorry."

"Ship, it's okay. You're doing a great job." Trillion paused. "I'm going to tell you something important. We're sending you coordinates for a target. Do everything you can to destroy this spacecraft."

Ship didn't argue, but he didn't come back with an affirmative, either.

"How do we know if he's doing it?" questioned Icarus.

Lex's orb in the corner flashed. The hapticgraphic battlefield in front of them expanded to encompass the whole several light-minutes of space. Lex continued replaying the battle in front of them. The scene played at one hundred times the speed, catching up to real time. Trillion marveled at how normal the sped-up battle looked. The battlefield stretched over several light-minutes, so even at one hundred times the speed, the assass-ANTs and spacecraft looked like they were cruising along.

As the projection got larger, zooming out to survey the battlefield, specific details disappeared. Individual objects were replaced with what seemed like a cloud. Nothing recognizable except a slight mist showing the greater density in space.

The front layer of Trillion's fleet moved forward, red laser light blasting out from the other side, shaving down her side one slice at a time. It looked like the front layers of Trillion's force were beginning to fade away. More and more of the front layers faded as they were destroyed by laser light, not even getting close to the enemy.

She pointed at her war fleet. "This is when Ship decided to focus his attack on the very front of the enemy spacecraft. The ones closest to me."

The army of assass-ANTs and spacecraft started to come together, getting smaller and narrower until it looked like one continuous line rather than a multitude of objects—becoming a snake once more. The line of assass-ANTs concentrated on the front section of the Starforce. The side closest to the moon.

Red laser light was still fixed on the frontmost assass-ANTs and spacecraft, but Trillion's army crept forward. It hit the enemy line and then punched through before it was hit with red light from the sides, utterly destroying everything that had crossed the front line.

"Okay, this replay is coming up to real time," Trillion said.

Trillion's army broke into two, the back half turning toward the middle of the enemy. It looked like half the train carriage splitting off in another direction. The back fleet narrowed even further, focusing on a single point. Then it froze in time.

Icarus squinted at the hapticgram. "Why is it frozen?"

Atlas looked over at Lex. "I think we've now reached real time."

The orb flashed green.

"Anyone opposed to changing our playback speed?" asked Icarus. "The battle looked much better when sped up."

Trillion shook her head. "We're not watching a movie. If this doesn't work, I might not survive. We need to be in real time to react to anything that happens."

"Well," Icarus said, "if we give Lex or Ship the ability to pull us back to real time, we should be fine. Their reaction times are much faster than ours."

There was a reluctant look on Trillion's face. "Okay. But Lex or Ship—if anything happens, no matter how small, pull us out instantly. Atlas's Ship, you have to wait in real time. No joining us at this playback speed, okay?"

The hapticgraphic image in front of them started to move again. Trillion's army snaked out toward the enemy. The red laser light shone bright as the front of her army was pushed back. Over two-thirds of Trillion's force was now gone. And more were dropping like flies. She didn't believe in a god, but at that moment she found herself praying to someone, something, anything that could hear her thoughts. For the briefest of moments, she closed her eyes and said a prayer. It wasn't herself she prayed for; it was her children. All the unborn embryos currently frozen in the fault of her ship—the nursery. She prayed if she didn't survive, they would. Prayer done, she reopened her eyes and pointed at a blue Starforce spacecraft. "Ship, focus everything we have on that one spacecraft. Kill it!"

She knew Ship couldn't hear her, but as if he was listening, Trillion's army started to come together, closer and closer, until they looked single-file.

Trillion walked toward the hapticgraphic projection and made an exaggerated pinch-to-zoom gesture. "I want to see up close." The projection increased. They could see individual spacecraft now. All of Trillion's spacecraft were in a row. They watched as hundreds of assass-ANTs jinked from side to side before being destroyed by lasers. But each assass-ANT managed to make it a fraction closer than the ones before it.

Trillion could feel her hands clenching. She looked around the room. Atlas and Icarus were stressed too. She breathed in deeply—she hadn't realized she was holding her breath. She didn't need to breathe, but it helped keep her in control.

Trillion closed her eyes for a moment. Then she opened them to see her army inching closer—one fried assass-ANT at a time. Her army was arranged in a pattern of about a hundred assass-ANTs and then a spacecraft, each one of them moving closer than the last. The spacecraft made leaps forward, while the assass-ANTs made steps.

Trillion took in the whole battle. She could see they were running out of spacecraft. There were ten left. Plenty of assass-ANTs, but the Starforce had worked out how to kill them faster so they weren't making any forward progress anymore—often, they lost ground.

Her last remaining spacecraft fired their engines on full and inched toward the enemy vessel—the master AI. They moved at a faster pace than anything before them, forming a tight line, like train carriages that were connected—so close, they were almost touching.

One by one, they were subjected to laser light. And one by one, they were destroyed or cut in half. Ten, then seven. Then six. Based on their progress, they weren't going to hit the targeted enemy spacecraft.

Icarus struggled to watch. "They're not going to make it," he fretted, covering his eyes with his hands.

"You can leave if you don't bring positive energy," chided Trillion, pointing to the door. But she was nervous too.

There were three of these fast-moving spacecraft trains left.

Boom! The closest spacecraft exploded.

Boom! The back one exploded too.

"Oh, no, what happened?" Atlas said.

Trillion couldn't see. She squinted. Then saw it. "They're all dead."

The back explosion boosted the middle spacecraft forward but also crippled it. It tumbled through space, toward the enemy ship. It looked like it was going to make it—but it didn't have any power. So, it would only take a course adjustment for the enemy AI to get out of the way. Trillion once again prayed that the Spaceforce AI wouldn't get out of the way.

Time stopped. For everyone.

The Ship of Atlas entered the room. "Trillion, I believe your Ship just ejected himself from the spacecraft."

Trillion looked at Atlas. "What does that mean?"

Atlas raced over to his computer and began furiously typing. "It means if we don't send something to intercept him now, he'll race right through the system without stopping."

Trillion didn't quite know what to do. She didn't have anything she could save him with. But she *needed* to. There was no way to save him if the enemy ships were still out there too. She had a thought. "Atlas, how hard would it be for you to hack into those spacecraft out there?"

He looked confused. "Impossible. Otherwise, we would have done that already. I told you—as long as there's a custom AI out there, it's impossible for us to override their instructions."

Trillion shook her head in frustration. Either her final spacecraft would connect with the enemy AI, or she would lose everything. She'd lose Ship, her best friend. And she would lose her children and maybe her life. It all came down to this moment, this one tumbling spacecraft needed to hit the enemy. Nothing else she did matter; slowing down time was superfluous to finding out her fate. "Lex, can you take us to real time?"

The projected battle in front of them progressed once more. Over ten long seconds they watched as the middle spacecraft tumbled toward the enemy, boosted by the explosion. It was tumbling out of control, but there was still a chance it could tumble into the enemy's craft.

The enemy spacecraft fired its engines hard, dodging Trillion's tumbling spacecraft, whose engines had failed to ignite. It was dead. The battle was over. Her final spacecraft tumbled away from the enemy, its trajectory meaning it would just miss the Starfleet master AI.

Icarus broke the silence. "Sorry."

Trillion pointed at the door. "Get out!" she said, not quite ready to accept defeat and forcing Icarus to leave.

Trillion's final spacecraft exploded, pelting the enemy's vessel with flying debris. With nowhere to run, moments later, the enemy craft exploded too.

Trillion jumped in the air in shock. "We did it!"

Atlas pumped his fist in the air, then pointed at Trillion. "No, *you* did it!"

Atlas turned to his computer and played the footage. "It's working. They aren't coordinated with their firing anymore." He pointed at the screen. "Look here."

Lasers still fired at the remaining assass-ANTs scattered around the battlefield, but only one per assass-ANT now. They fired straight ahead at assass-ANTs directly in front of them. Any that weren't on track to collide with an enemy spacecraft did not get fired at.

"They've gone back to using those lasers only as object avoidance, only firing at objects that could hit them," Atlas said.

Trillion held her hand up, pausing the projected battle in the room. She made an action like turning a knob, and the battle rewound. She pinched to zoom into one of the assass-ANTs and noticed it hadn't moved once.

She rewound it again. "Ship isn't controlling our side either. Can one of your two Ships get the assass-ANTs to aim down the middle of those craft? Then, at the last minute, curve into the enemy? Also . . ." Trillion paused. "How do we save Ship? Can you try and hack into the Spaceforce now that they don't have a master AI controlling them?"

The Ship of Atlas responded. "I think so."

Atlas's hands were moving so quickly, they were a blur. He disappeared for a moment and then reappeared. He flashed to the printer, then back to the computer before entering real time. "I think it's done. Once I launch this virus, we might be able to control some of the Spaceforce.

He crossed his fingers and pressed Launch.

CHAPTER 45

ATLAS

CLEANUP

The virus worked. It'd given Atlas control of a number of the
Starforce spacecraft. He was currently trying to take over the rest.
Hacking into a few was easier than he thought, but gaining con-
trol of the rest was going to be hard.

Atlas was typing away on his computer, exploiting vulnerabil-
ities, while Trillion stood behind him, tracking Ship on a large
screen. She did not want to lose sight of him.

"Icarus, can you send the Dottiens after my Ship?" Trillion
pleaded.

Atlas could hear from her tone that the idea she would survive but not have Ship was breaking her.

"Already trying," Icarus replied through the speakers because
he still wasn't allowed back onto Trillion's Ship.

Trillion's Ship was on a trajectory out of the Dottiens' system. He had attempted to make the ultimate sacrifice in order to save Trillion. It had worked. But now he might be lost forever.

Ship had pushed his spacecraft to the very limit of its ability, then ejected himself, meaning he was quickly racing out of the system, and if he encountered anything as big as a grain of sand, he would destroy his brain matrix. Out in deep space, traveling at the speeds he was traveling, it was only a matter of time before he hit something—and was gone forever. Meaning the team had to move fast—otherwise, he *would* be gone forever.

"The Dottiens are too slow," Icarus's voice came through the speakers. "I have no idea how they propel themselves through space. But whatever they've evolved for propulsion isn't powerful enough to catch up."

"Atlas, we need your new ships," Trillion pleaded once more.

"I think I have control of most of the Starforce now. Let me try something," Atlas said.

Atlas managed to get control of many Starforce ships. Any that were not under his control were destroyed. After the master AI no longer pulled the strings, hitting them became easy. The Starfleet was only using their lasers on objects on a collision course, so all they had to do was send an assass-ANT on a non-colliding trajectory, then at the last minute turn in to the Starfleet vehicle. And by then, it would be too late.

Atlas studied the data in front of him. He was looking at the relative speed Ship's matrix was traveling through space. It was going fast. Too fast.

His matrix wasn't accelerating, which meant catching up to him wasn't the problem—an accelerating ship would always catch up to one moving at a constant speed. It was the time it would take to catch him. If they didn't catch up to Ship, he would probably hit something—and hitting even a speck of dust would be fatal. Especially to his matrix, which was unarmored—basically a space tissue ready to be torn.

Atlas didn't think any spacecraft could catch him before his matrix encountered something. The g-forces required to catch up in a useful timeframe weren't realistically achievable. But Atlas knew he had to try anyway. Not for him but to give Trillion a sense of closure so she wouldn't regret and feel they didn't try absolutely everything. He knew what regret felt like. The feeling that you could have done something different—it was worse than failure. Even though the mission was futile, he wanted to give Trillion the gift of no regrets.

"Let's see how powerful the Spaceforce fleet is," Atlas said, instructing his new spacecrafts to move at full acceleration toward Ship. He hoped Trillion's Ship was lucky. Deep space was vast and the odds of hitting something in deep space was low. But Ship's matrix wasn't in deep space; it was in a star system busy dealing with a battle that just ended. Ship had to be really lucky if he was going to survive long enough to get saved.

Moments later, he was staring at the screen in disbelief. Atlas double-checked his playback speed, because he didn't believe his eyes. It wasn't until he double-checked the numbers and then had Ship confirm that he believed what he was seeing—because he hadn't seen anything move that fast before. Atlas was going to have fun, pulling a Starforce spacecraft apart and understanding how it worked. "For an army intent on staying in their own system, Sol has engineered some sort of rocket engine that can move faster than anything we have," he said before adding, "Or anything we could theoretically make." He thought about how long they had been gone. How big Sol's technology tree must be right now—far beyond anything they had. Atlas had a sneaking suspicion that it wasn't a battle fleet that was sent his way. Everything the Starforce used must have been built for defense, not attacking others. "Traveling at the speeds those ships travel, the lasers were probably designed for clearing a path for them as they traveled through space," Atlas said.

"What are you talking about? Trillion asked.

He turned to Trillion and smiled a happy smile. "We're going to catch up to Ship in no time."

Trillion let out a deep breath. Atlas didn't realize he was holding his breath either until that moment. He and Trillion hadn't thought the war was over until they had a clear path to rescue Ship.

The team was still waiting after a long time. But once Atlas had learned his new spacecraft would travel much faster than he thought possible, his worry that they wouldn't catch Ship in time was gone. Both he and Trillion had noticeably relaxed after that, and the tension in the room was dissipating.

"Atlas, how can we be sure that Sol can't just take over any of these spacecraft?" Trillion asked.

"We'll need to replace all the electronics and hardware onboard. Maybe more than that"

"I think I'll stay in this spacecraft—stuck on the moon or not. I won't risk putting myself in one of those."

"Good call," Atlas agreed. "But as a safety measure, I think we should also add a Ship AI into each of our new spacecraft. Just to ensure they aren't hackable."

Trillion shook her head. "Let's replace all the hardware. But I'm happy with my Ship. Is there a way we can use the Starnet so Ship can control all these spacecraft without light-speed delays?"

"I've been thinking of something like that. The one flaw with the Starnet is it only connects two points with each other. And it works best when those points aren't moving very much. With spacecraft, especially in battle, their movements are erratic. I've been playing with some new designs to enable that."

As Atlas began explaining how his new Starnet design might work, Icarus appeared in the room without his customary portal effect. He held out a bunch of flowers. "I'm sorry, Trillion."

The bouquet was comically big and made the room smell like spring. It was an arrangement of many different white flowers. Atlas thought some of the flowers were made up, because he hadn't seen them before. Icarus waved it like a white flag—showing he'd surrendered and was asking for forgiveness.

Trillion took the flowers. "It's okay. I know you were worried. I'm just glad you managed to get the Dottiens under control. You kept them out of harm's way."

"I'm sorry for doubting you, Trillion."

"Icarus, we've been friends for thousands of years—and we're going to be friends for the next thousand, too."

The two of them hugged it out. Then Atlas joined the hug. They had been through a lot together, and they were going to go through a lot more together in the future.

Icarus pulled out of the hug first. "Did we manage to get any information out of any of those spacecraft?" Icarus asked, looking at Atlas. "Do they know where Angelique is? Are we at risk of having a war fleet like this attack us?"

"I haven't pulled anything from those ships yet."

"That could be good or bad," Trillion said. "We need to assume they know where each of us is. We need to prepare for them attacking us."

"I might have something for that," Atlas said.

Trillion raised an eyebrow. "What is it?"

"I've looked into the design they used to make those lasers. We could make a bigger version. Connect it to a bigger power system. We could scatter them around each of our systems."

Trillion's eyes lit up. "Like a planetary defense system?"

"Exactly."

"I also have something that should help," Icarus said quietly.

Atlas could tell he was still feeling bad because of his lack of support. "What have you got?"

"You know how we've managed to communicate with the Dottiens? Well, their language is extremely efficient. The transfer rate of information is enormous. They've spent millions of years evolving a better form of communication to help them organize and keep their super colony running."

"Get to the point, man," Trillion snapped.

Atlas realized Trillion was still a little mad at Icarus, but his curiosity was piqued. "I'm interested, but you can tell me later."

"Okay, okay. The short version is we can use what I've learned to increase the Starnet bandwidth to. . ."

He was abruptly cut off as Ship appeared in the room. "Trillion, your Ship's matrix has been recovered. He's on his way back to you right now."

"Can I speak to my Ship now?" Trillion asked.

"No, there isn't a connection point for him to plug in to yet."

Icarus raised his hand, clearly still worried he'd get his head bitten off again. "Having our own Ships and calling them 'Ship' reminds me of my time in school. So many kids were called Hiroshi, we had to give them nicknames. Or call them Hiroshi One and Hiroshi Two."

"Whose Ship do we call Ship One?" Trillion laughed.

Atlas nodded in agreement. "Ship, do you want a new name? Want to be called something else?"

Ship shook his head. "I've been called Ship for as long as I've existed."

"Okay, team, I can't wait any longer," she announced, frustration mixed with excitement clear on her face. "My Ship, the one who saved me, needs to be part of this conversation. He's a hero and we should be celebrating with him right now. I'm changing my playback speed until he's here."

Then she froze in time, like the most realistic statue he had ever seen she just stood there, or at least it appeared that way to Atlas because he was still in real time—a subjective hour for him becoming a subjective second for her. One of her red curls looked like it was defying gravity—obviously falling at a glacial speed. He had never stopped to think about how changing playback speeds didn't actually change time, just their experience of time. Which, subjectively, he always thought was the same thing, but now he was seeing how it different it really was. Atlas winked at Icarus and joined Trillion in the future.

....

It felt like only a moment, even though it wasn't, that he was returned in real time. The Ship of Trillion was back in control of his own spacecraft. Icarus's control of the Dottiens was crucial in "unsticking" Trillion from the moon and keeping the Dottiens from placing more of the Starforce fleet there.

Everyone was on Trillion's ship now, and when her Ship teleported in, now fully connected to his spacecraft, the applause sounded enormous. It didn't sound like it was coming from only five people. Atlas clapped so hard. He wanted Ship to know how impressed they had all been with his fight.

Trillion ran over and hugged him. "Thank you," she said as she literally picked him up and spun him around. Atlas wondered if her tiny frame could do that before.

"You don't know how proud I am of you, Ship," Trillion said as she placed him back down, "the way you utterly destroyed that master AI. I'm so happy you're here. I'm so happy we all survived. You are my hero." She paused. "And don't you ever sacrifice yourself like that again."

The Ship of Trillion turned bright red.

Trillion studied him once more. "I like the new look, though. A fitting outfit for the winner of a war."

In the emotions of seeing Ship, Atlas hadn't yet noticed he had changed his appearance. He was dressed in a formal military outfit. Or, rather, it was based on a military outfit. Anyone would have thought he was the highest-ranking person, with the six stars on his shoulder.

Icarus walked over and shook Ship's hand. "Hi, I'm Icarus."

"Oh that's right," Trillion said. "You haven't met Atlas or Icarus yet."

"So, you managed to make FTL communication work," Ship said, looking at Atlas, then back at Icarus. "Why do you look like Donald Duck?"

CHAPTER 46

TRILLION

CHILDREN OF TIME

Trillion grinned from ear to ear. She looked up at the massive doors in front of her. She thought the nursery looked beautiful. "I'm a little jealous, you know."

She could see Atlas's grin, too. She'd never seen him that joyous.

Icarus jumped from foot to foot. "I can't wait; I can't wait!"

Atlas walked circles around the room. "Are you sure everyone has nine months they can spend with me?"

"Yes, yes. Neither of us would miss this moment," Trillion said.

"Yes, Atlas, we wouldn't miss this moment for the world. We will have many other children of time. But this is the first."

"Tchaikovsky. Nice reference. But are you saying Atlas is creating spiders?" teased Trillion.

Icarus glared at her. "Well, if the humans back on Sol are anything to go by, we might be better off with spiders."

Atlas stepped forward. "Calm down, you two. Don't ruin my moment." He placed his hands on the large hatch wheel in front of him and began to turn it. Then he stopped mid-turn. "Should we all do the honors?"

Trillion jumped forward, grabbing the wheel with two hands, Icarus teleported to the wheel and grasped it with one hand, and they all turned it together. Three large turns and the door made a loud *pop* followed by a hissing sound as air rushed out and the pressure in the two zones balanced out. The three of them pulled hard and the door swung open.

A smoky gas flowed out of the doorway and chilly air rushed over them, peppering Icarus's skin with goosebumps.

Trillion noticed Icarus's arm; she was impressed with the level of realism Icarus was putting into his avatar. "When did you add that effect?"

"You like it? I added it when I knew we were going to come in here. There's a few more you're going to see."

"Oh, like what?"

"You two," admonished Atlas, "focus on this moment. Please."

Trillion turned her head back to the open door. She looked down at the ground. Between the hatch and the inner doorway was a meter gap, then another door opposite. "Why the gap?"

"It's a room within a room," explained Atlas. "The inner nursery, where the embryos are, is connected to the outer room through shock absorbers so it can be protected against any sudden movements. It ensures no high g-forces are experienced by anything in here."

Trillion smiled. She had been slightly concerned that her fight with the Dottiens had damaged some of her own children. The worry disappeared and she concentrated once more on Atlas.

Atlas pressed a button on the side of the hatch they had just opened. The door opposite swung open. From where Trillion was standing the room looked quite large. She wondered just how big the space was.

Atlas took a couple of steps back. Then he ran forward and jumped, landing in the nursery.

A door to the left of Icarus appeared. He winked at Trillion before opening it and stepping through, then waved back at her.

Not to be outdone, Trillion pulled out a portal gun and shot it at the side of the wall. She walked through and appeared in the nursery herself.

Ignoring Atlas as he shook his head at the two of them, she looked around the room. It was enormous. The ceiling was at least ten meters high. There was row upon row of shelves. As she scanned the room, she noticed it was arranged into eight sections, all different sizes. Directly in front of her, the sign read HOMO DEUS. There was another sign to her right, a little further away. She strained her eyes to read it. It was the biggest section. It read ANIMALIA.

Atlas pointed at a red line circling them on the ground. "You can't go outside of this red circle."

As if to test it, Icarus began walking toward the line. As he came closer to it, he stopped moving forward. His legs were still moving, but he wasn't going anywhere.

"Are you moonwalking?" Trillion laughed.

Icarus shook his head. "No, I'm walking normally. It just won't let me go any further."

"It's not that you're not allowed to cross that line." Atlas laughed a little. "It's just that the hapticgraphic magnets all over this spacecraft stop at that line. It's to ensure the hapticgraphic engines can't be hacked in order to destroy any of the items in here."

Icarus stopped moving. He pressed his hand toward the line, trying to cross it. It looked like he was pressing against an invisible wall. "So, how do we get a sample?"

"Like this." Atlas pressed a button on the comm control on her wrist. A number pad appeared in front of him. "Turn away while I enter the code."

Trillion turned away, playing along with Atlas's game even though they both knew she could replay the event later if she wanted to learn the code. She heard buttons tapping.

Then a robotic arm dropped down from the ceiling and headed toward the section labeled Homo deus. It reached into one of the shelves and twisted a cylinder open, then pulled out a small metallic test tube about the size of a finger.

The arm moved toward Atlas in a quick, smooth motion before coming to a stop just inside the red circle.

"What's that?" Icarus said, pointing to the test tube.

Atlas pulled it from the robotic arm's grasp. "This is a single fertilized embryo."

Trillion turned her head toward Icarus. "How do you not know that?"

Icarus shrugged. "I haven't needed to look any of this information up yet. I will when it's my turn."

She reached her hand toward the test tube. "Can I touch it?"

"Of course," Atlas replied, handing it to her.

"I can't believe I'm holding the first ever human life to be born in another system."

The weight of the vial was noticeable. She could feel it was dense. "Should we name it?"

Atlas laughed. "I think we're getting a little ahead of ourselves. Let's grow it first."

"Okay, so, what next?"

"We'll seed the first child. Then Lex has an automated program that will seed the rest of them."

Icarus looked up. "Oh, that makes more sense. I thought we had to seed them all like this. That would have taken forever."

The three of them headed out to the hangar. Trillion and Atlas both felt the gravitas of this moment, so they took turns carrying the "vial of child," as she called it.

CHAPTER 47

TRILLION

CHANGING MINDS

Atlas's Ship was waiting at the airlock door, his gold skin sparkling as if he'd just been polished. There was an ANT next to him, waiting to take the test tube. Trillion noticed the ANT had wings; it wasn't like any she had seen before.

"What's that?" she asked Atlas.

"I call it a cormor-ANT."

"I love the name."

Icarus pretended to gag. "You two and your puns. I thought *assass-ANT* was bad enough; now this! Just stop."

Atlas patted him on the back good-humoredly. "Don't be jealous. Trillion, want to do the honors?" he said, handing her the test tube. "Give this to the cormor-ANT."

Trillion inserted the test tube into a compartment of the cormor-ANT. "Maybe we should have called this one a stork."

Icarus smiled, approving of Trillion's reference.

Trillion watched as the cormor-ANT closed the compartment.

Ship touched the cormor-ANT and glanced at Icarus. "You'll like this animation," he said, before fading into golden mist. The mist of Ship drifted toward the cormar-ANT and seemed to merge into it, dissolving into every part of it. At moments, it looked like golden glitter was falling on the all over the cormor-ANT before being absorbed into its skin. At others, it looked the cormor-ANT was breathing in smoke made of flecks of gold and fire.

Icarus looked at the cormar-ANT with a grin. "You're right; I did like that one, Ship."

The inside airlock door opened and Ship took control of the cormor-ANT, making it walk into the airlock. Each of the cormor-ANT's steps left a visible golden footprint. The door closed behind it, and it was launched out into space.

Atlas pointed to a large screen above the airlock door. "Ship, do you mind?"

The screen turned on. It showed a view from cameras on the cormor-ANT.

They watched as it dived toward the planet.

The planet looked inhabited. It was lush and green; clouds were in the sky. The night side of the planet was lit up with lights. It almost looked like Earth but with different continents.

As the cormor-ANT fell, the planet grew bigger and bigger, more details emerging the closer it got. They could see it had a slight green tint—even the water was green.

Their cormor-ANT adjusted its trajectory and headed toward the light side of the planet. Then it turned, angling itself toward the largest landmass near the equator. It turned on its engines, firing hard as it headed toward the planet at an increased speed.

The outside of the cormor-ANT started to glow red, and the atmosphere of New Europa became thicker. The cormor-ANT was pushing itself through the atmosphere, creating a lot of friction in the process. Layers of the cormor-ANT's liquid heat shield disappeared and was replaced by more of the nano-liquid material.

The view of New Europa expanded. More details emerged as it flew beneath the cloud layer. Trillion could see buildings. Even skyscrapers started to emerge on the planet.

Trillion pointed at the screen. "Is that a city, Atlas?"

"Yes, I made some replicas of Earth's biggest buildings." Atlas pointed at one on the corner of the screen. "That small one there is a copy of the Burj Khalifa."

As the cormor-ANT drew closer, the city came alive. Even more details emerged. There were roads, skyscrapers, suburban streets, and railways.

The cormor-ANT began to glide, its wings helping it stay afloat. As it flew, it started weaving in between tall buildings. It flew past several statues.

Atlas looked at the other two. "Those massive statues are us. And I included our Ships in there, too."

Atlas's Ship's voice came through the speakers, sounding mildly braggy. "Mine is made of real gold."

The orb in the corner flashed.

"Oh, yes, and I included you, too, Lex," Atlas said. "We can do a flyby of those statues later."

The cormor-ANT flew through the city. It flew over buildings. It turned sharply and fired its thrusters suddenly to avoid a tall skyscraper, then continued on to the edge of the metropolitan area, where the view opened up on to a large field. Low trees and a patchwork of flowers covered the ground.

The cormor-ANT flew over fields of lavender, gliding closer to the ground, the purple flowers shaking in its wake. It continued on, over a hill of poppy fields, the bright red sea of flowers bursting with vibrancy.

Trillion's eyes were glued to the screen. "Credit where credit is due. This is beautiful, Atlas," she said, clapping a little.

"Just wait," Atlas said, his attention focused on the view. "You haven't seen the best part yet."

"It gets better?" Icarus asked. "And you tease me about being ostentatious!"

Atlas pointed to the screen. "It's coming up."

The cormor-ANT continued to fly low over the poppy fields, ruffling the flowers beneath. As it reached the top of the hill, they could see the vast planet open up to a sunset overlooking the water.

Icarus started to clap. "Wow, this is incredible!"

Atlas smiled. "I timed it so that you'd see this sunset right here at this very moment."

Trillion wondered how much effort Atlas had put into the choreography of this moment. The sunset wasn't just happening around then; it started right then. With the sun hitting the ocean, it created a mirror image of the sun—as if two suns were touching each other. As she stared, her eyes started to water. "You know, this is the first time I've missed Earth."

She stepped forward and put her arms around the two men's shoulders. "Thank you, Atlas."

Atlas wiped a tear from his own eye. "Why am I so emotional?"

The cormor-ANT turned its engines on hard, pausing all forward momentum. A wide, flat concrete building lay just below it, overlooking the water. It had a large BIRTHING UNIT sign on the roof. Ship guided the cormor-ANT toward a mezzanine and through open sliding doors. It landed in a room that resembled a hospital ward, only it had no beds.

In the middle of the room, a robotic nurse waited with arms stretched out. The cormor-ANT opened up its inner compartment. The nurse carefully took the test tube out of it, seemingly unaware of the wild journey it had just been on.

"Are there hapticgraphic engines in that room?" Icarus asked.

Atlas's face lit up with excitement. "Yes. Yes, there are. We are going there next." He teleported out.

"I guess we go too," Trillion said, before she teleported out.

Trillion and Icarus joined Atlas in the birthing unit ward. Trillion thought the ward looked bigger in person.

Atlas's eyes were closed. He couldn't look up at the machine. He knew what was happening. "This is the moment I've been working toward my whole simulated life."

Trillion pulled him close to her in excitement.

Smiling, Atlas said, "My children will be here soon."

The nurse carried the test tube to a square-shaped machine along the wall. It had an opaque compartment filled with a sack, and a clear compartment with lights and tubes running in and out of it.

"What happens next?" Icarus asked.

Atlas could barely talk. "This"—he sniffled—"this machine will defrost the embryo, then act as a surrogate mother, nurturing the baby for nine months until it's ready to be born."

"I'm so proud of you, Atlas." Trillion squeezed him even tighter. "And a little jealous."

"So jealous, old man," Icarus agreed. "I can't wait to have this moment with my children soon."

Trillion let go of Atlas. "Now we wait."

Atlas shook his head. "I can't wait."

Icarus raised his eyebrow. "What then?"

"We change our playback speed," Atlas said.

Icarus nodded. Then Trillion nodded, and nine months raced past them in a few moments.

Trillion saw a flash of movement. She assumed it was Atlas. Maybe he had normalized his playback speed early. She resumed real time too.

She saw Atlas holding a baby drinking out of a bottle. She smiled. The baby's chocolate skin was so perfect.

"It's a boy," Atlas said, holding the baby out for her to see.

"Can I hold him?" asked Trillion.

Atlas handed the baby over.

Trillion beamed. He smelled like pure joy. "He's perfect. Does he have a name?"

Atlas pondered for a while. Trillion could tell his mind was working overtime. "His name is Atreus."

"I think that's quite fitting," Trillion said while not taking her eyes off Atreus. "Peter started this journey. And now the first baby ever born away from Sol is named after him,"

Icarus joined real time. "I can't believe this is the first baby born away from Sol."

Atlas bit his lower lip. He walked around in a circle. "I don't know what it is, but I don't feel right. I feel sad. I feel lonely. I miss my family."

Icarus placed a hand on Atlas's shoulder. "You've just seeded your first world. It's okay to feel a bit emotional."

"No, it's not that. I can feel a rush of emotions coming back into me. Like I was somehow too stoic. And now my emotions are colored."

"Are you okay, Atlas?" Trillion asked, comforting the baby while feeding him.

"No. I don't understand why I wasn't sad about Peter dying until now. Where's the rest of the crew we left behind?" He raised his hands over his head.

Atlas started pulling his hair. In a panic, he tried to speak. "Oh my God. Angelique!" Fear flooded his face. "What happened to Angelique? Where is she?"

Trillion took Atlas's hand and held it. "What's going on?"

"I don't know. But I'm starting to panic," Atlas said, and began to hyperventilate.

Icarus tried to calm him, placing a hand on his shoulder.

Atlas slid to the ground and curled up into a ball, rocking from side to side.

"Hmm," Icarus said, looking at Trillion. "This might have something to do with our programming."

"What are you talking about?" Trillion asked.

"Atlas will have a better grasp than me," Icarus said, trying to remember what he had learned back on Mars. "Basically, the one change that was made to us when we were uploaded was a deep desire to create children. It's a desire greater than anything else. It keeps us focused on this one task."

Trillion sat down beside Atlas, the baby still in her arms. "Yes, I remember learning about that. Basically, we now live forever, so this programming is designed to keep us following the mission, not getting distracted."

Icarus looked down at them. "Ship, do you have anything to add?"

The Ship of Icarus appeared in the room. "Only that that piece of coding disappears once you've seeded a world. Once a colony is established. I think that's what's happening to Atlas now."

Atlas was sobbing. He started to shiver. He was curled into a ball so tightly that Trillion wondered if his avatar was breaking.

Ship looked down at Atlas. "I think it's the emotions coming back all at once. It's too much for him." Ship looked up at Lex floating in the corner. "Lex might be able to implement a piece of code that acts like an antidepressant. At the very least, it might slow down the rush of emotions."

Atlas looked up. "Do it. I can't bear this pain."

The orb flashed.

Trillion watched as Atlas's shoulders relaxed. She handed him his child, hoping it would help calm him further. "Talk us through what you're feeling?"

Atlas started to breathe normally again and his sobbing subsided. "It's like I can feel again. Think again. I was so obsessed with building this world. Seeding it. But now that obsession is gone. And now I can see clearly."

Icarus sat down next to the two of them. "What does *seeing clearly* mean, Atlas?"

"Haven't you noticed how myopically obsessed with our children we are? Trillion almost destroyed an alien species because she feared they were going to stop her raising children."

Trillion nodded slowly. "I can sort of see what you're talking about."

The baby started to stir. Atlas stood up, gently moving from side to side, rocking the baby back to sleep. "I wonder if we can remove that piece of code in each of your matrixes."

Ship put his hand up. "I can answer that. The short answer is no. You can't make that sort of change to a custom AI. That's what makes us unhackable. Here's a look at each of your matrixes," he said, holding up a tablet. It looked like an interconnected mess of fiber-optic cables. "There's a physical node in each of your matrixes that has been there since you were each switched on."

He swiped at the tablet, changing the screen. "This is Atlas's matrix now." There was a small part that was blacked out. "This section here has now been switched off."

"Does that mean it could be switched on?" Atlas asked.

"Manually switching off just that section would be impossible to"—Ship was thinking it through—"impossible to do without potentially turning off something that wasn't meant to be turned off."

Trillion looked closer and could see it wasn't just one section turned off. There were tendrils reaching out from that section that were blacked out, as if a very complex puzzle piece had been switched off.

Ship added. "The code was always designed to be turned off once each of you completed your mission. So, completing the mission would be the safest way to do it."

Trillion put her arms out. She wanted to hold the baby again. She took him into her arms and stared into his eyes. "Okay, so, what next?"

Atlas looked back at Trillion and Icarus. "We need to seed your children. Then we need to go looking for Angelique."

Trillion smiled, holding the baby and daydreaming about what Atlas had created. "Atlas, you've built a new Eden."

AUTHOR'S NOTE

Now that you've read Book 1, take a look at the artistic drawings with all the spoilers on them! My favorite shows what Icarus looks like as a duck-human anime character. They're totally free, so you have nothing to lose. Go check them out on my website before you forget—MenilikDyer.com/eden.

ABOUT THE AUTHOR

Menilik Henry Dyer is the author of *A New Eden* and its sequels, *A New God* and *A New War*. He is also writing a series he calls "the Bobiverse meets Children of Time." Visit his website at www.MenilikDyer.com.

DISCOVER
STORIES UNBOUND

PodiumAudio.com

Made in the USA
Las Vegas, NV
03 February 2024

85249910R00184